THE WILI

M000028433

AN ANTHOLOGY
OF
STORIES ABOUT THE
SOUTHWEST IN THE
1850s & 60s

By
Doug Hocking

BUCKLAND ABBEY, L.L.C.

The Wildest West

Devil on the Loose
Copyright © 2016 Doug Hocking
All rights reserved.
www.doughocking.com

Published by
Buckland Abbey, L.L.C.
Sierra Vista, Arizona
Cover Layout and Design
Copyright 2016 © Goose Flats Graphics
Cover Photo Credit
Wyatt's Hotel, Coffee House and Saloon Theatre

ISBN: 978-0-9907619-4-5
LCCN: 2016901028

BUCKLAND ABBEY, L.L.C.

The Wildest West
Other Books by Doug Hocking

***Massacre at Point of Rocks*, 2013.** The story of Kit Carson and the White wagon train massacre. Ann White and her baby daughter were taken captive by Jicarilla Apache in 1849. The Army recruited a reluctant Kit Carson to get her back. The trail was three weeks old and it had snowed, but Kit followed it for over 200 miles. The story takes the reader into Jicarilla Apache camps and ceremonies and explores what life was like in 1949. Available from www.doughocking.com , Amazon.com and Ingram.

***The Mystery of Chaco Canyon*, 2014.** Four friends, an Anglo, two New Mexicans and a Jicarilla Apache are set on a quest after a fabulous treasure. The trail will lead them all over the Southwest of the early 1860s, and through Civil War battles as they are pursued by Penitentes, Danites and Knights of the Golden Circle all seeking the same long lost power. The story starts at a rock in Los Lunas, New Mexico, where the Ten Commandments are inscribed in an ancient Hebrew dialect. Available from www.doughocking.com , Amazon.com and Ingram.

***Devil on the Loose*, 2016.** Bray St. Gnomebray seeks a new life, fortune and love in 1860 Arizona. He falls for a fairy princess, founds a cattle ranch and a succesful mine only to have outlaws take it all away, including the girl whom they plan to send to slavery in Mexico. 300 miles from the county seat, Arizona was a haven for outlaws on the run. The Devil really was on the loose.

The Wildest West

***Tom Jeffords, Friend of Cochise*, 2017.** Jimmy
Stewart played Tom Jeffords in 1950's *Broken Arrow* to
Jeff Chandler's Cochise. He rode alone into Cochise's
Stronghold to make the peace. The real Jeffords was
equally brave and became fast friends with the chief. The
history books got most of it wrong. The true story is even
better.

Dedication

To my wife Debbie Erno Hocking who is still putting up with it all and trying to help,

And to my editor, Adele Brinkley, who helped get this out on short notice,

And to Carol Markstrom and Van Fowers who got me interested in Tom Jeffords

Table of Contents

Historical Fiction

Articles from History & Ethnography

Maps

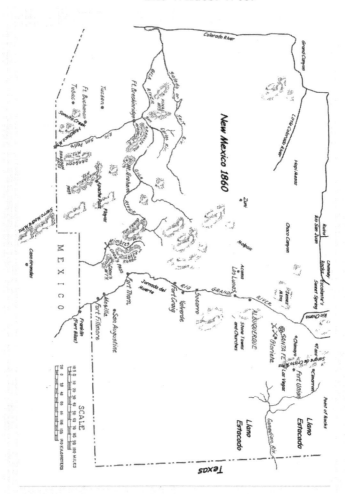

The Wildest West

The Wildest West

Preface

Everything was different before the railroad came. Transportation and the mail were slow. The Southwest was wild in the 1850s and 60s. The United States had only recently taken the Southwest from Mexico, and American law and order did not yet extend to the new lands. Justice was what a man could make of it. When it formed in the 1880s, the Arizona Pioneer Society recognized the distinct difference between their experience and that of those who came later. The Pioneers limited membership to those who had arrived before 1870. They knew there was something different about men of that era. There were no cowards among them. There couldn't be. Everyman was a hero capable of defending himself. Not all were good. Many were on the run and found the Southwest to be a place where the law couldn't touch them.

Enjoy these stories with my assurance that they are interesting, teach a bit of history, and are safe for children. I wanted an anthology of short stories of which I could be proud. While many of my friends write excellent stories, sometimes they wander into realms not suitable for the young, and others miss the mark by repeating worn-out plots. Moreover, I wanted a volume that I could be proud to put into the hands of church friends and teenagers knowing they won't encounter ribald tales or unnecessary bad language. In other words, I wanted a book in which I knew and loved every tale.

One element in which I take pride is that every one of my stories is set against a realistic background. If I say a town was there, it was, and the same goes for trails, streams, and hills. More than that, I've tried to get the

1

cultures and historical events in the background the way they really were. I hope that the reader will learn a little history from every story.

I am an historian, and I pride myself upon going back to primary sources wherever possible. Primary sources are the accounts of people who were actually there and witnessed the events. Comparison of many sources allows us to draw conclusions about what really happened separating them from those accounts that are colored in various ways. I am not a post-modernist. I believe that only one thing happened, and that the truth of it is knowable or at least approachable and it is the historian's job to try and find it. When Ike Clanton calls Wyatt Earp a villain and murderer, I look to who their friends were and note that the upstanding people of the town stood with Earp, while Ike's friends were rustlers and outlaws.

My amiable friend asked in her book, *Who Were the Cochise County Cowboys?* She told us they were all "handsome young men who never done a wrong thing," I mentioned to her that all of them were dead within two years after the Gunfight Near the O.K. Corral, were shot and killed during holdups or by posses, explaining that I suspected they weren't as pure as she insisted.

At the same time, I am an artist of letters, and as such, I pluck ideas from history in an attempt to present you with its reality. While I try to stay true to history, I'm not writing history; I'm writing about it. Many of my stories fall into the realm of historical fiction. I took the real story and tried to make it come alive by putting words into the characters' mouths. Elsewhere, I've merely tried to present the shape, smell, texture, and taste of what it was like to live in the frontier west.

The Wildest West

I've included in this anthology a number of short historical and ethnographic stories, some of which I released to and had published in other anthologies. They focus on the mid-nineteenth century, and I hope they will help you understand that era better. Others have enjoyed them, and I hope you will, too.

I trained for five years as an ethnographer and as an historical archaeologist. More than that, I grew up on the Jicarilla Apache Reservation in the Rio Arriba, the land north of Santa Fe. As a child, I came to know the alien cultures of the *Indio* and *paisano*, the Mexican-Americans of the Rio Arriba, in ways no adult ever can. The adult comes to the reservation fully formed, trained in being an American. I arrived half formed and learned from my peers. The adult arrives and socializes with his peers, mostly other Anglo-Americans, viewing the Indian and paisano as something different, something less. Both he and they have learned to guard themselves from exposure and hide much cultural material from each other. Children are not so guarded and share more of themselves and their culture. I hope I accurately convey something of these cultures in my stories. I don't know the people of the Abajo, the area south of Santa Fe, of Chihuahua or Sonora as well as those of the Rio Arriba. I only know enough to know that there are very real and deep distinctions among them.

Reading my stories, you'll learn about the Southwest and its peoples, cultures, and towns. You'll learn about what it was like to live on the frontier between 1846 and 1875. You'll know the guns, the tools, the animals, and the modes of transportation. I hope you'll come to understand the economics, the conflicts, and the reasons why people acted as they did. Most of all, I hope you'll enjoy the stories. My first and highest aim, like that of Louis L'Amour and Tony Hillerman, is to be a good storyteller.

"The Power of Fox and Snake" continues the story of Peregrino Rojo, whose name means the Red Pilgrim. Rojo is a Jicarilla (Hick-a-ree-ya) Apache renaissance man excited by the world and interested in everything with a desire to learn anything he can. At heart and soul, he remains an Apache. He learned Spanish and English along with the customs of those peoples by hanging around and taking jobs in Santa Fe and Taos. Now in his mid-twenties, he has travelled east with the Skimmer of the Plains, Francis Aubrey. Fascinated by a river bigger than all the water he has ever seen combined with a steamboat floating upon it bigger than the Taos pueblo, he lingers. His people love to gamble, and soon he boldly enters into the world of riverboat gamblers and stays a while for the adventure.

"The Lady Was a Gunfighter" picks up on a similar theme. What if Ann White's baby daughter, Virginia, (see *Massacre at Point of Rocks*) had lived and been passed from tribe to tribe as a slave? In my story, she ends up with the Mojave, arguably one of the most violent tribes with habits not in keeping with Victorian standards. What would she have been like as an adult? Would she have known the quality of mercy or love? I pair her with Doña Tules, New Mexico's gambling courtesan, as her teacher and mentor. Purists will note that Tules was already dead at the time of my story and would have been in her late 50s. The story is fiction, so I guess I can fiddle with history a bit.

"Can We Still Collect the Bounty" is, of course, a bounty hunter story. A friend asked me to write a story and put him in it. Be careful what you ask for. The next day a publisher called me for a story to add to an anthology. The theme was to be Dead or Alive, so my friend became the man wanted dead or alive. His wife, reading the story for the second time, suddenly looked up and exclaimed, "Hey, wait a minute! He's wanted for killing me!" I've recreated Cimarron after the Civil War and included Lucien Maxwell and Clay Allison. The era is a bit late for the one and early for the other, but hopefully I give some idea of who they were and how they impacted the town.

In 1855, the governor of New Mexico accused Kit Carson of cowardice. No one was sure what he was talking about, though an incident where Kit told the governor to take cover during treaty negotiations with the Ute and Jicarilla Apache came to mind. Kit understood Apache and knew they were ready to kill the politico. "Showdown at Echo Amphitheatre" is my version of how that council might have gone. This story appeared in the La Frontera anthology *Broken Promises*, **True West Magazine** selected as the 2014 Best Western Story Anthology.

When Congress ordered the Overland Mail north to the Oregon-California Trail in March of 1861, the Overland Mail company left men and equipment behind in what soon became Confederate Arizona. Butterfield had hired northerners as his hostlers, stationkeepers, conductors, and drivers. Many of them were men who had worked for him in New York, Yankees to the bone. Stranded, they hoped the mail would soon run again. In April, J.J. Giddings assessed the line for the San Antonio and San Diego Mail, a Confederate line and ended his life a guest of Cochise, hung from a tree, head down, over a small fire. The Butterfield men continued to hope and hang on, despite increasing Southern harassment and growing Confederate power. Finally, seven of them stole a stagecoach and fled westwards toward California. I've taken everything we know of the character of these men and of what became of them and blended it into "Escape from Mesilla."

Wind Wagon Thomas was a real person. He heard about the sea of grass that was the great western prairie and knew that men could sail it in boats. He built them with great wheels and sails. It would be a wonderful and inexpensive means to traverse the Santa Fe Trail. He set out to prove himself. According to newspaper accounts, one of his proto-types made it 40 miles before capsizing in a crosswind. What if, embarrassed, he'd continue his work in secret and made it across the plains to New Mexico with a cargo? "Pirates of the Llano Estacado" tells how he might have been received.

By 1860, people were starting to call the area centered on Tubac and Tucson Arizona. It was a haven for outlaws and men on the run from committees of vigilance in California. The county seat of Dona Ana County was 300 miles away in Mesilla on the Rio Grande. Fort Yuma was 300 miles to the west in California. There was no marshal. The court was supposed to come to Mesilla from Santa Fe once or twice a year but seldom did. Congress denied Tubac law and order. The citizens tried to fend for themselves without having the law on their side. There could be no prison and no court. All sentences would have to be corporal or capital. The good citizens of Tubac tried hiring some law officers but soon found their brand of justice too strong to swallow. "Marshal of Arizona" asks what folks are to do when there can't be law and order.

In 1854, Jicarilla Apaches nearly wiped out two companies of dragoons near a place called Cieneguilla (see-en-eh-gee-ya). Two very different versions of what had occurred emerged. In one, the Apache ambushed a gallant lieutenant and his command and nearly wiped out the dragoons. Only the courage of the young officer saved the day as his men inflicted heavy casualties on the hostiles. In the other version, a head-strong lieutenant who thought he could whip the whole Apache nation with a company needlessly attacked a peaceful village, charging up a slope too steep for his horses. The counterattack had him surrounded in a bowl where the Apache fired down on his men until the young officer panicked and cried, "Save yourselves. Every man for himself." The command retreated leaving their wounded. The Apaches suffered only two casualties. The Apache spared the remainder of the command, which was by then out of ammunition. The Jicarilla broke contact and departed when they could easily have killed every soldier without loss to themselves. In "Letter from Fort Burgwin," a soldier tells what he saw that day. One of the companies that fought there was wintering down from Fort Massachusetts. Later that year, they were shorthanded due to losses at Cieneguilla and due to a high rate of desertion. There was also a mutiny in Taos. All of these difficulties of morale can be traced back to what happened at Cieneguilla. Having heard the story from the Jicarilla themselves and having looked into the battlefield archaeology, my version reflects the story told by Apache.

I'm not one to rewrite the history of Cieneguilla or to disrespect the honor of the dragoons needlessly. In search of food and aid from their government agent, band of Jicarilla under Chacon came in voluntarily to Camp Burgwin. They'd had a rough winter. The commander there tried to confine them, and they fled. The commander of Cantonment Burgwin sent Lieutenant Davidson out to gain and maintain contact. Instead, he attacked their camp choosing an impossible approach. The counterattack pinned his men down, and he lost courage and told them to flee. He left his wounded to the mercies of Jicarilla squaws. He regained his courage and rallied his men as they ran out of ammunition. The Jicarilla broke contact or his command would have ended like Custer's. Lieutenant Davidson told a version of the story that makes him a hero ambushed by the Apache. Some of his men supported him apparently because of the courage he showed when all might have been lost, but the breakdown in morale became obvious later.

Another version emerged, picked up from the men by Lieutenant Bell who wasn't there but whose version is supported by the archaeology 150 years later.

"Penitent Child" is about understanding life and religion in nineteenth century Rio Arriba, New Mexico north of Santa Fe. Life was hard and frustrating, and *paisanos*, as the local Mexicans called themselves, stood in danger of being pronounced a *brujo*, a witch, if they failed to conform to community standards. There were witch trials as late as 1775 and murders well into to the 1880s and perhaps later, though they are spoken of in other terms. Talk to the paisanos and you will know that they still worry about witches and about what can happen to an outsider in some of the small towns. The Penitentes remained powerful well into the 1960s and may remain so. With a secret society, it can be hard to tell.

I've included a number of short historical articles that have been published in other places. "Fandango at Fort Massachusetts" appeared in *Wild West*. It is the story of the Fourth of July Celebration in 1856 at the most isolated fort in the United States. The guest roster was a Who's Who of the Wild West.

The Wildest West

"The Black Legend of Lieutenant George Bascom" is about the misinterpretation of history and how it can be difficult to correct. I delivered a paper on this subject to the Arizona Historical Society in 2015 and it was published in *True West* that year. Meaghan Saar did a wonderful job of editing. In the story, Bascom stands accused to starting the Apache Wars by insulting Cochise. The legend does justice to neither man.

"The Life and Times of Tom Jeffords" is an attempt to encapsulate the life of Tom Jeffords in a very short form for the Arizona History Convention 2016. I am working on a biography of Tom and want to present some of the information I've learned. I found no one had ever completed a biography of Jeffords. I thought everyone would know his name. After all, in the 1950s he had his own television show, *Broken Arrow*, and in 1950 Jimmy Stewart played him in the movie of the same name against Jeff Chandler's Cochise. My thanks goes out to Van Fowers who does an excellent "living history" presentation on Jeffords. He inspired me to look more deeply into the subject.

Wild West Magazine published "Padre Antonio Jose Martinez, New Mexican Hero." Martinez was a remarkable man in every respect. He owned the first printing press, was the first New Mexican ordained as a priest, was spiritual head of the Penitentes, served in the Mexican and then American legislature, and started the first school and first seminary in New Mexico. When New Mexico was made a diocese of the United States, French priests and bishop were sent, and they tried to stamp out New Mexican religious culture and the memory of Padre Martinez. Bishop Salpointe even left him out of his history of the church.

9

The Wildest West

"Sailing the Great Lakes" started as an essay in understanding Tom Jeffords's life on the Great Lakes. The Lakes were very different from the salt seas and called for a different kind of sailor. The experience helped to mold Tom Jeffords into the man Cochise would respect and befriend.

I published "Go Jii Ya" in **Wild West**. It is about the Jicarilla Apache's most important ceremony. An extended recounting of this celebration is an important part of *Massacre at Point of Rocks*. If you are interested in what life was like for the Jicarilla Apache in the mid-nineteenth century, you can't do better than to read my book.

I wrote "Tom Jeffords, Sutler" for the newsletter of the Sierra Vista Historical Society. Sierra Vista was founded in 1957, and the historical society tends to see history as beginning in the 1950s when Sierra Vista was first incorporated. I'm interested in the middle years of the nineteenth century, so I know what came before. Sierra Vista was built over the remains of the Babocomari Ranch, Old Camp Wallen, the McLaury ranch, the Hog Ranch, Fort Huachuca, and the Fry and Garden Canyon settlements. Tom Jeffords, who made the peace with Cochise, took up the job of post sutler and post master. The sutler was the post trader, an early version of the Post Exchange, PX.

I hope this book gives you an idea of what life was like in the middle years of the nineteenth century in the American Southwest. This book presents themes that I think you may not have encountered before.

Many times people have asked me how I unravel history from fiction in a historical novel. There's no one good answer. It's difficult. The definition of historical novel is broad. Some works claim to be historical because the background is real. *The Homesman* was one such. Glendon Swarthout explored a real aspect of the old west, those who lost the battle, but the story itself was totally from imagination. Some would say that if historical persons are present, they should be doing what history tells us they did. In a historical fiction, the author has the literary license to put words in their mouths and explore their feelings and character.

"Escape from Mesilla" is such a story. The story tells what we know of the facts and explores the character of the men involved from what we know of them. From this story, you could speak with confidence about the history of the Freeman Thomas party. "Marshal of Arizona," at the other end of the spectrum, sets an absolutely real stage with a few historical characters, but the story is invented to explain the real situation in Tubac in 1860 and the problems it caused. It's not easy to know what's history and what's not. Perhaps the stories will pique your interest enough to look into the history. But be warned. Although I go back to primary sources and many secondary sources, popular histories, don't have the true story. Many are more fictional than my historical fictions.

Showdown at Echo Ampitheatre

Spanish culture stalled at Red Wall Canyon, just northwest of Abiquiu, for almost two centuries. It was the gate to the castle of the *cimarrones*, the wild Indians. The Old Spanish Trail to California ran through the canyon, but it was a trail for horses and *mulas*, mules. *Carretas*, the heavy-wheeled carts of the Mexicans, went no further than Abiquiu. No one dared to farm this wild country. Navajo, Utah, and Jicarilla brought stolen goods and slaves to trade with the *brujos,* witches of Abiquiu, for the *vecinos*, the people of New Mexico, thought anyone who dealt in such commodities was a witch. They whispered, but none too loudly lest they be overheard and given the *ojo malo*, evil eye. "The people of Abiquiu are *brujos*. It is a bad place. They do not keep their word, even to friends."

At Red Wall Canyon, one passed beyond this last vestige of civilization into the wild.

As the party exited the canyon, the distant walls of the *Piedre Lumbre*, the Rocks Aflame, rose above them, like a blazing bonfire red, orange, yellow and fiercely white-hot. They were led by a small but powerfully broad-shouldered man in buckskin, his dark red hair sticking out from under his wide hat like straw on a scarecrow. His rifle resting across his pommel, he raised his hand in greeting to mounted Jicarilla Apache and Utah warriors who bade him follow. Behind him two riders shifted in their saddles to talk.

Dan Trelawney was dressed in buckskin like his boss, Indian agent, Kit Carson. "Roque, do you think Congress and the governor will keep his word this time? This is the third time a governor has offered this treaty, and the first two times Congress wouldn't even consider it."

Roque Vigil, tall and powerful, was dressed in Mexican finery. The seams of his black pantaloons, which could be closed with silver *conchos*, were open to the knee, revealing colorfully decorated *botas*, rawhide leggings, above his moccasins. A red sash at his waist concealed a knife and *pistole*. His vest was black with silver brocade above a white shirt with full sleeves.

"Do you think Chacón will keep his word this time?" Roque asked. "Kit is still furious that he left Cantonment Burgwin when he promised he would stay. He is angry that Chacón then killed most of two troops of dragoons."

Dan countered. "He could have killed them all. He claims now that he lost 60 men, but we know he only lost two."

Behind them, by prearrangement, Sergeant Pengelly called a halt so that his men could adjust their uniforms and break out their guidon and pendants. The governor turned himself out looking quite splendid in top hat and tails. Governor Meriwether, the personal representative of the Great White Father, wanted to ride in a coach as suited his rank, but Indian agent Carson had explained the unsuitability of the carriage to these trails.

Pennants fluttering, adjustments were made to reveal the splendor and majesty of the governor and of the United States. The party allowed braves of the Utah and Jicarilla tribes to lead them to an alcove in the flaming walls. They entered an amphitheater hundreds of feet high that threw back each sound made. There, standing atop a hill that rose like a pulpit, Chacón of the Jicarilla and Lobo of the Utahs saluted the arriving entourage, their speech booming from all directions. It was a fine beginning. Behind the military trailed pack animals and a flock of sheep in the care of Mexican boys.

Governor Meriwether rose in his saddle. "We owe them a twenty-one gun salute as leaders of sovereign nations."

Dan closed one eye, and cocking his head, said to Roque, "My, is he ever puffed up, a regular bantam rooster."

Meanwhile, Sergeant Pengelly, an experienced Indian fighter, protested to the governor. "Sir, it's not their way."

"It would start us a fine war," Kit demurred.

Yielding, but not mollified, the governor told Kit, "Give each tribe ten sheep each day we are here. That should be enough to feed them. I'll make a formal presentation of blankets and military coats to the chiefs when we gather."

A fine gathering of tepees stretched away across the low, rolling hills of the plain enclosed by bonfire cliffs. Dan figured that the governor's estimate of the number of people there and what it would take to feed them was not inaccurate.

The governor pointed and then insisted on having his way. "I want our camp there, on that knoll." That particular knoll was south of the encampment of the combined tribes.

"Governor, that hilltop will catch the wind," Pengelly told him. "It is too exposed."

"The better to flutter our banners, sergeant," Meriwether replied. "We must look official, even regal. We must impress."

Kit turned away so that Dan couldn't tell if he was laughing, crying, or rearing back to spit.

Meetings would take place in the amphitheater seated around the base of the shell facing outward toward the "pulpit" hill.

Kit called Dan and Roque aside. "The tribes consider it a place of great power."

"What kind of power?" Dan asked, understanding a little of Jicarilla mysticism.

Kit whispered in awed tones. It was easy to get the feeling that God himself presided at this natural cathedral. "Earth Power or Mountain Power, I think. It is hard to break promises bound in earth and mountain. They are meant to last.

Kit breathed in deeply. "Can you feel it, lads? This place is the work of the Great Architect of the Universe."

A fine, cool, swiftly flowing mountain stream ran to one side of the encampment. Under steep banks, the water flowed sweet and clear.

Thoughtful, Dan pondered Kit's religious leanings, which stood, he thought, somewhere off toward the mystical between Indian and Freemason. God was vague, though wonderful, powerful but distant. He had rejected both Protestant and Roman Catholic teachings. While God's handiwork was clear enough, Kit didn't seem to understand how some men could claim to know so much about what God wanted people to do, especially when it always seemed to turn to their advantage.

On the second morning, Dan noticed that all of the sheep the governor had brought along were enjoying the water up beyond the Indian camp. Finding Roque, Dan asked, "We been raided in the night?"

Before Roque could answer, they heard Governor Meriwether shrieking, "Mr. Carson, Mr. Carson. Dammit, where are my sheep?"

"Please call me Kit. I gave them to the chiefs to distribute."

"This is gross insubordination. I told you to give them ten per day," the governor roared.

Kit's calm voice answered. "*Indios* don't think like that. They expect a big gift right off. If we'd held back, they'd have thought we were treating them like children or worse."

"Still, I gave instructions!" Meriwether thundered. "And I expected them to be followed to the letter."

Magnificent and frightening when roused to anger, Kit managed to control the impulse to throttle the governor. He continued patiently trying to explain. "The chiefs would have thought we were holding the sheep as cheap bargaining chips. The gesture would not have been well received."

Governor Meriwether spun on his heel and stalked back to his tent.

"He's got a lot to learn about negotiating with Indians," Kit said mildly. Dan blushed, and Roque hung his head. Until then, Kit had not let on that he knew they were eavesdropping. "This will be the third time this same treaty has been negotiated with these same chiefs. Chacón is to get land around Abiquiu, this land. His people are to get farm implements and we will teach them to farm, and the government will feed them until the farms are up and running. And the government gets the Llano Estacado, all of the Jicarilla lands east of the Shining Mountains. The Utahs give up the San Luis Valley and get a similar deal. Twice now the government hasn't kept up its end."

"Kit," Roque asked, "does this mean you aren't angry about Cieneguilla?"

Kit's features clouded. "That's a separate matter. I got Meriwether to agree to feed the Jicarilla even though Congress hadn't approved the treaty. But Chacón didn't wait. He went on the warpath."

Dan couldn't hold his tongue any longer. "He moved his people away from the captivity a drunken major tried to impose and set up a peaceful camp. A hot-headed lieutenant attacked the camp without provocation and got his backside handed to him."

"If he'd waited like he promised, his people would have been fed. I looked the fool, and it makes this negotiation all the harder." Kit snarled and walked away.

Servants the governor had brought along prepared Meriwether's dinner in the evening. He had a chef, a butler, and a couple footmen. Dan supposed he intended to invite guests and impress people with the fine dining. The chiefs and Kit didn't work out quite as he'd expected as dinner companions. He was still angry with Kit, and Sergeant Pengelly, Roque, and Dan were too far below his station to invite to dinner, so he ate alone.

The rest of the governor's escort ate at two campfires. Pengelly's men seemed to prefer to be away from the sergeant, so Peng, as they called him, Dunn, a corporal, Roque, Kit, and Dan dined together. The second night *Peregrino Rojo*, the Red Pilgrim, joined them.

Lithe and athletic, Rojo, son of Chief Vicente, was about Dan's age. He dressed in white cotton trousers, knee-high moccasins and a red shirt, looking more like a Chiricahua or a Pueblo than a Jicarilla. He had traveled widely and lived among whites, Mexicans, and Pueblo Indians, learning their languages rapidly and well.

Since he was *N'deh*, Dan could not imagine Rojo apologizing for holding Dan and Roque at gunpoint while the three of them watched the Battle of Cieneguilla from a hilltop. Rojo knew enough of *gavachos* and *Mexicanos* to expect Roque and Dan to be upset. The present slight ruffling in his poise was as close to nervous as Dan had ever seen him. Dan understood that Rojo could not let them join the Cieneguilla fight. The way he'd handled it was best for all concerned.

"There's *chili con carne* on the fire," Dan told Rojo. "Grab a bowl and some tortillas. Coffee's over there." Roque handed Rojo a bowl.

Rojo gathered his food and laced his coffee with half a cup of sugar. *Indios* like sugar and take their coffee very sweet and didn't seem to notice that others didn't add quite as much sugar.

Rojo smiled. "If a thing is good, enjoy as much as you can get."

"What will the chiefs ask for?" Kit inquired.

"Same as what was in the Lane treaties, only more food and sooner," Rojo replied. "They need food and farm implements now. This is the starving time, and the next moon is planting time. We can't survive another year like this."

Kit nodded. He knew.

"The chiefs are nervous," Rojo continued. "Blood has been shed on both sides. *Americano* soldiers pursued and killed the People White and Mexican hunters shoot at them for sport or fear. The *Americanos* have a wrath they have never experienced. They fear you will punish them further.

"Two tribes are called to council. There is a third tribe with whom you make war. They fear your governor has invited the Navajo. The Navajo are our enemies. They are especially the enemies of the Utah. It would not be good for them to come here.

"The Navajo are many," Rojo said. "We are few. The Jicarilla are concerned. Chacón has word of a large party of Navajo braves at Cañon Largo, a day's ride away. He worries. They know you often use one tribe to fight another."

Rojo, often serious, usually poker-faced but playful, was as grim as Dan had ever seen him.

Kit responded, "We come to make council, not war." Thus reassured, Rojo departed to his own camp. "Sergeant Pengelly, are your men ready to defend the governor and those who have come to council?'

"Aye, and I'll have them saddle their horses and prepare their weapons every day. The horse-holders will always be nearby and ready."

It was not a night for storytelling or music-making. Circumstances were bleak and they all knew it. In the morning, the conference began in earnest. Broken promises left much distrust on both sides.

They met the chiefs on the hill in the amphitheater while their people gathered below to hear what was said. Kit and the chiefs embraced briefly.

"*Gidi*," Chacón greeted Kit using his Jicarilla name. "I am glad you have come."

Kit replied sadly. "Chacón, we have almost exterminated the *N'deh*."

It was true, and it saddened Kit, though he thought it Chacón's fault for failing to wait for him to bring food to Cantonment Burgwin. Kit also supported Lieutenant Davidson's report of having been ambushed at Cieneguilla, although Dan doubted he believed it. Nonetheless, in Kit's mind, Chacón's action had forced Davidson to pursue and participate in killing many Jicarilla. Only Kit could find them when they didn't want to be found.

The Wildest West

The governor kicked off with a long speech about goodwill between peoples and helping each other. It seemed to Dan, though he was sure the governor never actually said it, that the phrase "our little red brothers" had been repeated over and over in the governor's discourse. The governor and the Great White Father were going to help the Indians and teach them and guide them on the path to a bright, civilized future. He would help them advance by teaching them to grow crops by scratching in the earth and to live in houses with leaky roofs and no windows. He didn't say leaky roofs and no windows, but what else could he have been referring to? He was offering them the chance to live in villages that stank and crawled with vermin and disease. The Indians had seen the Mexican towns, and with the materials on hand, cramped, adobe hovels were all that could be created.

As Dan saw it, and as he suspected the Indians saw it, they would have the chance to starve when the crops failed. The government would allow the filth to grow around their lodges while they dwelt in fetid, airless hovels. The People would live in squalor as the Mexicans did. That's not how Meriwether put it, but the chiefs knew a treaty of degradation was coming. They had seen how *gavacho* and *vecino* lived. They were giving up tepees full of light and clean air. They were giving up the chance to move away from their garbage and filth. They were giving up the chance to move in search of food when local sources failed.

Lobo of the Utahs spoke next. Dan couldn't recall much of his speech because he didn't speak Utah. Kit translated. He waxed eloquent and went long. Dan guessed politicians everywhere had a similar notion of how best to use hot air.

The Wildest West

Lobo's last few words stuck with Dan. "More than anything we want peace. We will give up much to get it. But you must not starve our people. They starve now. Running from your soldiers, they cannot hunt. Your people hunt on our lands, and there is nothing left for us. We are desperate. We need sustenance. We will farm, but you must feed us until the farms produce. We will not die like beggars. If you do not treat us fairly, as you have promised in the past, we will fight you proudly until none of us are left. I have spoken."

Chacón, Vicenti, and all the surviving chiefs of the Jicarillas spoke as was only right. They were free men, free to follow Chacón's lead or to set out on their own. Dan translated the Spanish that they spoke and was even able to help a little when there were words in *N'deh* speech whose equivalent in Spanish the chiefs did not know. Dan played his part as "translator" as best he could.

There were some memorable statements from the assembled chiefs. The governor had told them they must not steal sheep and cattle. Several chiefs agreed while suggesting that the government should not allow *gavachos* and *Mexicanos* to steal the *N'deh's* deer, antelope, elk, and buffalo. There was mention of the hunting lands already taken and of game already lost. *N'deh*, the People, starved. The government should compensate the Indios for their losses already incurred. Mexican and Anglo took the food from the mouths of their women and children. The government should provide food. They brought up the treaties Governor Lane had made with them. They expected the whites to abide by these. The government had made treaties with the Indios, which they accepted as fair, and the Jicarilla and Ute had kept to them until starvation drove them to hunt because the government did not follow through on its promises. Congress refused to consider the treaties.

Chacón spoke, saying, "I have always known freedom. I am a man. If I wish to go there, I go as I please. I have done nothing for which to be confined.

"We farmed here," he continued, "on the Rio Puerco awaiting tools and supplies. None came. The promise was broken, but we farmed until the drought made the water level fall below our irrigation ditches and the crops died. We waited for the promised food, but none came, so we hunted. Then your Long Knife soldiers told us we must go to Cantonment Burgwin to be fed. We did, but we received no food. When they tried to make us prisoners, we left. We are free people. They followed and attacked our camp. We defended ourselves and could have killed them all, but showed mercy. Now you say we have broken our promises. It is a lie! I have spoken."

Governor Meriwether stood there on the hill in the middle of the magnificent amphitheater flame, frozen in the band shell curve behind him. He stood there reduced to tiny insignificance, his words heard by all the assembled chiefs. The Lane treaties stood before him and between him and promotion. He needed an accomplishment to win a job in the east. The Lilliputian governor boomed forth his response.

He spoke, and the echoes accused him. "The Lane treaties are no more. They were imperfect. The government has kept up the white man's end as far as was legal. The agent could not provide food and supplies before Congress approved the treaties. The treaties waited approval at the house of the Great Father until Jicarilla and Utah had violated them."

Governor Meriwether proceeded to list the Indian's felonies against the treaties. They had stolen livestock intended for the Army from Anglos. They had raided along the Santa Fe Trail. They had ambushed and almost wiped out two troops of dragoons at Cieneguilla. The governor continued with the misdemeanors. The Indians had ravished Mexican women at Las Vegas and stolen Mexican livestock and children. This last was apparently the lesser offense.

"And finally," Dan whispered to Roque, "there was the naughtiness of killing Pueblo hunters, a trifling matter among friends."

Meriwether continued his oration. The Army had punished Utah and the Jicarilla. They could now be forgiven. If they wanted it, there would be peace. The assembled chiefs could make new treaties with Governor Meriwether.

Within the amphitheater, an *N'deh* voice boomed from everywhere, "We are betrayed! Navajos attack our camp!"

Then came the cry in Ute that was soon echoed in Jicarilla, "Kill the governor. Kill the betrayer!" The war cry was followed by "Slay him! Kill Meriwether! He has tricked us! We are doomed!" The words boomed and echoed in the great amphitheater. Men ran. Riders appeared.

Chacón, cool and calm, thundered. "Protect the camp!" He dropped into the war language, the abrupt, shortened form of speech known only to Jicarilla men trained in it since youth. Dan understood no more.

Pandemonium descended as a bugle blew. Pengelly called his men, and they mounted, as the sergeant looked to Kit for instruction. The governor stood confused. And useless, Dan thought.

Pengelly heard Kit cry, "Find the Navajo. Stop them!" Kit pointed south toward Pedernal and Red Wall Canyon.

Mounted warriors rushing to and fro separated Dan from Kit who called, "Dan, protect the governor. I'll meet you below the river bank." He pointed. Negligent of his own safety, Kit would provide them cover by running parallel to the pair toward the bank.

Dan grabbed the governor's arm. "Come on, Meriwether. We've got to run to safety."

The governor jerked away. "We must remain calm and restore the conference to order."

"Governor, the Navajo are attacking, and the Jicarilla think you set them up. You are in danger! Come with me."

Behind the governor, who was now separated from Dan, a mounted Jicarilla charged down on him lance poised to skewer the representative of the Great White Father. Dan yanked his revolver, knowing his shot would come too late.

Speeding to catch up with the dragoons, Roque turned and charged his horse into Governor Meriwether's would be assassin, knocking horse and warrior to the ground. He doffed his hat and continued on his way.

Meriwether was oblivious to this gallant action. He walked away from Dan back toward the hill in the amphitheater. He raised his arms above his head calling for attention and silence. There were no chiefs to pay attention or sit in silence. They had rushed off to defend the camp from the attacking Navajo.

Off to Dan's right on the ridge, a warrior drew bowstring to ear aiming at the governor. The range was too great for Dan's pistol. He ran toward Meriwether, but hope of saving him died in Dan's heart. Appearing from the far side of the ridge, a mounted warrior came too close to the bowman and bumped him, spoiling the shot. Rojo grinned at Dan who continued to run toward the governor.

Nearing him, Dan yelled, "Governor Meriwether, we have got to seek safety. We have to run for cover."

Governor Meriwether who had not understood the calls for his execution stood his ground. "Hear me, friends," he echoed and boomed to an audience long gone. Unaware that he had twice been nearly assassinated, he thundered, "Return and let us talk and be friends."

Had the Indians heard or understood, he would have been assured safety, Dan thought. Indians believe the mad have been touched by the gods and are not to be tampered with. But there was no one to translate and no audience to listen.

Dan hit the governor once in the belly and threw him over his shoulder. Thus burdened, Dan ran toward the river bank where they might find concealment and cover from stray shots. Kit, though separated from the pair, was still guarding their flank. The famous scout ran along raising his rifle to ward off any who looked as though they would interfere with Dan and the governor. Too heavily burdened Dan, the way seemed long. On his shoulder Meriwether struggled making the passage even more difficult. Indians were still rushing to find their horses. Others ran to join the fight on foot. Dan headed east. Indians crossed his path going south. A few paused to menace them with their weapons. Kit's presence held them at bay. Kit jumped down under the bank of the river as Dan ran the final yards, still struggling with the governor.

Just short of the river and safety, Governor Meriwether regained his wind and kicked away from Dan, who slid down under the bank.

"Governor," Kit called, "don't hazard yourself. They will kill you! Get down here with us."

"Coward!" Meriwether screamed at Kit. "We must go back and restore the meeting. Get out here and do your job."

"Governor!" Kit yelled, "You are in danger. Get down here." Meriwether's words stung Kit to the bone, and he was angry.

"Kit Carson, you are an insubordinate coward!" Meriwether shrieked. "You're fired, relieved of duty! I will not have an insubordinate coward working for me as Indian agent."

In the distance, a bugle sounded recall.

Roque rode up, followed by Pengelly and his dragoons.

"It was a mistake," Roque told them. "Some shepherds bringing the sheep up here to graze raised a lot of dust."

"A Jicarilla saw it," Sergeant Pengelly reported, "and panicked since the dust was near the trail from Cañon Largo."

Rojo arrived and hearing that the Navajo were not upon them said, "They were afraid they had been led into a trap. They feared attack by a large force. Navajo aren't coming, but I think the peace talks are over."

"Coward!" Governor Meriwether thundered at Kit Carson. "Your cowardice has ruined my peace talks. You're lucky I don't have the sergeant arrest you. You are fired."

"I'll show you that you can't fire me!" Kit scowled as mad as Dan or Roque had ever seen him. "My appointment is from the President, not you!"

The Wildest West

Governor Meriwether and the dragoons were the first to depart, heading south back toward Red Wall Canyon and Abiquiu where they would arrive about dusk.

Roque spat. "Let the governor spend the night among the *brujos*. They will give him the *ojo malo*."

Kit signaled Dan and Roque to follow him to Chacón's tepee. They dismounted and entered. Inside they found Rojo and his father, Vicente, Guido Mundo, and Chacón who offered to have his women bring dinner. They ate lamb stew in silence.

When they were full, Chacón said in Spanish, "Leave us now," and indicated he would talk alone to Kit.

Outside in the dark, Dan, Roque, and Rojo huddled close where they could hear the conversation inside. The tepee glowed like a Chinese lantern.

Chacón spoke first. "Gidi, my old friend, it is good that you have come."

Kit said nothing.

Chacón continued. "I did not break my promise to you. I waited. We waited until Drunken Long Knife tried to make prisoners of my people with rifle and bayonet. They would not let us wait any longer, and my people would not. So they left."

Kit understood that leadership among the Jicarilla was a matter of respect, not abstract authority. When rifles, bayonets, and prison compounds frightened his people, Chacón had little choice but to go with them.

Carson finally spoke. "I begged for you. I went to the governor and made him give up food for your people. When I returned, I found you gone and many pony-soldiers dead. I felt disgrace, for I had vouched for you, and you slew the soldiers."

Chacón looked into Kit's eyes so the frontiersman would know he spoke the truth. "The long-knives attacked our camp. They did it foolishly with a bad plan. I stopped my people killing them when they were beaten, and we were once again free men, free to go our own way. You are a great reader of signs. You have read the ground and know it is so."

For a long time, Kit said nothing. Both men were comfortable with long silences, though silence was a rare thing among whites. Finally, Kit spoke. "The leader of the pony-soldiers is my friend. He is a brave man."

Chacón nodded. He understood.

Kit spoke again, bringing an accusation against Chacon. "You say that the pony-soldiers slew 60 of your braves. This is not so. Only two died."

Chacón said nothing for a long time. "Why does this Little Father of the Whites," he referred to the governor, "bring this same treaty for the third time? We have kept our promises until we were starving. He has not kept his."

"Men far away," said Kit, "make decisions we must follow."

The chief accused, "These decisions would kill my people."

Kit tried a new tack. "You traded Lobo Blanco's land on the Llano Estacado for peace and control of your lands near Abiquiu and the Piedre Lumbre. You had no right. They were not yours to give."

Chacón remained as calm as Buddha.

"By this," the frontiersman continued, "you made a false promise."

The chief spoke slowly. "You cannot farm Lobo Blanco's *llano,* and your Great White Father says the Jicarilla must become farmers."

Outside, Roque whispered to Dan and Rojo. "The land was already promised by the Treaty of Guadalupe to the holders of land grants from the Mexican government."

"By Mexican law," Dan replied in hushed tones, "such lands must be developed within ten years and must not be occupied by Indians. The grant is invalid on both counts."

The three friends looked at each other, guessing correctly that the government would decide that the grants were valid.

Inside the tepee, Kit smiled. "It's okay. The land wasn't the governor's to give anyway. There is a land grant, and it has a Mexican owner."

Outside Roque hissed. "Spanish! We are Spanish, not Mexican!"

"I wonder if they can hear us," said Dan, and the trio fell silent.

"What will happen now?" asked Chacón.

"The Utahs killed everyone at Pueblo on the Arkansas. The Army blames your people, too. The army will hunt for you, and I will be their scout."

"The *N'deh* will hide," said the chief, "and you will not find the Jicarilla."

Kit replied. "I found you at Ojo Caliente and again at Fisher's Peak."

"This time you will not find the people."

Kit Carson nodded. "I will not find your people, so the army will not see them either."

Chacón rose, and so did Kit. The chief approached and threw his arms around the scout. "Goodbye, Gidi, my friend. There is truth and a promise between us."

Can We Still Collect the Bounty?

Dan Trelawney tightened the cinch around his mule's belly. He was a big man, broad shouldered, and dressed in a beaded elk skin coat against the spring chill, duck trousers, and knee-high moccasins, topped by a broad, flat-brimmed straw hat. He checked over his weapons: a Sharp's breech loading rifle, two Colt-Walker pistols, a Bowie knife, and a tomahawk. His wife, Sebriana, brought his saddle bags and bedroll.

"I will miss you, *mi esposo*," she said.

He smiled down at her. "I'll miss you too, Doña Loca. It's been a good winter."

She snuggled closer.

"*Muy caliente*," he said, and she giggled. "But Don Lucas Bonaparte has summoned us to the palace."

Beside them, Roque Vigil was finishing up with his fine stallion as his wife, Maria, brought him food for the trail. He dressed in fine New Mexico style, a black vest embroidered in black and closed by silver buttons over a white shirt and britches open along the outer seam and closed down to the knee with silver *conchos*. Tied at the knee and showing through the opening were tooled leather *botas*, a protection like chaps, worn above his moccasins around his lower legs. A red sash around his middle concealed a Colt pistol and a large knife.

Maria pulled her husband's head down, kissed him passionately, and reaching up placed a broad-brimmed, flat-topped black felt hat on his head.

Roque mounted and turned to Dan. "Come, we must ride. Don Lucien Bonaparte Maxwell has summoned us to Cimarron."

Dan mounted and replied, "I don't like it, being summoned. I'm not his serf."

"Ah," said Roque, "like it or not, he is the *patron y alcalde.*"

"Yes, and lord of all he surveys."

Maxwell did indeed own most of northeastern New Mexico from Las Vegas into Colorado and east to Texas. He was the biggest landowner in the country.

"He is also our *amigo,*" said Roque.

"Yes, he's our friend, and if it weren't for friendship, I'd be home in bed with Sebriana."

Roque laughed. "You may yet die happy with *mi prima* as did many of her former husbands."

"Yes," said Dan smiling, "but they were old and weak."

They arrived in Cimarron just as the setting sun was coloring the sky in shades of red and violet over the Sangre de Cristo Mountains. In the west, the peaks hovered over the little town, and the Llano Estacado stretched away east farther than the eye could see.

They tied up at the St. James Hotel.

"It's big," said Roque, "bigger than *El Palacio* in Santa Fe and two stories high!"

Dan nodded. "And fancy too. The cook and owner was chef to President Lincoln, and this place is almost as fancy as the White House. Think we'll find Don Lucas here?"

They entered a lobby paneled in dark wood and lit by a crystal chandelier and turned into the saloon and restaurant. Lucien Maxwell stood at the bar drinking with two men. One they both knew, bearded Clay Allison, a rancher. Clay was well thought of, but he could be vicious when drunk. The other was a stranger in clothing almost as fancy as Roque's but dark with a holstered pistol tied down low. His face was pocked, his eyes deep set and darting, his mouth grim and ugly.

"What do you think, Roque?" asked Dan indicating the stranger. "Gambler? Regulator?"

"Something worse, I think."

Maxwell saw their approach in the lavish mirror behind the bar and turned to greet them, smiling broadly through a mustache worthy of a monarch. The broad-shouldered, former mountain man was clothed in a black suit and black boots that came to his knee. He talked around a cigar anchored at the corner of his mouth.

"Roque, Dan, here you are at last!" Gripping hand and forearm, he greeted his guests in turn and without preamble explained the situation. "You know Zanna, who danced here in the saloon."

"*Si*," said Roque. "How she could twirl, her skirts lifting high, and such legs . . ."

"She's a good girl," said Dan. "Dances well but doesn't flirt with the customers."

"She dances no more," said Maxwell with dire finality. "She's been brutally murdered, sliced from neck to navel, scalped as well, and worse."

As shock set in, Maxwell continued. "She was popular. Folks collected $100 as bounty for her killer, dead or alive. As hideous as the crime was, they don't think he'll let himself be taken alive. I put up another $400 if they'd let me choose the hunters. Kit Carson is still in the Army, a general now, so you two are the best I know that are available."

Danny nodded. "Sounds like you know who done it."

"Gen Bäcker was paying her court. French, from St. Louis, small man with wavy hair, a carpenter. He was seen walking with her about an hour before her body was found. He seemed a nice enough sort, teaching carpentry skills to the Mexicans, changing the way they build their houses, adding gringo blocks, doors, windows, and porches. But they say he had a vicious, unpredictable temper, a wild temper. Zanna must have rejected his suit. She had other suitors. He hasn't been seen since."

From behind Maxwell, Clay Allison broke in. "Mr. Maxwell, I told you I can do the job. I liked her too and want to see that monster dead!"

A disturbance at the end of the bar distracted them. A slap resounded through the room. "Let me go!" a female yelped. "You can't touch me there."

"Come here, whore," the dark stranger demanded.

"I am not a whore!" she said in words of ice.

The stranger grabbed her and pulled her to him. "Oh, yes you are."

"Jack," pleaded Allison, "let her go!" His foot wounded in a recent gunfight, he limped over to separate the girl from his dark friend.

"This whore's gonna make nice with me!"

Dan stepped in. "That's enough of that," he said closing in on Jack, getting within range of knife or fist.

Unexpectedly, the stranger's elbow flashed up and into Dan's face, stunning Dan, and knocking him off balance.

Recovering, Dan gripped the stranger's left wrist and wrenched it away from the girl. The lights went out, the stars came out early, and the world closed in on Dan.

Climbing up from a deep pit, his jaw afire with pain, his head throbbing, Dan opened his eyes in an unfamiliar room. "Where am I?"

Roque looked into his face grinning. "He awakes."

"Must be hell," mumbled Dan.

"To be precise," said Lucien Maxwell offering Dan a whiskey, "you are in my office."

"Hell it is," said Dan. "What happened?"

"Jack had a very big knife, I think," replied Roque, "with a knuckle guard like a saber. He hit you with the guard between jaw and ear, and you hit the floor. You got a lump that bleeds a little."

Maxwell nodded. "I've never seen anyone move so fast. Like a snake striking. You've been out for a while. We dragged you over here to my house."

Dan noticed Roque had changed into buckskins. "Did you agree to Mr. Maxwell's terms while I was asleep?"

"*Si.*" Roque nodded.

"Five hundred dollars to bring Gen Bäcker in dead or alive, is that right? We don't usually do this sort of job." Dan looked pointedly at Roque. "Hunting your fellow man is too much like pursuing runaway slaves."

"This one is a monster, not a man, and I much prefer you bring him in alive. That's why I wanted you two. He deserves a trial and a hanging."

"Alive then. Which way did he go?" asked Dan. "How will we know him?"

"It seems he took her scalp and *rebozo* as souvenirs. Probably still has them. He was seen earlier today in Elizabethtown," said Maxwell. "You need to leave right after supper. I can't hold the other would-be bounty hunters back much longer. They will be a danger to you."

Their horses moved quietly through the dark along the trail up into the Sangre de Cristo beside the wild Cimarron River.

"You could have turned him down, amigo."

From the dark, Dan replied. "You'd already accepted. I figured you had a reason."

"Her murder was so terrible, and she was so beautiful and kind. We can't let a man like this escape to kill again."

Snow stood on the high country hills as they approached Elizabethtown in the afternoon. The newly founded mining camp was a jumble of hastily erected shacks and tents. Dan and Roque made their way up the muddy street to a building marked General Store and Post Office.

As they tied their horses, Dan said, "As good a place to start as any."

They entered the dark interior amidst the smells of piñon smoke, spices, and turpentine. A pot belly stove added feeble warmth. A heavyset man in apron and a shirt with gartered sleeves smiled and called out, "How may I help you?"

Keeping his reply casual, Dan said, "We're looking for a man called Gen Bäcker, short man, wavy hair. Some think him handsome. You might notice a slight accent."

A boy Dan hadn't noticed scuttled out the back of the store.

"Why?" The room got suddenly colder.

"He killed a beautiful girl," said Roque.

"Don't believe it," said the storekeeper. "Anyway, ain't seen nobody like that. Don't care for bounty hunters neither, so git out!"

As they collected their horses, a woman in gingham and a bonnet approached, accompanied by a boy of about twelve years. Dan noticed a greenish stain on her cheek and eye, an old bruise, and fresh ones on what he could see of her wrists and forearms. The boy walked and moved stiffly.

His eye was black, his nose bent, and his lips puffed and bleeding slightly.

"You the ones lookin' for Gen?" she asked without preamble.

"Si," said Roque. "Have you seen him?"

"You leave him be! He's a good man!"

"He killed a woman," said Dan.

"He saved my son!" the woman replied. "His stepdad was beating him something awful until Gen stepped in."

"What happened?" Dan asked.

"Gave the boy a penny for a peppermint. His stepdad saw and 'cused him of stealin' it. Told him no. Said the boy was wastin' his money and commenced to beatin' him."

Roque looked puzzled. "Why don't you leave him?"

The woman looked startled. "He's my husband! He's okay when he's not drinkin'."

Dan asked, "So how did Bäcker get involved?"

"The boy was on the ground, and his paw was kickin' him. Gen told him to stop. My husband swinged on him. Gen hit him, and my old man went down. Boy and me, we run. Be okay maybe when he stops drinkin'." She shuddered, and Dan thought she crossed her fingers. "Don't go after Gen, please. He's a good man. He didn't mean to, but my old man woulda kilt the boy if Gen hadn't stopped him. An' Gen's so small."

The boy said, "Come on, Ma," and pulled her away down the street.

"He's been here," said Dan.

"Bet he left in a hurry," replied Roque.

"Still think he's a monster?"

"Maybe he just likes to hurt people," said Roque, a hint of uncertainly in his voice.

They continued up the muddy way to a large framed tent with a wooden false-front and a sign reading Delmonico's.

"Classiest saloon in town," said Dan.

They entered and stood at the rough planks between barrels that passed for a bar. Even at this early hour, the place was crowded and stank of unwashed bodies, tobacco smoke, alcohol, and drunks who'd been sick.

"What'll ya have?"

Dan turned to the bartender and saw a man in filthy apron with puffy, bloodshot eyes, and a chin in need of a shave.

"What have you got?"

"Whiskey and cactus juice," the bartender replied.

"Whiskey," said Dan. Tasting his drink, Dan turned to Roque. "Grain alcohol, colored with tobacco spit, flavored with chili, molasses, and just a hint of rattlesnake head."

Roque smiled grimly. "What did you expect?"

"We'll have to wait for a break in the crowd to get the bartender's attention."

Dan turned to survey the crowd made of owl-eyed miners, prospectors, investors, and speculators in suits, slovenly girls, gamblers in fancy clothes, and filthy men who moil in muddy streams for gold.

"*Bendejos*," spat Roque. "They are stealing Mr. Maxwell's land and gold."

"His land grant comes this far?"

"*Si*," said Roque, "to the spine of the *sierra* Sangre de Cristo."

"Look! Over there in the corner," Dan whispered. The crowd reshuffled itself blocking his view for a moment.

"What?"

Dan looked again. "I was sure I saw Clay Allison, but I don't see him now."

A huge man parted the crowd as he approached them. A head taller than Dan, he wore dirty work clothes and had heavily muscled shoulders. Even in this environment, Dan smelled the booze on him before he arrived, but what Dan noticed first was a bloody, busted mouth and missing teeth.

"Oo da ones look 'or Acker? Sum'its hi' me in da mouf mid a hamma! I kill him. Go mid oo!"

Roque looked at Dan as the stranger pushed into the bar between them. "*Que paso*? What'd he say?"

Dan translated. "Apparently, he's met Gen Bäcker who hit him in the mouth with a hammer. He wants to go with us and kill the little carpenter."

Roque's eyes got big. "This is the one Gen saved the boy from? He's got courage that one!"

The big man growled.

"And a hammer," replied Dan. "Mister, you belong home in bed until you heal."

The big man's head swiveled to glare at Dan.

"I goes mid oo!"

Dan nodded. "He's insisting on going with us."

"No!" hissed Roque. "I don't like *borrachons* who beat womens and *chicos*." Roque turned his back on the big drunk.

The big man pulled a knife from his belt and moved to plunge it into Roque's back. Dan struck the man's wrist with his tomahawk, stunning the hand that held the knife but not breaking the bone as he'd hoped. The man turned on Dan as the crowd cleared space for them. Dan tossed the tomahawk to Roque.

"Hold that for me."

The Wildest West

The man swung, and Dan ducked under the huge fist, in return jabbing his own left with all his might into the monster's stomach. It was like hitting a tree. Dan's arm went numb as he danced away from the man. Blocking blows seemed out of the question to Dan who found it surprisingly easy to duck and dodge the huge fists.

"Stop playing with him, Dan! If he connects a punch, you're dead."

"I don't want to knock him down!" yelled Dan. "If he falls on me, I'm dead."

To Dan, it seemed unfair to hit him in that badly injured mouth or to strike him with an object, but blows to the man's body had no apparent effect, hurting Dan more than they did the drunk.

"Schtop 'ancin' roun'! Hol' schtil so I can hid oo."

Dan danced out of the way of a blow that narrowly missed its mark.

"Schtop!" The big man grabbed a chair and threw it at Dan, striking him a glancing blow.

Dan closed and swirled behind the man, kicking him in the back of the knee. The man partly collapsed on that side but did not fall. It was enough. The big man had used a weapon, so would Dan. He drew his Bowie and with the man's head now low enough, Dan smacked him smartly behind the ear with the hilt. The big man crumpled and lay in a heap on the floor. He snored loudly and peacefully.

The crowd cheered as a few lucky souls collected their bets at 10 to 1.

"We'd better leave," said Roque smiling.

They found dinner, stabling for their stock, and a room for the night. Before sunup, a woman's scream a woman's scream awakened them. Grabbing their gear, they rushed into the street and ran toward the gathering crowd. At its center, lay one of the slovenly girls from the saloon, or so Dan thought. It was hard to tell. She was cruelly gutted and part of her face was gone.

"The fiend," proclaimed a voice in the crowd. "He's scalped her and taken her *rebozo*. Musta been an Injun!"

"*Bendejo!*" yelled Roque. "He did not run. He was in the *pueblo* with us all night. We've got to stop him, Dan!"

Someone in the crowd called out, "I saw someone running his horse on the Mora Road right after I heard the scream."

"*Vamanos!*" yelled Roque, and he and Dan ran to get their stock.

The trail led south toward through the high valley between the mountain peaks.

"How we gonna follow this trail, *amigo*?" asked Roque. "Lotta peoples rode this way."

"It ain't easy. Wish we had Peregrino Rojo with us."

"*Si*. That Apache could track a mouse up a rock wall."

"A horse went through here at a gallop," said Dan. "The shoes are very long and narrow. If we're lucky, where the trail divides between Mora and Santa Fe, we'll have been the first to pass, and we'll see which way he went."

"*Bueno*," replied Roque.

They were in luck. The rider ahead of them had gone west toward the High Road between Santa Fe and Taos.

Below the peaks, Peñasco wasn't much of a town—a chapel, rarely visited by a priest, a shuttered building of uncertain purpose, and a few houses sharing common walls around a tiny plaza. More houses were strung out along the *acecia madre*, the mother ditch. The people who lived Peñasco formed more of an irrigation cooperative more than a town. Mountain pine and the aroma of onions and chilis cooking scented the air.

Pointing to the shuttered building, Roque shivered. "*Morada*, meeting place of the brotherhood of *Penitentes*."

"Here? In a remote village?"

"They are strong in the mountains," replied Roque.

A woman's scream disturbed the sleepy village.

"He's here!" proclaimed Roque.

"Ride!" yelled Dan, spurring his mule toward the disturbance.

A middle-aged couple clad in the ragged clothing of the poor held each other and wept. A skinny girl not yet in her teens wailed and pleaded as a heavy set man with a large, drooping mustache tried to drag her away. Four others in clothing not much better than that of the weeping couple supported him. Two of the men carried yucca whips. Another began playing on a *pito,* a tiny flute.

"*Que paso?*" demanded Roque as he rode up. "What's going on here?"

"Please help us, *señor*," said the sobbing man. "*El Gordo* would take my daughter for his wife. She is very young and does not wish to go. He says I owe him money, but he has been paid."

"I do not accept this payment," said *El Gordo*, Fatso, "It came from *Gringo Guero*."

Roque turned to Dan. "The whips, the *pito*, they let us know these are *Penitentes* of the *Hermandad*, the brotherhood. They will have others backing them up."

"The *Hermandad* is a religious order," insisted Dan. Turning to the five brothers, he said, "Have you no morals to take one so young against her will after you have been paid? Has your *morada* no shame that you represent it in such a way?"

"They have no shame!" said the ragged man hugging his wife and spitting. "They are banditos from Truchas!

41

Their *morada* does not care what they do to people outside their *pueblo*."

Addressing *Gordo*, Roque said, "Is it true you have been paid?"

"Only by the *Gringo Guero*, the blonde American," sneered *Gordo*. "It does not count."

"Let the girl go," said Dan in a voice that did not allow argument.

Startled, *Gordo* let go of the girl who crawled to hug her mother's leg. Two of his friends drew long knives. Unhesitating, Dan spurred his mule into them, kicking one in the belly as he did so and striking the other with the barrel of his pistol. Both crumpled. Dan turned his mule to see Roque with his pistol drawn.

"You had better never come back here again," Roque said. "Never. No more Peñasco for you. *Quien sabe*? You understand? I'll come back. If I hear you been here, I'll find you and kill you."

A wet spot appeared in *Gordo's* trousers.

"Now run along," said Dan, "or I'll start killing you right now!"

When they'd gone, the little family dried its tears as more children and an old man appeared from their *casa*. The old man hobbled, clearly suffering from injuries.

"*Viejo*," said Roque addressing the old man. "Are you hurt?"

"*Si*. But it is no matter. You have helped us. *Gracias*."

"What can we do for you to repay your kindness?" asked the younger man. "My wife will make you dinner."

"Thank you," said Roque.

After the woman and her daughter had bustled away to fix dinner, Dan explained their mission to men. "Can you help us? We seek a very bad man, a small man with wavy blonde hair, a carpenter. We followed his tracks here. He has murdered two women."

"We have not seen him!" snapped the woman from where she worked.

"He went south to Truchas, I think," said the younger man.

Waiting for dinner, as they attended to their mounts, Roque asked Dan, "Do you think he went south?"

"Only three ways to go from here," replied Dan, "south to Truchas, north to Taos, or west to the Rio Grande. I expect he didn't head for Truchas."

After a dinner of enchiladas, beans, and roasted lamb, the four men sat back to smoke and talk. The three Mexicans lit *cigaritos* while Dan lit the little pipe he called his nose warmer.

"He helped us you know," said the younger man whose daughter Dan and Roque had saved. "*Señor Guero* stood up to the banditos when they came before, and he gave them money to pay my debt. He said I could pay him when I see him again. He is a good man."

"These men have helped us as well," said the old man.

Dan nodded. "It seems our villain is a good man. Señor Maxwell wants him brought in alive."

Roque picked up the thread. "There are others hunting him. We have seen them on the trail. If they find him first, they will kill *Señor Guero*, I think."

"This is bad news," said the old man. "The little carpenter was very good to us. A bearded man and his friend, *El Diablo Prieto*, the dark devil, came this way looking for the little man. The dark one beat me badly until my son pleaded with him and finally told him the small carpenter had gone to Taos. The evil ones rode out hours before you got here."

"Gracias," said Dan. "We will see that the carpenter gets a fair trial before an honest judge. More than that I cannot promise."

"This is confusing," said Roque. "How can one who commits such evil deeds be so kind to others? He doesn't act like a man on the run."

"Allison and Jack are ahead of us. We need to ride hard for Taos."

Roque and Dan descended along mountain streams through pine forest until the sunbaked adobe plaza of Taos stood above them on a small rise.

Dan spotted one of the distinctive hoof prints they had followed. "Looks like he's headed for the plaza. Can't be far ahead, or the print would have been wiped out."

"*Si*. I'll go 'round that way, and you come in from this side."

Dan dismounted and tied up his mule.

As Dan rounded the corner into the plaza, people ran past him seeking cover.

Gen Bäcker faced Clay Allison. "Bäcker, you devil, go for your gun. You've got a chance; otherwise, I shoot you where you stand."

The little man with the wavy hair held saddle bags in his left hand. He held something, maybe a gun, on the side away from Dan.

Roque stepped into the plaza across the way, his gun holstered. "That's enough, *Señor* Allison. We take him in alive."

Allison spun around, drawing as he did. Roque drew, but Dan could tell Roque's hand had been too slow. Bäcker's thrown hammer hit the gunman in the side of the head. Allison collapsed on his face. Roque stood, startled to be alive.

His back to Dan, Allison's dark friend, Jack, stepped out, his gun raised to have a clear shot at Bäcker. It was a long shot for a pistol, so he took careful aim. Dan charged and knocked Jack to the ground. As they arose facing off, Dan kicked Jack's gun away.

Jack straightened from a fighting crouch. "That's okay then. We can share the bounty." Approaching Dan, he smiled crookedly.

With blinding speed, Jack drew his small sword and swung at Dan.

Ducking under the sword, Dan struck him a hard blow to the stomach. "You don't get away with that twice," he said drawing his tomahawk.

Jack slashed at Dan's belly. Bringing his own weapon down, Dan caught the blade with his tomahawk, wrenched it from Jack's grip, and threw both weapons aside. They circled, each striking out time and again. Dan dodged most of the blows, and Jack was tiring. A hard blow to the jaw brought him to one knee. He arose, grabbing a handful of dust and tossing it into Dan's face. Momentarily blinded, Dan jumped back out of Jack's range.

This was the opening Jack had hoped for. He dove for his pistol. Grasping it, he cocked the hammer, rolled, and aimed at Dan.

Dan's .44 shot flame as a small hole appeared in Jack's forehead. Jack fired, but the movement was only the last twitch of his dead fingers.

As Dan picked up his tomahawk, Roque picked up Allison's gun and Bäcker's hammer, keeping his pistol trained on the small man the whole time.

"What you got there, amigo?" Roque said to Bäcker.

"Proof! It's Jack's saddlebags. Look what's in it."

Approaching Bäcker, Dan said, "Give it here." He took the leather bags and opened them. "Ugh!" Dan dumped the contents. On the ground law two bloody scalps wrapped in *rebozos*.

"I recognize Zanna's scarf," said Roque.

Dan growled deep in his throat. "You've got these things. They must be yours."

"No, look," pled Bäcker. "My horse is there. The saddle bags are still behind the saddle." Pointing to Roque, he went on, "Isn't it enough I saved his life?"

"Not to seem ungrateful, *señor*, but that hammer saved your life as well."

"Where'd you get these?" asked Dan.

"That horse, there," said the small man. "The one the man you killed rode in on."

"Blood leaked out of the bag," said Dan walking over to the indicated horse. "There's dried blood on the flank as well."

Clay Allison, coming to, felt for his gun but didn't find it. Rising he said, "Hey, I saw him first. That's my bounty."

"You were going to kill him," said Dan. "We were told to bring him in for trial."

"I never killed a man who didn't need it! This one needs it."

"How do I know that's your horse?" Dan asked Bäcker.

"My tools are in a bag rolled up on the horse's flank."

That's where Dan found them. Picking up Jack's knife, a shortened saber, Dan found it caked with blood.

Looking at the knife, Roque remembered something. "There was a Colorado Volunteer at Sand Creek who was accused of doing such awful things to Cheyenne women that even that vile crew wanted no part of him. They broke his saber in two and exiled him."

There were ample witnesses to attest to Dan having killed in self-defense. A meal and a place to bed for the night seemed in order.

Allison joined them at dinner. "He's my prisoner. I'm staying with him. Roque, give me my gun back."

In the morning, they tied Bäcker's hands to the pommel of his saddle and tied Jack across his horse's back. It would be a two-day ride back to Cimarron.

Joining them Allison insisted, "He's my prisoner!"

Dan turned on him. "One more time, Allison, and I will shoot you even though Roque still has your pistol."

At Maxwell's house, Dan cut the bindings and let Jack's body fall to the ground. It was already starting to ripen. They let it lie, helped Gen down, his hands still bound, and walked toward Maxwell's door.

Maxwell emerged, looked over the four men, and said, "Release Bäcker at once!"

"What?" asked Roque. "You gonna shoot him?"

"Hold on, Mr. Maxwell!" Dan protested. "We went through a lot of trouble to get him here alive."

"He's my bounty," said Allison.

"Hello, Mr. Maxwell," said Bäcker. "I found Zanna's scalp and *rebozo* in Jack's saddle bags. Dan killed him."

"This here's my bounty," said Allison again pointing to Bäcker.

"He's nobody's bounty," said Maxwell. "Gen Bäcker came to me right after Zanna was killed and offered to serve as bait in a trap for a monster."

Roque sighed. "Sounds like we'll be sharing the bounty with Bäcker."

Marshal of Arizona

The sunset blazed red and orange over the Tumacacori Mountains west of Tubac. Just enough light was left in the day to draw a bead on a large target. From the town's lone cantina, two men emerged onto a dusty street. The day had been hot, and men early sought the dark interior of the cool adobe pub. Now tempers flared hot as well.

Men thought of the larger man, dressed in worn, black, woolen clothing, jacket, and vest, as a "fast gun" or at least a man fast enough to use his gun. That he was a belligerent drunk and still alive seemed to indicate that his gun hand was fast. His gun, a .36 caliber percussion cap revolver, short barreled and light for quick handling, was tucked in the belt that held up his trousers. "Poker Jack" had wandered in from California and was reputed to head the list of a committee of vigilance. He undertook no known occupation but always seemed to have money.

His opponent, the stranger, dressed in fringed buckskin wore what was then a rarity, a belt supporting two holsters and a Bowie knife. The holsters, black, military issue, rode high and leaned forward. The flaps had been cut away and replaced with leather thongs tied in loops that slipped over the hammers to keep the guns from sliding free. He slipped both loops off the hammers of his pistols, so that he could draw them swiftly. The holsters showed the outline of Colt Dragoon .44s. The only fast way to pull the guns was a cross-draw, right hand to left pistol.

"I don't really want to kill you," said the man in buckskin, "and I don't think I've done anything to insult you, but if I have, I apologize."

The Wildest West

In the cantina, the stranger had jovially claimed to be able to snuff a candle flame at 30 paces with a shot from his pistol. It was a foolish thing to say, but, as with the wearing of his pistols, he intended to let people think he was dangerous so that none in this perilous country would think him an easy mark. Two towns, Tubac and Tucson, the Sonoita Creek farming area and Fort Buchanan, were beginning to be called Arizona. The region was 300 miles from the nearest court when it was in session once a year and just as far from the nearest town of Mesilla. Arizona was 600 miles from Santa Fe where the judge made his home. Tucson was a haven for men who had little use for law. Tubac was headquarters for the Sonoran Mining and Exploration Company, owner of the Santa Rita Mines and others.

Belligerent, if not intoxicated, Poker Jack had growled, "Don't mock me, boy!" His pretensions as a gunfighter and marksman were well known.

"I'm not mocking you," replied the stranger civilly enough.

"You callin' me a liar!" blurted Poker Jack. It wasn't a question.

"I've no wish to fight," said the stranger, backing away toward the door.

Out in the street, people dodged into doorways, seeking cover from bullets that soon would fly. They guessed the stranger would die, for such was Poker Jack's reputation, but they feared one or the other's shots might go wide.

"But I want to kill you," said the man in black. "It is an affair of honor!" Poker Jack edged around slowly, ensuring that the setting sun was behind him.

The Wildest West

When he saw the stranger squint, Poker Jack drew his weapon, or tried to draw, but it hung up on his vest. He'd cocked as he drew, and now his hand, pulling upward against the impeded pistol, jerked forcefully against the trigger. There was an explosion, a pistol firing, and Poker Jack fell screaming onto the dusty street. There was a hole where the inseams of his pant legs joined.

The stranger stood, both pistols in his hands, his feet braced, and ready for action. The word went up and down the street that his draw was lightning, so fast that no one had actually seen him pull his guns.

"The stranger shot the wick off Jack's candle," someone yelled, and the stories began as each claimed more knowledge than the next about what had occurred and the stranger's prowess with a gun.

Bastyan Clegg, the stranger, glanced about in the gathering dark. "Get that man to a doctor. Where are his friends?"

"There's no doctor here," someone replied. "And he hasn't any friends here."

"Let's take him to Ehrenberg," suggested another, and with that, several of the people now emerging from doorways and alleys grasped Poker Jack under the arms and began to drag him down the street as he screamed and bled.

Clegg entered the cantina, ordered a drink, and then stood with his back to the wall watching the door. A well-dressed man of medium height and build entered. His energy and self-confidence reflected in the way he scanned the room, unafraid to meet any gaze, willing to look any man in the eye. Locking onto Bastyan, he strode across the room and stood next to him at the plank between two barrels that passed for a bar.

"Buy you a drink?" he asked. "I'm Charles Poston." The new arrival extended his hand.

"Sure," the stranger replied taking the soft, slightly greasy hand. "Bastyan Clegg." Soft, he thought. This is a politician and a schemer. Bastyan would count his fingers later.

"You shoot Poker Jack?" Poston asked.

"Nope," Clegg replied without explanation.

"They say you did!" insisted Poston.

"That's what they say," replied Clegg.

"I need a man with your kind of reputation," Poston said, "a man who's fast with a gun and not afraid to use it, who wears his guns where folks can see how fast he can get them out."

"Why?" asked Clegg. "I'm no mercenary for hire."

"I should explain," said Poston. "I've been appointed *alcalde* here. That's a New Mexico term for something like a justice of the peace, but it's a lot more — mayor and captain of militia. I want to see Arizona made into a territory with some government. Right now, we're part of Doña Ana County, and the county seat is over in Mesilla on the Rio Grande. There's no law or court here, and while I'm a kind of judge, I'm no sheriff."

"What's in it for you?" Bastyan asked rudely.

"Fair enough," Poston replied. "I own and am developing several mines in the Santa Rita and Cerro Colorado Mountains. Without government and without law and order, I can't find investors willing to risk their money. Thieves and murderers come up from Mexico and troublemakers down from Tucson, which is no more than a nest of men on the run. And Apaches raid right up to the corrals at the edge of town." Seeing alarm in Clegg's face,

51

he quickly added, "But Captain Richard Ewell of the 1st Regiment of Dragoons is attending to that problem."

"I'm thinking," Bastyan Clegg said, "that when Poker Jack is fixed up, he's coming after me and might well go for my back. I think I might not want to be here for that."

A fortyish man in a bloody apron showing the prints of hands recently wiped of gore entered the cantina, and seeing Poston, he approached the pair at the bar.

"Will he live?" Charles Poston asked the newcomer.

"I ist ze mining engineer, Charles, not ze docktor!" the man said.

Poston introduced his chief engineer. "What do you think, Ehrenberg?" asked Poston.

"I think ze news is badt und gut," Ehrenberg replied. "Ze badt news ist dat I think he hast nicked the artery deep in his leg, und I cannot schtop the bleeding zo he vill die. Ze gut news ist dat if ve had a Hebrew zemetery, he could be buried in it." Ehrenberg smiled at his presumed humor.

"So you can shoot the flame off a candle at 30 paces!" exclaimed Poston. Not stopping to hear Clegg's protest, Poston went on. "With a reputation like that, no one will want to tamper with our new marshal. You're perfect for the job!"

"I have to think about it," said Clegg warming to the idea. He needed a job. "What's the pay? And what will my authority be? Where's the jail?"

"Why there is no jail," replied Poston. "You'll have to tie lawbreakers to a tree. But your real job and only authority lies in intimidation. I want you to intimidate rough characters into leaving Tubac alone and going to Tucson to play. We've no justice court and no prison. You just scare them off. It's all image, my good man. Come, we'll talk about it over dinner."

The Wildest West

En route to Poston's casa, they encountered Missouri Anne hurrying home in the dark. Light from a doorway showed her to be quite handsome in all respects. Her name, Poston told Bastyan later, was a testament to the pilgrimage of her father, an itinerant preacher. Her siblings bore similar testaments—Mississippi Jim, Texas Tim, and Arkansas Sally. Introduced to Bastyan, Missouri Anne looked up into his eyes in a way that melted his heart and told him he was her hero. Having encountered only Mexican women in the last several years of his travels, Bastyan Clegg was intrigued enough by Miss Missouri Anne to stay in Tubac a spell.

With no badge or official authority, Justice of the Peace Charles Poston made Bastyan Clegg marshal and called a town meeting confirmed the appointment by unanimous consent. The town allowed a salary of $50 per month in U.S. dollars, which would be paid by voluntary subscription from merchants and mining companies. There being no official government apart from that in distant Mesilla, there was no authority to collect taxes. The people of standing in the town felt better knowing they finally had law and order.

"Marshal Clegg, come here, we need your help!" cried the owner of the cantina the next evening.

Entering, Bastyan came face to face with a Goliath of the desert. He towered at least a head over Clegg and was a yard wide across his broad, powerful shoulders. The big man stank of raw alcohol laced with tobacco for color and other secret ingredients, rattlesnake whiskey, as well as of sweat and animal butchering. The man looked at Clegg and couldn't quite focus his eyes. Bastyan ignored him and headed for the bar.

"I'm gonna tear this place apart if that barkeep don't fetch me a drink right now!" yelled the big man. He raised a chair over his head and smashed it through a table. Both objects were local rarities in Tubac, being there was no sawmill for hundreds of miles. "Then I'm gonna tear this town apart. Where's your new law dog? I'll start with him."

Then, for no particular reason, he turned and punched the man closest to him, knocking the man to the ground as he stood laughing. The big man's distraction with the man he'd just clobbered gave Bastyan his opening. Approaching swiftly from the man's left flank, he hooked a foot behind the man's ankle and hit him a hard left upper cut to the jaw. The big man tumbled to the ground as Bastyan drew his left pistol with his right hand and stepped over the giant. There was no need. The blow to his jaw and the fall to the floor had caused the drunk to lose focus and close his eyes. As so often happens with a drunk already unstable on his feet, he fell and passed out.

"Get me some rope and a horse," said Clegg.

"You're not going to hang him are you?" queried a tremulous voice.

Securely tying the man, Bastyan used the horse to drag him to a cottonwood tree that grew along the wash on the south side of town and secured the big man to it.

"Jail tree," Bastyan said turning to the barkeep who had come with him. "We'll leave him there overnight, and in the morning he won't know who or what hit him."

And so life went for several weeks. Subduing and disarming drunks proved easy for a man who tried to approach unseen. Drunks had been a big part of the trouble in town. Men found that there were only three options for entertainment. Drinking and gambling led to arguments, and the other option to jealousy, though men with their pants down around their knees were almost as easy to subdue as drunks were. No one sober wanted to face the man with the fast gun. Those reverse holsters were intimidating, especially when everyone else carried their pistols tucked into their belt or a pocket. There was no way anyone could beat his draw by pulling a pistol out of the folds of their clothing. Besides, the marshal could snuff a candle at 30 paces.

"Apache!" came the cry one evening. "They're stealing Poston's stock."

Bastyan Clegg grabbed up his plains rifle, powder horn, possibles bag in which he kept bullets, patches, and percussion caps. Although he was fleet, by the time he arrived at the corral, the Apaches were already departing with Poston's horses. Clegg raised his rifle and without much hope of hitting anything fired off a shot. It nicked his target's ear. Lucky shot. The Apache turned his horse about and couching his lance charged Clegg.

Caught in the open, Clegg saw nowhere to hide or run. He thought himself a dead man. Calmly, because the dead do not hurry, Clegg reloaded, pouring powder, driving home a ball without patch, and mounting a percussion cap. He raised his weapon. With the Apache's lance tip almost at his muzzle, Clegg fired and jumped to the side. The Apache fell, a black hole oozing between his eyes. Bastyan picked himself up and ran for cover in case any Apache might try for vengeance. None did.

Finding her man, Missouri Anne wound her arms around one of his and looked longingly up into his eyes. They stayed that way in the twilight until the "militia" had been raised. The few intervening moments passed slowly for Bastyan. The girl was warm, and where her body pressed against his arm, he could feel her fluttering heartbeat. The girl squeezed tight, setting the hook. Bastyan had drifted through the southwest deserts searching, though he couldn't define that for which he searched—home, purpose, a job, wealth. He hadn't given it much thought, thinking he'd recognize it when he found it. Now, liking this new sensation, he thought Missouri Anne might be the undefined "it."

"If we go after them now," said Poston, "they may turn the stock loose to delay the pursuit."

"You picked us a good marshal," said one of the militiamen. "Can't miss and just as cool as you please under fire."

Bastyan recovered some of Poston's stock that evening without further incident. The Apache had melted into the desert, and Bastyan Clegg's reputation grew along with his fondness for Missouri Anne.

The summer monsoon blew in, bringing humidity and a daily hour of fearsome thundershowers during which the heavens flashed with lightning, and black rumbling clouds displayed their displeasure with the presumptions of humankind. Gripping his hat against the wind, Bastyan tilted the brim to release a torrent of water and then looked around the lantern-lit room. A muscular man was beating a Mexican girl; blood was already oozing from her nose and lips. No one paid the pair any mind.

"You filthy whore!" the man yelled. "You've taken my poke! Give it back!" He slapped her so hard Bastyan was sure the blow would take off her head.

"No! No! Señor. Please," Juanita whimpered. "I took nothing!" Smack! The man struck her again.

Bastyan looked askance at the bartender who said, "You know Joe. He's our blacksmith. Lives at the old ruined mission Tumacacori. He's a pretty good guy. We need him. If he says she took something, she probably did."

"No man should hit a woman like that," admonished Clegg.

"She's new," countered the bartender. "Just down from Tucson. Probably picked up evil ways. Besides, Joe's everybody's friend."

Unnoticed by Joe, Bastyan stepped in behind him and assuming he was drunk, kicked Joe's feet out from under him, following through with a smashing blow to the chin. Joe went down, but with surprising speed and agility was back on his feet, crouched and stable. His first counterpunch—a near miss—bounced off Bastyan's shoulder and impacted the back of his head, making his ears ring. The marshal knew he was in trouble with a very tough opponent. He wasn't here for the pleasure of a fight but to enforce order. Avoiding fierce blows that, though crudely aimed, came in rapid succession, Bastyan feinted with his left as he drew his right-side pistol right-handed. Finding his moment, Clegg smashed Joe in the side of the head with his heavy Colt. The man collapsed.

Released by her assailant, Juanita darted out the door never again to be seen in Tubac. Her kind was all too readily replaceable.

"That hardly seemed fair," declared the bartender.

"Wasn't fair," replied Bastyan. "He was beating a woman."

"*Puta ladron*, thieving whore," said a voice. "She weren't no good."

"Somebody fetch a rope," said Bastyan. No one moved.

"Get it yourself!" said one of the men who'd watched the fight.

The Wildest West

Bastyan did and after securing Joe dragged him over to the usual cottonwood jail-tree. The storm abated, and Joe spent the night cold and wet. Releasing the blacksmith in the morning Clegg noticed that one eye drooped and that the muscular man's speech was slurred. He staggered a little as he walked.

The morning was bright and the sky blue. Rain the night before had washed away all trace of dust and haze. For now, the sky was clear, but clouds would gather during the day as fresh moisture blew in from the Sea of Cortez and simmered off the desert floor. Bastyan walked the streets without a friendly greeting anywhere. Conversations stopped as he neared, and eyes turned hostile to stare. Even Missouri Anne hurried to the far side of the road.

Reporting to Poston for his week's pay, Bastyan found more disappointment.

"I had a hard time coming up with your pay," admonished Poston. "The cantina owner refused to pay his share. He says you're a menace to good business. Says you didn't give Joe the chance to explain and that you should've been helping Joe get his poke back."

"I saw a strong man beating a woman," responded Bastyan. "I thought he was drunk. I acted to protect her."

"Ehrenberg says the blacksmith may never fully recover," replied Poston. "We need our blacksmith. Right now, he can't see straight or steady his tools. He's the only one we've got. Besides he's really a nice guy. Everybody likes him"

"Except Juanita," mumbled Bastyan.

"You were hired to protect the people of Tubac!" insisted Poston. "Joe, the blacksmith, is one of those people. You had a duty to protect him."

The Wildest West

Bastyan almost quit right then and there, but thoughts of Missouri Anne kept him lingering. Besides the work was usually easy and the pay reasonable. He might be able to settle down, even get married if Missouri Anne could just see past his reputation as a brutal man, one quick as lightning with a gun.

He practiced with his guns daily firing them to ensure that he always had a fresh load. In the summer humidity and storms, moisture could get through the cylinders and wet his powder. So, he kept his powder dry by constant practice, drawing, and firing, proving that he could shoot the flame off a candle at 30 paces. Clegg was quite public with his practice thinking this the best way to further his reputation and intimidate would be evildoers.

The blacksmith's speech improved a little, and after a week he could hold his tools properly, but he was never quite the same. Bastyan's relations with the people of Tubac followed a similar route; they were never quite the same. He had been a beloved hero. Now, outlaws and citizens both feared him. Men who used to buy him drinks edged away when he entered the cantina. They were afraid to rile him and even to drink near him for fear he'd give them the "drunk treatment." Hostility ended, but love did not return.

It took weeks, but as the rains became less frequent, Missouri Anne no longer crossed the street to avoid him, and Bastyan was able to invite her to picnic. Taking her down by the slow moving Santa Cruz River, he spread his blanket on a grassy spot under a walnut tree. As she spread victuals on the blanket, he could see that either the girl was a poor cook or her heart wasn't in the food that she'd prepared. Even the cold chicken smelled burnt, the biscuits were misshapen, and the adoring looks were also long gone.

"*Pollo quemado*, my favorite," he joked smiling. She either didn't understand or was ignoring his "burned chicken" comment.

"My father said we're headed for California soon," offered the pretty girl.

Stunned by this prospect, Bastyan blurted out, "Are you going with him?"

"Of course," she answered icily. "What's to keep me here?"

"I thought perhaps..." he stammered.

"The men hereabouts are entirely too brutal to make good husbands," she said haughtily. "Though Mr. Kirkland seems nice."

"Why is your father pulling up stakes?" Bastyan asked, trying to turn the conversation away from rancher Kirkland.

"He's the first protestant minister in New Mexico Territory," she stated proudly.

"But this is Arizona," Bastyan responded, trying for levity.

She graced him with a frosty stare. "Arizona isn't a territory, isn't anything but a name. It's still New Mexico."

"He's the only kind of a preacher around here in a very long time," said Bastyan. "There hasn't even been a Catholic priest in over 30 years. Folks need him. All us brutal sinners need him."

"More sinners in California," huffed Missouri Anne.

Bastyan also suspected there was more gold for the offering plate. Arizona had some new mines but was still cash-poor. Wisely, he said nothing. The girl might be frosty, but she was talking to him, was alone with him, even if they were only yards from the town. Playing on a woman's vanity, he complimented the poor food, her hair, her eyes, and as the afternoon progressed, she softened a little. The girl got lots of attention being part of an, if not elite, at least, very limited sorority, but the men to which she was accustomed were laborers, farmers, ranchers, miners, and teamsters, all lacking in sophistication and the ability to ply a smooth tongue. He flattered her, and she enjoyed it. On the way back to town, she looped her arm through his and leaned on him just a little.

This isn't my old life, Bastyan thought, but it is getting better. Things are looking up.

"Mornin,' marshal," said a storekeeper the next day.

After a moment's surprised hesitation, Bastyan replied, "Good morning."

The icy stares were gone. If they didn't always greet him, people at least didn't stop talking as he neared. Even the cantina owner began paying his share of Bastyan's salary again, but with the admonition to Poston that Clegg had better watch his step and not be mistreating good customers. As the storms passed, a warm September was born, and life in Tubac seemed good.

With the passing summer, stories came in from outlying districts. Tucson played host to a former Southern Congressman who shot and killed an Irish headwaiter in the Capitol for refusing to serve him breakfast after the stated hour. German mining engineer Brunckow, along with his associates, was murdered at his mine near the San Pedro River. His killers had tossed Brunckow, pierced by a star-drill, down the mineshaft. The others had been bashed to pieces with picks and sledgehammers by the Mexican members of the crew who then fled for Sonora. Further north, Mexicans murdered the crew building the Butterfield Overland Mail Station at Dragoon Springs as they slept and then disappeared south. Some of the young men who ranched and farmed along Sonoita Creek took it upon themselves to beat up Mowry's Sonoran workers in reprisal. As far as anyone knew, Mowry's men hadn't been involved in either set of murders. Stock thefts and marauding Apaches along Sonoita Creek were commonplace. In a region haunted by Apaches, Mexican banditos, and California bad men, Tubac was at peace. Folks believed marshal Clegg's ferocious reputation kept evil doers at bay.

"Help! Murder!" screamed the man running up the street toward the adobe casa near the cantina that was Bastyan's home and office. Blood covered the man.

"What happened? Are you hurt?" Bastyan demanded.

"No. Not my blood," replied the man panting hard from exertion and fear. "I found Henry Smith at the edge of town. It's awful. He was hacked to pieces, just all cut up. Machetes, I think." A crowd gathered around them.

Poston came trotting up the street toward Bastyan. "Mexicans, two of them," he cried. "They were seen hacking Henry with machetes. Just now! I gave Henry the payroll to take out to the Santa Rita Mine. They must have known."

"Saddle me a horse, please," said Bastyan turning the man who kept the stable. Ducking into his adobe, he picked up his rifle and accoutrements and his saddlebags. "Get me some jerked meat and trail bread," he said to the storekeeper when he emerged. "How long ago?" he asked turning to Poston.

"Minutes!" replied Poston.

Clegg tied down his equipment and mounted the horse that had been brought. "I'm on their trail."

"Wait!" cried Poston. "You'll need a posse!"

"Good," replied the mounted marshal. "You get them together and send them after me."

"But there's two of them," insisted Poston.

"Armed with machetes," replied Clegg, "and riding hard for Mexico. I've got guns."

"Bring them back for trial!"

Bastyan Clegg looked at him and shook his head in bewilderment as if trying to clear his mind. He wondered what Poston was thinking. A trial was impossibility because of the distance to the annual court in Mesilla. Poston lacked the authority as alcalde to bring in a death sentence, and nothing less would satisfy anyone. He was distancing himself, Bastyan thought, from the inevitable. It was unlikely the Mexicans would allow themselves to be taken alive. Poston didn't want to get his hands dirty. He wanted his payroll back, too, though it couldn't be more than $500. He had only eight men at the mine.

"I'll do my best," replied Bastyan. Some in the crowd smiled at his vow. They knew the fast gun's reputation for brutality.

Bastyan Clegg rode to the south and soon spotted a dust trail in the distance. He followed the dust as it veered eastward toward the river. Soon there was no dust to follow, though it didn't take Bastyan long to locate two sets of tracks in the soft earth under the trees along the river.

They must know someone would follow them, Bastyan thought, as the trail veered west into the desert and disappeared again.

He didn't push his horse hard. That would wear it out all too soon, although the horse was well fed. Equally matched in horseflesh the chase could go on forever. Bastyan had to hope he had the better horse. If he were patient, in time he might overtake them. Unfortunately, the border wasn't far away. Pursuing his quarry over the border, he was apt to find himself the prey. He needed to end this chase in the next few miles. He hoped they had ridden far before stealing the payroll and now rode jaded horses or that they would make a mistake. Perhaps they would stop and try to ambush him.

Ahead of him, the dust trail thinned out. One man had stopped, perhaps doubled back. In any event, one man was still giving him an easy trail to follow.

Clegg came upon a horse, saddled and bridled and sweating heavily, its sides heaving, feeding on a patch of grass by a shallow arroyo. The horse stood out in the open. Perhaps the horse was lame and abandoned. He had to go closer to check. One thing was obvious: whoever had left it was certain he would see it. They might lure him in close and then emerge from ambush in the arroyo as he dismounted. As he approached, he could see that blood spattered the horse. Henry's, he thought. He scanned the terrain looking for anything that might conceal his quarry. The small arroyo beyond the mare might hide a man. A mesquite thicket might offer cover, but surely mesquite thorns would discourage entry. Nothing moved among the boulders to his right. The arroyo seemed the most likely hiding spot. Wary, he drew a pistol, cocked it, and then with his attention on the animal rode forward toward it.

A boulder towered above him. As he rode passed, a blood-curdling scream startled Bastyan. A Mexican leapt from a stony perch bringing his machete down with violent force. At the sound, Clegg turned and raised his pistol. The move saved his hand, but the machete impacted with heavy metal, knocking the revolver from his grip and briefly paralyzing his arm. The falling body knocked him tumbling from his horse with the Mexican on top. Suddenly shifting his weight and thrusting upward, he dislodged his assailant and found his feet. Crouching, they faced each other. Bastyan tried for his off-hand pistol but found his arm still too numb to grasp it. With his left he drew his Bowie. Facing a machete, he felt that he was unequally matched and could only dance about yielding ground to avoid the other man's blade. He could not hope to parry, but the big knife was heavy and slow in the man's hand. Bastyan could duck and dodge the blows, and he could close in as the blade swept to one side or the other.

The heavy blade swung by, and Bastyan leapt in, flicking his smaller blade at the Mexican's eyes, and taking a nick out of a heavy eyebrow. The man flinched and backed away. Clegg danced out of range. Blood ran into the man's eye. The side with the wounded eye would now be his weaker side, his vision restricted. But it was also Bastyan's weak side, his right arm still numb but gaining feeling. The Mexican began another broad swing, and Bastyan, judging its pass began to close in again. As he thought, the Mexican wasn't strong enough to redirect the blow once it began, and reaching over the arm and grasping the machete, Bastyan neatly removed the end of the man's nose. The man screamed hideously and bled copiously. The fight continued, but the advantage was now with Bastyan.

To and fro they fought. Bastyan Clegg left his mark on cheek and chin, hand and arm, and a deep cut across the man's belly. Bastyan continued to flick and dodge as feeling returned to his right arm. Cutting the man across his right eye and cheek, he left the Mexican blinded by his own blood. The man backed away, wiped his eyes, and then unexpectedly charged, the machete held high overhead and descending. Able to use his right again, Bastyan drew and fired, catching his assailant between the eyes. A neat round hole appeared at the bridge of his nose as the Mexican fell.

Bastyan grabbed the man's hat and stripped off his jacket. Donning both, Bastyan went after the horses. Catching his own, he was able to catch up with the other Mexican. Leaving the body where it lay, Bastyan mounted the Sonoran's horse and resumed the chase, leading his own mount. Tumacacori lay behind him, and the Portrero, Pete Kitchen's fortress ranch, was not far ahead. Clegg suspected that the other Mexican might seek refuge there. Pete was all right, but his family and ranch hands were all Sonorans, and the man he pursued might be a relative, thereby complicating matters. It occurred to him the man he chased might be ahead somewhere waiting for his partner to rejoin him, hence his disguise.

Perhaps a quarter mile ahead, a rider emerged from concealing mesquite wearing a broad sombrero. Bastyan waved and the stranger returned the greeting. Clegg held his rifle aloft showing his "accomplice" that he'd killed the hated *gavacho* and had captured his arms as well as his horse. The distance closed. At 100 yards, the Sonoran began to suspect a cheat. At 50, he was sure of it and departed at a gallop. Close enough, thought Bastyan, spurring his horse after the man.

He allowed his horse to run full out as this was the final chase. They were just beyond pistol range, so there was no point wasting ammunition. True, Bastyan's dragoon Colts had greater range than most pistols, but aiming from a galloping horse, he was unlikely to hit anything 50 yards away. He could dismount and use his rifle, but the range would increase, and Bastyan, in losing the advantage of close range, would only get one shot. So they would ride hard until one man or the other's horse proved the fleeter or gave out, or one of them made a mistake.

The mistake came when the Mexican's horse stepped into an arroyo—one of those odd little things born of the violence of the last storm no more than a foot wide, hidden by overhanging grasses, but several feet in depth. The horse tumbled brutally breaking its leg and rolling over the Sonoran who didn't get away in time. Bastyan thought the man might have died. As he neared, he saw horse still quivered, barely alive, and there trapped under the dying beast, was the moaning Mexican.

"*Señor, por favor*," he whimpered, "you must save me. The *caballo*, he crushes my chest, I can't breathe. *Un bondad!*"

Bastyan looked down at the man. "Did you show Henry Smith any kindness when you hacked him to pieces?"

"*Señor*, I beg you, please," wheezed the Mexican.

"Tell you what." Bastyan said. "Tell me where you hid the payroll, and I might help you."

"Have you looked in my amigo's saddlebag?"

The cash was there, and good to his word, Bastyan helped the man out from under the horse, a process that became quite gruesome, and left the Mexican covered in blood. The horse could not rise, and its efforts nearly crushing the man under him. Clegg put the beast out of its misery and then dug into earth and horse to open a path. Disarming the man, Clegg assessed his injuries. Ragged breathing suggested a few broken ribs. A broken collar bone seemed to be the cause of an arm that wouldn't move. He was bruised from head to foot and appeared to have landed on his face, for a great deal of skin had been scraped away. The Sonoran's nose was broken—more blood and black eyes.

Tying the Mexican and allowing him to ride his compadre's horse, Bastyan mounted his own and led them back to his partner's dead body.

"Time to get off," Bastyan said. "From here you walk, and your friend rides."

"But *señor*, I am stiff from my wounds. I can barely move."

Pulling and leveling a pistol, Bastyan replied, "You'll find a way."

And so they went, the Mexican stumbling and begging the long miles back to Tubac. Each time the Mexican fell, he removed more skin from his elbows, palms, and shins. Late in the evening, they arrived in town, the man looking more like a beaten corpse than a human. Bastyan gave him water and tied him to the jail-tree before heading to Poston's casa. There he stopped by the doorway and cut the bindings that held the dead man to his horse, letting the body drop unceremoniously to the ground.

Bastyan knocked, and when the door opened, he handed Poston the payroll. "Here's your money. It's been a long day. I'm going to bed." He turned and walked in the direction of his home.

"You can't leave that body here!" Poston cried.

Not responding, Bastyan continued his walk to home and bed, too tired even for food. Things were bound to look better in the morning.

The October morn dawned unseasonably cold and crisp. At mid-morning Bastyan emerged in search of a large breakfast to find the dead Mexican propped against the side of his house looking ghastly. Passersby whispered and pointed. Damn Poston, thought Bastyan. He overheard the word, "tortured."

At the jail-tree, he found Missouri Anne kneeling beside the Mexican cleaning his cuts as she fed him tortillas, eggs, and *refritos*.

"Oh no, *señorita*," squealed the Mexican taking sight of Bastyan. "Here comes *el diablo*. He will beat me and torture me as before. Surely, he will make you go away, leaving me here to starve and bleed!"

Missouri Anne rose and slapped Bastyan, causing his head to snap sharply to the left. "How could you? How could I ever have thought I loved you? The word is out. You tortured them both! You're inhuman! Everyone knows your evil reputation. They only stole a few dollars. How could you be so cruel for just a few dollars?" Apparently she was overlooking the murder.

Saying nothing, Bastyan turned and walked toward town. The hostility will pass, he thought. Continuing on his original mission, Clegg went in search of breakfast. No one greeted him; instead, they crossed the street to get away from him. Conversations stopped at his approach, and the good citizens of Tubac blessed him with icy stares. He caught snatches of conversation—"murder" "torture" "brutal" "bad reputation" "cruel."

Entering a café, the host looked up and said, "We're closed!"

"But, there are people here," replied Bastyan.

"Closed."

"Look, I only need a few tortillas, eggs, bacon, whatever you've got," said the marshal.

"Fresh out!" said the host with finality.

Rolling his eyes, Bastyan turned and went back out into the street. From behind him, Bastyan heard words hurled by people he could no longer see—"beast" "monster" "son of a. . ." "*puto*" "*cabron!*"

The dead Mexican was still propped against his house; he was starting to stink. I guess he's not going anywhere, Bastyan thought and then headed for Poston's. Perhaps the alcalde would offer him breakfast . . . or lunch. The morning was fast passing.

Poston came to the door but didn't invite Clegg in. Instead, he handed the marshal some money. "Your pay up through today and I've thrown in two weeks' severance. That's more than I should do, I believe, but . . ."

"What?" asked Bastyan.

"The town decided this morning," said Poston. "You're fired. They refused to put up any money for your pay, so this is out of my pocket."

"Why?"

"Isn't it obvious," Poston replied. "This is a nice town, good people, not Tucson. They won't stand for torture and murder. They can't take your brutality!"

"What are you talking about?" asked Bastyan.

"The Mexican told us everything," replied the alcalde. "How you captured them, tied them, beat them, cut them with knives as a lesson. Then you murdered his compadre. You told him how you had to as we had no authority to hang them and no *juzgado* to lock them up. So, all you could do was torture them as a lesson and kill them. But you wanted people to see the lesson."

"This is nonsense!" insisted Clegg. "Nonsense. I shot the one because he tried to kill me. The other had his horse roll over him."

"The dead man is all cut up," replied Poston. "It's pretty obvious how you tortured him before he died, just like the other Mexican said. And as for him, making him

70

walk was torture! Especially after what you did to him. What a fine lesson in intimidation you've made. It's too much. You're fired."

Bastyan Clegg saw the futility of further argument. Poston's mind was made up. So apparently were the minds of everyone else in town. Missouri Anne would marry rancher Kirkland, he guessed. Oh well, he sighed. He had no deep investment in this town, his home for only a few months. Walking back into town, he gathered his possessions and his horse. Mounting his steed, Bastyan considered his options.

Tucson was out. He'd been the marshal of Arizona. Likely as not, that crowd would kill him, shooting him in the back if they feared his fast draw and prowess with a gun. There was nothing for him along Sonoita Creek. Butterfield had a string of stations stretching from Tucson back to Mesilla and was always looking for help. Two or three men manned each station. Tucson to Mesilla was Chiricahua Apache country. Three men alone twenty-five miles from the next station and over a hundred from military help were not odds Bastyan cared for.

Santa Fe then, Bastyan thought. There were plenty of possibilities in the Rio Arriba, especially if he didn't brag about his fast gun and ability to shoot out a candle flame at 30 paces. He'd find something, and the Mexican girls up that way were right pretty. Bastyan rode east, the setting sun behind him.

Pirates of the Llano Estacado

Wind blew through his long black hair as the young man gazed out over the railing across the undulating swells. He was handsome with sun darkened skin and high cheek bones, well made, and muscled with powerful shoulders. Unlike the other sailors who did their hair in a ponytail, he tied his in braids to keep it out of his eyes and then bound it to his head with a red scarf. He wore white duck pants cut at the knee and a red sash at his waist concealed a knuckle-guarded Bowie knife. One ear sported a large, gold hooped earring. In New Orleans, he'd learned from the sailor men and adopted their mode of dress. He'd even been amused to acquire a parrot from one. So when he set out on the current voyage, he looked a sailor even if he still had much to learn. There was time on a cruise, lots of time, and the captain had to find ways to keep the hands busy and out of trouble. When a deck hand was required, the need would arise suddenly and the crew must deal with it before disaster struck. A sudden shift in the wind could easily capsize their craft if not handled efficiently. He looked away forward where another hand was polishing a small, brass, 3-pounder cannon attached to the rail and picked up his own can of vinegar and sand.

Three small brass cannons weren't t much to defend the ship. Polishing them kept the deck hands busy. Three deck hands weren't many to defend the ship either.

"'Tis enough," said Captain Thomas. "Three hands are enough to raise, lower, and set that big fore'n'aft sail. 'Tis enough. Two officers to stand the watch and a good cook to keep us all happy. 'Twill be fine. You'll see. Fewer hands, fewer to divide the profit. And we shall make a great profit. The voyage hasn't been done before."

"But what if we're attacked?" asked the young man.

"The cannons sweep both sides. 'Twill be a surprise to boarders. We shan't anchor in any harbor we don't trust. We'll keep her moving day and night and make it hard for them to keep up."

Adapting to his captain's language, the young man said, "But, captain, we'll be on shoal shore the entire time. How can we dare run at night?"

"We'll reduce sail just a bit to slow our progress."

The young sailor had thought a wind-driven ship would be silent. Of course, there would be the hum of the wind in the rigging and the sails snapping like the canvas on a prairie schooner on a blustery day. He hadn't expected the constant deep rumble and grumble of the ship making its way west. Nor had he foreseen the frequent, bone-jarring jolts that felt like they must tear the vessel apart. He could not become used to them. At night, swinging in his cot, he dreamt horrors of the ship breaking up.

The ship made good progress. The captain had his charts and steered them clear of rocks and shoals. A man at the masthead was constantly calling out the landmarks and warning of shoal waters. A crewman or an officer stood watch at the wheel. The young man took his turns on watch and aloft. He sprang up through the rigging, nimble as a squirrel, graceful as a hawk on the wing, silent as an owl.

From the masthead, he could see for miles.

"Boy," the mate told him, "you have the sharpest eyes of any in the crew. You can see twice as far as they can."

The young sailor said nothing. His father had trained him in the hunt, and when the safety of his family demanded it to see the finest details and interpret them.

From aloft, he reported on what he could see and called it down to the captain and helmsman. "Shoals to starboard, half a league."

He'd hear the answer from the captain ordering the helmsman. "Hard aport! Adjust your sails there."

The great ship turned but slowly, so maneuvers had to begin early. The slow turn allowed the crew plenty of time to adjust the sails.

Captain Thomas had explained the winds to him. "The prevailing wind comes from the southwest, and that's the direction we are bound. We've a good ship, and she can sail very close to the wind's eye. The fore 'n' aft sail allows that. We pull her in close to the line of the ship. See how the wind causes the sail to spread its belly? When it does that, the wind pulls us to it. If the wind were from behind us, we'd let the sail far out to the side and let the wind push us. You see?"

He didn't at first, but as the weeks went by, he came to understand. He learned about tacking where the ship turned away from her true course to work with the wind and beat back toward it by stages. A lot of ground was covered, and very little headway made. Fortunately, they did not have to tack very often. The ship was weatherly and sailed close to the wind's eye.

From the masthead, the keen eyed young man sang out. "Buffalo off the port bow! Half a league."

Captain Thomas cried back, "How close can we approach?"

"Close. Gunshot. Steer one point to port."

The captain was elated. "Fresh meat! Load the cannons."

The two on the port were loaded. The captain aimed one and the mate the other. "On my command. . . fire!"

The Wildest West

Two buffalo dropped, hit hard by 3-pound solid shot.

"Lower the sails. Drop anchor. We're going ashore."

They butchered the meat on the spot and brought it aboard along with heads, hoofs, and hides.

"Waste not, want not." The captain was a New England man and frugal.

There was a raised poop deck aft, which was the cover to the captain's cabin where he and the mate stayed. It was also where the crew took their meals together with the officers who found they had to remain cordial but distant, affable though stern. Their orders must be obeyed instantly so they couldn't be true friends or too friendly, but the atmosphere at meals still had to be comfortable and inviting to the crew.

The cook worked in a cookshack amid ships by the mainmast and the crew slept forward in the fo'c'sle. Below decks were packed with goods to sell at their next port of call.

"Captain," said the young sailor, "if we attach a bit of red cloth to the rigging by the gunnel, I think the antelope will approach to see it."

"What?"

"They're curious, sir."

It was done and provided many a fine meal as the animals came within easy rifle shot.

From the masthead came the cry, "Raiders off the starboard beam!"

The raiders approached, making all the speed they could and came briefly within arrowshot.

"Shall we load the cannon, sir?"

"No need. They'll soon fall behind."

The relentless wind drew the ship onward, and the raiders soon fell away aft.

The Wildest West

March of 1853 was unseasonably warm and wet. Days were as hot as the dry bricks of the *horno,* the adobe oven. Unseasonable heat drew in great thunderheads from the southwest across the desert. Dan Trelawney watched as clouds built high and menacing through the afternoon. On a hot day, he knew, the longer rain holds off, the higher the cloud peaks would build. When they'd built up lofty enough, they crashed onto the land with tremendous force. When the clouds gathered their strength all day, as they were doing, they broke with fury after sunset. Lightning flashed all around, and thunder boomed like the sea breaking on a rocky shore. The wind swirled, blowing all lost things before it. Rain would come down as if God were emptying His *olla* directly onto the world. It rushed to the earth in great, huge drops. Then the sluice gates opened wide, and the rain came right at you like waves and spindrift across the *llano,* the grassy plains. As the lightning flashed, you can see things in the tempest, ragged bits of rain and cloud mixed with things blown on the storm. It wasn't surprising that *vaqueros,* cowboys, told folks that in the storm they could see damned souls chasing the devil's stampeding herd. Sometimes, they could see treasure galleons of old tossed on hurricane seas.

Sometimes Dan missed the sea and missed Greenport far Out East in New England on Long Island, where smugglers avoiding tariffs and whalers came and went from ports around the world. He'd grown up with the smell of the sea all around. He'd known the sailors before he made his way west to New Mexico and partnered with Roque Vigil on a ranch south of Rayado along the Santa Fe Trail. They hoped to make their fortune by being the first to meet and barter with the wagon trains as they arrived.

The Wildest West

Roque and Dan feared that thunder and lightning would frighten their herds and start them running. They could scatter across the llano for Indians to steal or seek shelter in *arroyos*, dry river beds that would soon be flooded. Roque and Dan had planned for stormy disasters to their herd in the layout of the ranch. The smaller side canyons had been prepared with brush fences so that livestock could be driven in and easily penned. These were places where the water would not, they hoped, run deep. The rain was early, but they were ready. With dusk fast approaching, they had to work swiftly and separately, each driving livestock from distant pastures to the waiting corrals. Dan arrived first back at the buildings that constituted their ranch headquarters. There he raced from building to building shuttering and battening down and making all ready for the coming, storm which looked to be a violent one.

The storm broke with rising fury before Don got to their adobe ranch house. Rain was already falling in cascades, the lightning flashing, and thunder sending a continuous drum roll before Roque returned. Roque stumbled in looking dazed. Dan started to ask about their stock when he saw the confused look in his partner's eye and began to worry if he'd been injured by a falling limb or flying debris. A near lightning strike can have strange effects. Dan had heard of men whose eyes glowed, who had strange visions, and whose fingers crackled with wicked sparks a yard long for days or even months afterward. Roque's hair stood on end and his eyes were large and round, glowing in the dark of their cabin.

"Roque, are you all right?" Dan cried, "*Qúe páso?*"

"Danito, I have seen it," he rumbled in sepulchral tones, "*el barco.*"

"A ship?" Dan queried.

"Aye, Danito, a ship with sails set racing across the llano. A ship like in the days of my ancestors, the *conquistadors*, carrying *oro* to *Espania*," he nodded.

"A ship? How could a ship be here?" Dan worried that his partner had come too close to the lightning and was having visions.

"Aye, Danito, and there was a *pirata* at the masthead," Roque referred to the pirate he'd seen as if proved his case. "I saw him in the flashes of the lightning. He and the mast glowed with *fuego de San Yelmo*."

"A pirate? Saint Helmet? Oh, Saint Elmo's fire. You've seen Saint Elmo's fire? I've only heard sailors speak of it. What would a pirate be doing here?"

Pirates held more terror for Roque than for Dan, and the Mexican was more inclined to see them as minions of the devil. Dan's Trelawny ancestors were pirates from Cornwall who preyed on Roque's ancestors until they'd saved enough from their misadventures to start a ships' chandler's store at Greenport, Long Island.

"What would a pirate be doing here?" Dan repeated.

"He was crew on *el barco del Diablo*, the devil's ship," Roque pronounced in triumph. "And the ship fired a cannonball at me."

"Would you like a nice cup of tea then?" Dan asked. Their friend Doña Luna, a Jicarilla shaman, had showed Dan an herb she said would put a buffalo to sleep. As powerful as Roque was, Dan hoped she was right. Sharing a cabin far from civilization with a madman was not safe. Outside the storm raged with a fury seldom seen. After Roque fell asleep, Dan brooded worrying about his health. Finally, he opened a shutter to view the storm and was shown vision after vision in the flashes of hell and worlds beyond. In the night, the little stream beside their house raged above its banks.

In the morning, the skies had cleared. Fallen branches and debris were strewn all about. Dan stepped outside to do his business, but found his water suddenly stopped when he realized what lay at his feet. There at the edge of the high water mark of the creek lay a soaked and apparently dead pirate. He lay face down, clutching the edge of dry land. His long black hair was bound to his head in a red scarf. He wore white duck pants that came to the knee with a red sash around his waist and white shirt with great loose sleeves above.

"Roque, come quick," Dan called, "and bring your gun. I've found your pirate."

When Roque arrived, Dan rolled the pirate over on his back. The pirate coughed and burbled water from his mouth and nose. A large knuckle-guarded Bowie knife was secured in the pirate's sash. Roque crossed himself several times mumbling '*Madre de Dios, Madre de Dios.*' A red and green parrot fluttered down and landed on the pirate's shoulder, pecking at an ear adorned with a large hoop of a gold earring.

"Roque, I think we know this pirate. Teresina and I made the hole for that earring not three years past," Dan stammered. Teresina was Kit Carson's teenaged niece who often stayed with Kit's wife when he was away.

"Ow," said the pirate as the bird nipped at his ear. He sat up.

"It's *Peregrino Rojo*?" said Roque in surprise. The Red Pilgrim, son of Jicarilla Apache chief, Vicenti. His true Jicarilla name was known only to his closest family and would never be told; that would give the possessor of the name power over him. The tribal cousins may have their own nickname for him, but it would be unpronounceable, so Rojo would have to do. He'd spent years around the settlements, fascinated by everything and learning to speak flawless Spanish and English. Dan thought of him as an Apache renaissance man. Rojo had been missing from the scene for a while. It was rumored he'd gone east with Francis Aubrey, Skimmer of the Plains, a wagon master and trader.

"If you two are here, I must have drowned and gone to hell," said Rojo. He coughed up some more water.

They stumbled together into the house and filled themselves with coffee and a breakfast of tortillas, eggs, potatoes, chili, *queso*, that is, cheese, and bacon. As he recovered, Rojo's story began to emerge.

"I went east with Captain FX Aubry," Rojo told them, "and then followed the Mississippi down to New Orleans. I met, loved, and lost a girl. I sailed with pirates trying to get her back."

Roque cut in. "See? I told you I saw a pirate," The big Mexican felt vindicated.

Rojo continued. "I pretended to be a Spanish grandee, Don Manuel Armijo, and gambled at the tables on the great steamboats of the Mississippi."

"Wait!" cried Roque. "Don Manuel Armijo was the governor!"

Rojo smiled an evil grin Dan was sure he'd seen before on a shark. "Yes, and they always thought the name sounded familiar; therefore I must be very great and well known, so I was always welcome at the tables.

"I came to miss my mountains and sought to make my way home," Rojo told them. "Near Independence, I learned of a man who was seeking sailors for a trip to Santa Fe.

This seemed strange so I looked him up, and that's how I met Captain Thomas.

"Captain Thomas had built a great ship of twenty tons on wheels. That's not so big for a ship, but huge for a wagon. The wheels alone were fifteen feet high. And above it all was a great mast with triangular sails.

"They mockingly called him Wind Wagon Thomas, but his idea was sound. The big wheels would carry us across water courses and arroyos with little difficulty, and the sail would drive us forward. Being on wheels, we'd have little leeway. The forward wheels were geared to turn and allow us to steer. We had three swivel mounted three-pounders for Comanche, but mostly, we could just sail away from them. We'd stop at night in bad weather when we couldn't see, but usually we sailed through the night in the moonlight. With a crew of six, we mounted watches to make sure no one came aboard.

"Captain Thomas wanted to leave before the grass was up so he could get to Santa Fe first and reap the highest prices for his goods. So we sailed on a night a week before the full moon just thirty-five days ago. We saw not a soul except a few Comanche all the way across the plains. All went well until we were cast on a lee shore by that Diablo storm. Our ship lies broken not far from here smashed on the rocks. We fired our guns to sound the distance to the shore in the storm and dark to no avail."

Roque interjected, "I told you the *pirata* fired cannon at me."

"Our ship is broken," Rojo continued. "She'll not swim again. Our first mate died when the mast fell on him. Captain Thomas sits there saying he's goin' down with his ship. I saw your cabin from the masthead before we wrecked and tried to make it up here in the storm, but the stream thwarted me."

Dan looked at his friends. "We need to make plans. There's a treasure in salvage to be had! I've seen it Out East when ships went aground."

"Ah," said Rojo, "but this ship's not abandoned. Captain William Thomas hasn't abandoned his ship. That's the law of the sea. You'll have to ask him to cut you in for a share. It's not fair salvage. Captain Thomas and what's left of his crew are still with the ship."

"All right then," said Dan nodding his head. "He'll still need help. Roque can you find wagons?"

Conestoga wagons came by the hundreds to New Mexico each year. There being little to carry, few traveled back to Independence. Most were broken up for the finished wood and metal they contained. "Sure," said Roque. "I can find some at Rayado."

"Rojo, can you find drivers?"

"My cousins are always near."

"Good," said Dan. "We can haul things to Fort Barclay and some to Santa Fe. We can't let on the size of the cache. We don't want to drive prices down. Will your captain go along with this?"

Rojo nodded. "I think he will."

They saddled mounts and rode over to survey the shipwreck. She lay among the rocks below the bluff with her rigging tangled about her. Her mast was snapped and her back broken. It was clear she'd never swim again.

Rojo introduced his friends to the captain who looked into Dan's eyes most curiously. He was a man of dark coloring, under medium height, and dressed in a dark blue naval jacket with brass buttons. He wore a captain's hat and tall black boots.

With the help of the crew, they cut the rigging free and tied it down to protect the cargo from the elements. They helped the Captain bury his first mate under a cairn of rocks on a low hill. Then Rojo and Roque set out on their missions. Roque would find wagons and draft animals and Rojo would meet him in two days with the drivers. All the while, Captain Thomas kept looking at Dan most intently.

Finally, he said, "I know you, Danny Trelawny; I know your father, boy."

And Dan realized he knew the captain, too. They clasped their arms about each other and greeted one another as long time neighbors should. Dan told the captain of his father's death and brought a tear to his eye. William Thomas hailed from Greenport where Dan's family had known him as a miller, vendor, valued neighbor, and friend to Dan's father, but he was much more. A man of agile mind, he was a true Yankee inventor who'd taught himself to work in iron and wood and to understand the mechanics of all sorts of machines. In his youth, he'd gone to sea serving 'before the mast,' that is, as a common seaman. According to Dan's father, he lacked 'vocation' for the sea and soon returned to land. There he provided Dan's family with his inventions to simplify the lives of sailors. Many, perhaps most, were quite good and were still in use when Dan went west. Perhaps Dan's family should have known when Thomas named his son Rocky Mountain that something distant was calling to him. When Dan was ten years old, Captain Thomas sold his property, packed up the family. and left for parts unknown.

The ship was built around the dimensions of the wheels which were fifteen feet high. Her length from forward edge of the front wheel to rearward edge of the back wheel was three times the diameter of the wheel or forty-five feet. That is to say, this was the length of her main hull. Beyond the forward and rearward wheel, the hull tapered another ten feet to a proper prow. Her hull was curved like that of a ship, and she rose fifteen feet above the truck that carried the great wheels. Her beam from hub to hub was twice the diameter of a wheel or thirty feet, though her deck in order to accommodate the wheels was only twenty-five feet wide. Her main mast rose sixty feet above the deck. She was a gaff-rigged cutter with mainsail and staysail. A jib could be rigged to take advantage of fair winds. The wheel was forward and turned the forward road wheels through a system of pulleys and levers. There was a great lever for her brakes. Below the deck was the hold, and it was all for cargo.

"'Twas a fine ship, Danny. With a good wind and over level ground, she made good time."

Rojo told Dan the ship was faster than a galloping horse.

"In light airs," Captain Thomas went on, "she still gathered enough wind to move more swiftly than a man running. Because of the shape of her sails and because her wheels would not allow leeway, she could sail within a point of the wind's eye. 'Tis to say, she could sail almost directly into the wind. With her great size, she was able to carry a small forge and supplies to make her own repairs. She was me darlin.'"

Captain Thomas paused a moment before continuing. "I never planned to get further west than Barclay's fort or perhaps Las Vegas. Glorietta Pass over to Santa Fe would have been too much for my fine vessel. It's a steep and narrow climb. I would have sailed her back to Independence carrying passengers and the mail, a wealthy and proud man. The scoffers would have been ridiculed. I'd have been commodore of a fleet of wind wagons. But my dreams are dashed." He hung his head. Dan didn't think Captain Thomas cried, but he couldn't be sure.

"Captain," Dan began, "You were able to travel faster than the conventional wagons on the trail with no livestock to feed and only a tiny crew and no fear of outlaws and Indians or Texians. You'd be able to travel in winter when the trail is closed to all others. You've got to build another!"

Dan knew the captain would have been able to make more trips than the caravans could because he did not rely on the grass. He would make a fortune with a fleet of these ships.

"No, Dan," the captain said. "She didn't stand up to the gale but went on the rocks. She was ill-behaved in strong and uncertain winds."

Dan wondered if the ship or her skipper's lack of skill as a sailor was at fault. He said nothing. The man was his friend and should be encouraged. He'd done something wonderful.

The captain murmured. "If the wind suddenly shifts direction, an ocean going vessel will heel over on her beam ends and spill wind from her sails. She will also slide sideways through the water away from the direction of the wind." Dan knew the sideways motion was called leeway. "A keel redirects some of this sideward energy into forward motion. The Wind Mill, for so I've christened her, made no leeway. Sitting on four wheels she could not go sideways. The Wind Mill was designed to be so broad abeam that she could not heel over, which would have been a disaster. A change in the wind, easily dealt with at sea, must be translated instantly by the Wind Mill and her crew to forward motion or to spilling the air from her sails. Failure, as you can see, results in a vessel dumped on her side with a broken back and shattered mast. It's a problem of her nature that I cannot fix."

"Captain," responded Dan, "you could try. You're a genius with these things."

"The hard wind out of the east blew us west off the Trail. Try as we might, we could not beat back into the wind fast enough. We should have hove to, but I wanted some shelter from the storm. As we came closer to the hills," said Captain Thomas, "I was at the helm and Rojo at the masthead looking for shoals. That left the mate and two hands to trim the sails. The wind shifted suddenly, and as the mate tried to spill it from the sail, it shifted again. The mate became bound up in the sheet, and another shift took him overboard hanging by his leg. The wind shifted yet again still more fiercely and smashed him into the hull. He became tangled in the taffrail, and the sail unable to spill wind dragged us over on beam ends. The mast cracked, and we came up hard on the rocks over on our side."

Roque had no trouble coming up with six wagons while Rojo found a trio of Jicarilla teamsters. The sailors rigged a hoist to bring goods up from the hold: satin, velvet, flannel, muslin and cashmere, silk stockings and handkerchiefs, tools of all kinds, brandy, rum, and tins of oysters and sardines. In New Mexico, the stores brought over the Santa Fe Trail represented vast wealth, and wealth draws wolves as surely as carcasses draw buzzards. Word spreads even when there are no towns nearby.

They made a camp, a careless camp, a sailor's shipwreck camp. The wagons were drawn up haphazardly and partially loaded. Boxes were stacked along the tall sides of the ship where they'd been hoisted over the side. The ship, broken back and mast, rested against a rocky hillside. In the center of all, the sailors made a joyful bonfire. Spring evenings were cold near the mountains on the high plains, and the sailors wanted to enjoy the warmth. They were shipwrecked, and it was their due.

Rojo pulled Dan aside. "This makes me nervous. Too much light and noise." Dan could see that the Jicarilla teamsters were restless as well.

Dan nodded. "Me, too. They're all night blind."

From far beyond the circle of firelight came a screeching, unearthly howl. One of the sailors, apparently an Irishman, leapt to his feet. "'Tis the banshee sure, come to take us! We should have drowned in the shipwreck. Now the banshee comes!" The howl grew louder and closer.

Now Captain Thomas was on his feet. "What is that?"

Dan looked around. Rojo and the Jicarilla had disappeared. "Captain, get everyone aboard ship and load your cannons with grapeshot!"

The Irishman cried out. "Ye can't hope to fight the banshee with cannon!"

"Get aboard!" ordered his captain.

Captain Thomas ordered weapons issued and began to hand them out.

Dan watched as three rifles went to cook and sailors followed by cutlasses and pistols. Rojo and the Jicarilla reappeared as silently as they'd disappeared and drew weapons as well. They swarmed over the side resting against the hill.

He took Dan and the captain aside. "Comancheros. Somehow they have found us. They've brought *carretas* to haul your goods away. That was what you heard. Those big, solid wood wheels are ungreased."

"Comancheros?" said the captain.

"Yes, sir," said Dan. "They're pirates who go far out on the Llano Estacado, the Staked Plains, to trade with the Comanche. The Comanche raid Texian towns, farms, and ranches and steal everything, taking women and children as white slaves. The Comancheros sold their slaves down into Mexico. The Comancheros supply them with guns, powder, and *aquardiente*, fire water. It's a blood trade, a slave trade."

The captain's bushy brows knit. "I thought Mexico abolished slavery! They brag about it and point a finger at the United States."

"I guess Texians and Indians don't count, nor peons neither," said Dan quietly. "They're dangerous. They're thieves and killers as well as traders."

There was a time deep in the night when all good and honest men slept soundly. It was quiet and dark after moonset with only the stars to give faint hope that light would come into the world again. On board, all were sleeping with their guns as bedpartners. Only Roque was awake. Why? Wasn't he a good and honest man? Perhaps his conscience bothered him, and he was pondering whether or not lying with another man's wife was a mortal sin.

As he paced, in his consternation, he whispered to himself. "It wasn't like Carlos was a friend, more of an acquaintance and not even a *primo*. And Consuela was so beautiful and so willing. That must count for something. It's natural for a man. It would be unnatural to refuse her, and Padre Martinez said I could go to Hell for unnatural acts." A sound drew his attention, something no louder than a mouse scratching himself. "*Raton*," he grumbled, but he looked that way and sensed motion in the dark. "To arms!"

The captain was up in a flash. "Prepare to repel boarders!"

Excited, the cook and the Irish sailor each fired a cannon. In the flash that stole night vision, they glimpsed writhing figures even before they heard the screams.

"Reload, you fools!" cried the captain.

There was scrambling below. Dan called out, "They are trying to come up through the cargo we left alongside!"

A sailor leaned far out and fired down. There was a scream from below, and then he was skewered like fish by a lance and toppled over the side.

"Don't lean out!" yelled Roque. "You're too exposed."

Mice scurried in the dark, and then there was silence except for the moans of the dying below. No one slept. Time moved slowly before the dawn arrived. The dead sailor and four others lay below.

"Drat." The captain frowned. "Poor fields of fire blocked by the wagons and cargo. We should have killed more. What are their arms?"

Roque replied. "A few rifles and pistols, spears and lances, bows and arrows, and knives like small swords."

The banshee screeching started again. Something was coming out of the sunrise, but the blinding light concealed it. Soon a *carreta* full of hay came into view. There were men pushing it from behind, but the cart concealed them and cow hides.

"They mean to use it as a siege tower," said Dan.

The cook fired his cannon into the cart with no effect.

"They've wet the hay down so it won't burn," said Dan.

The cart thumped against the side and men swarmed up on top concealed by the side of the ship. The cook swiveled his gun as far as it would go and fired into the cart. There were screams, and the cook became a target as he reloaded.

The cart wasn't tall enough for the purpose. Still, the crew couldn't fire down into it without exposing themselves. The men in the cart had a long reach to the rail. One showed himself and received a bullet for his trouble falling back on his comrades. The crew, Rojo, Dan, Roque, and the Jicarilla were drawn amidships to face the challenge although it wasn't amounting to much.

A cry came from the Irishman who swung his gun around, standing out over the rail to do so and firing across the stern deck to the rock strewn hillside. There were screams including that of the Irishman as the men in the cart fired and brought him down. From the rocks and hill, Comancheros were swarming over stern onto the deck.

"Cookie, keep the ones in the cart from coming over the rail!" cried the captain. "Everyone else with me!"

They thundered down the deck firing into the mob as they went. Dan and Roque fired their pistols until they were empty. The captain's cutlass served the enemy out well. Too close for spears, the captain had a longer reach than the big knives of the Comancheros. Rojo was enjoying the use of his own cutlass, a new weapon for him. With their bows, the Jicarilla thinned the rear ranks of the enemy. Dan and Roque worked with tomahawk and Bowie.

Behind them there was a boom as Cookie fired his cannon again.

And then, as swiftly as the siege had begun, it was over. The enemy withdrew. Captain Thomas's crew reloaded and bound their wounds. Cookie made breakfast. They were alert and watchful.

Some of the enemy lying wounded stirred. The Jicarilla put arrows into them.

Dan turned to his friend. "Rojo, tell them to let them go."

Rojo disapproved but gave the instruction. A few more crawled away leaving them with nine corpses of Comancheros and two of their own dead.

After midday, the banshee screeching started up again and receded slowly into the distance. The Jicarilla rode out and returned with the news that the Comancheros had left.

They spent the next several weeks unloading the great ship and taking loads of goods into Barclay's Fort, Santa Fe, and Las Vegas. They remained watchful, but the Pirates of the Llano Estacado did not return. Being the first into Santa Fe for the season, Captain Thomas sold his goods at premium prices. Finally, they broke up the ship itself. Its oak timbers were valuable in hardwood starved New Mexico. Even the iron tires of her wheels went to the blacksmith shops. In the end, there was nothing left but the cairn of rocks that marked the last resting place of the first mate and two sailors. Only Captain Thomas, Cookie, Roque, Rojo, and Dan knew of the epic journey of this modern Admiral Drake.

Captain Thomas looked sternly at his crew, Dan, and Roque and said, "Tell no one."

"But, captain," protested Dan, "you've done a wonderful thing. You made it this far, and you made a fortune."

The captain snorted. "No fortune. I've paid for the ship and paid what's left of the crew. No more. The wreck ends my dream. Too many have died. I don't want anyone to know. I'm embarrassed by my folly."

With the work done, they gathered in the common room of Barclay's Fort on the Mora River where the

Mountain Route and Cimarron Cut-off of the Santa Fe Trail come together again.

When they were well in their cups, Captain Thomas spoke to his friends and surviving crew. "A toast, gentlemen, to work well done with my thanks." They raised their glasses and even the Jicarilla teamsters joined in with rare smiles. "Now swear to me you will tell no one of the ship or the wreck. No one must know. Swear!"

Reluctantly, they swore. No one would know the tale of the Wreck of the Wind Mill or of Captain Thomas's great success and failure or of the battle with pirates. It would be lost to history.

"Whither, Captain, does your wind blow?" asked Dan.

"For the States and Independence. I'll find a new project."

And so, the story was lost. The world only knew Wind Wagon Thomas had built two wind wagons at Independence but had been unsuccessful because they wrecked nearby. As everyone had suspected, and the newspapers scoffed, men can't sail the prairie sea in wind driven boats on wheels, even if they have a pirate at the masthead.

Letter from Fort Burgwin

In the days before the Civil War, the Jicarilla Apache were the terrors of the Santa Fe Trail, which passed through their hunting grounds and disrupted the herds of game. Although armed primarily with bow and arrow, they were excellent warriors. Attacked by two troops of U.S. Dragoons, 60 soldiers, an Apache force about equal in number killed or wounded every soldier with little loss. The Battle of Cieneguilla is almost forgotten today. It was an Indian victory, so there was little press to report it. New Mexico was far off, and the Army didn't want the story told. They accepted the lieutenant's version that made him a hero.

April 18, 1854

At Cantonment Burgwin
Near Taos, New Mexico Territory

Dear Josiah,

Sorry I haven't written for so long. I've finally got a little time as I'm confined to the hospital. I don't want to worry you; I am on the mend. In March, I took an arrow in a fight, a little battle I bet you haven't heard about anywhere else. Hickareeya[1] [Jicarilla] Apaches nearly wiped out two companies of dragoons at a place called Seeyenagheeya [Cieneguilla], the little swamp. Those few of us who survived were all wounded and out of

---

[1] Note: Private Joseph's somewhat eccentric spellings of names have been replaced after the first occurrence with more conventional forms.

ammunition. It was only through the kindness of the Apache that any made it back to camp. There was nothing to prevent them finishing us off.

The report our lieutenant turned in made him look quite the hero. I don't hold that view and need to tell you what happened. The Army will not question his report. "Large force of dragoons wiped out by small party of peaceful Apaches" doesn't sound nearly as good in the annuls as "Small party of dragoons, ambushed by huge war-party of blood-thirsty Apaches, survive by skill and daring of their leaders."

Nor does the Army want the world to know about the problem of dragoon weapons. We carry a saber. Unlike out firearms, it stays loaded all the time if we can just get close enough to use it. The pretty jingling sound it makes as we ride ensures that Indians will hear us coming miles away even if they miss the flash of polished metal. Next, we have the horse-pistol. It is a single-shot percussion cap pistol usually fastened to our saddles. It isn't a bad arm, but lacks range and isn't much fun to reload under fire. It is accurate to about 25 yards. Enemies can cross 100 yards while you're reloading, so they are usually on you before you finish.

If we were fighting proper, civilized armies instead of savages, we might be able to turn to them and say, "Excuse me. I find myself embarrassed by the lack of a ball in my pistol. Would you mind terribly waiting while I reload?"

And they, being civilized, would respond, "Not at all. Go right ahead." But since we are facing savages, this doesn't work. In fact, the Apaches seem to take a certain glee in finding us thus temporarily disarmed. Oh, for Colt's six-shooter. Six shots between reloads would be an advantage. One trooper could shoot keeping the enemy at arm's length while the other reloads.

Lastly, we are armed with musketoons, a shortened musket. It has little more range than a pistol with no rifling for accuracy. The ball rides so loose in the barrel that it can roll out. Like the pistol, it has but one shot. We reach into our belt-pouch pulling out a cartridge - powder and ball wrapped in paper - bite off the end, pour the powder down the barrel, follow it with ball and ram it home. Next, we half-cock the hammer and insert a percussion cap on the nipple. You can see this takes time, and in that time, because the range is so short, the enemy is upon you. At Cieneguilla, I saw nervous troopers dropping cartridges. Cartridges are large compared to the tiny percussion caps that soon carpeted the ground. Under fire, men drop them.

Disciplined fire can overcome some of these problems. One man fires while two reload; that should be the way. Even when fire is controlled, reloading is a close run thing because the range is too short. That's what I saw in battle with the Apache at the Little Swamp, not disciplined fire, but the results of dropped ammunition and short range.

The Jicarilla fought us with a few rifles and cheap trade fusils, but mostly they were armed with bow and arrow. I know it sounds primitive, but their range is 50 to 100 yards, making it greater than our own. The arrow, fired at high angle, comes down on you where you crouch behind cover. The savage can put six arrows in the air while we reload one round. "Aha!" you say, "at that rate they'll soon run out of arrows." If the Indians are in possession of the field, they simply gather up their shafts and reuse them. At Cieneguilla, Jicarilla women gathered them for their warriors.

95

The Wildest West

Near the end of the battle, when we had but a few rounds left, one bold woman gathered arrows in full view of the dragoons. She was bold as brass not 100 yards away. A dragoon fired on her. "Cease fire!" yelled the lieutenant, "We're out of cartridges, and she's out of range." The hussy turned her back on us, lifted up her skirts and spanked her buttocks at the U.S. Dragoons.

It amazes me how men idealize an officer for bravery. They like a man who is aristocratic and aloof and one who has graduated from West Point. But mostly they like bravery even if it isn't accompanied by any more military sense than a new corporal ought to have. Lieutenant Davidson was brave, no doubt. Some dragoons say his bravery saved us, but to my mind, it was his bravery and stupidity that almost got us all killed.

Let me tell you how the battle went, and you can judge for yourself. First, I should tell you about the people we fought and how we came to be at odds with them. Jicarilla see themselves as members of two bands. Oyairoh [Ollero] live south of Taos along both sides of the Rio Grande. They farm a little and make pots and baskets to sell in town. They come in to trade so we know many of them by name. Yahnairoh [Llanero] live on the plains in tepees across the mountains from our fort. Both bands used to hunt buffalo together. Their enemies, the Comanche, are more numerous now and keep Jicarilla away from the buffalo herds. Mexicans and Americans hunt on Apache lands. Jicarilla are starving. The Indian agent at Abbey Que [Abiquiu] showed the Ollero how to irrigate and farm last summer, but a drought killed everything. The Indian agents are asking the Governor, who is Indian commissioner, to provide food for the Jicarilla. Without food, the Llanero will continue to steal sheep and cattle and to raid caravans on the Santa Fe Trail. The starving Ollero will be forced to join them.

The Llanero were already stealing cattle and sheep in January. The dragoons from Ft. Union have been in the field fighting them. Jicarilla are hard to catch. Kit Carson, Indian agent for Taos, has told me some of the things they do. They have a plan to defend every camp they stay in. They camp in many of the same places year after year, so they have developed these plans over generations. On the trail, they always have a plan to come back together at a specific place. If they are surprised, they scatter like quail, but always know where they will meet up. Pursuers are left with many small trails to follow.

Mr. Carson says they have caches of supplies all over. Apaches don't need to have wagons or supply mules to slow them down. They just ride to places where they have things stored. They will ride a horse to death, eat it, steal another, and ride on. That makes it hard for dragoons to keep up. We're not supposed to ride our horses to death.

Kit Carson, Indian agent, yes, that Kit Carson. He lives at Taos with his wife, a Mexican lady. He's a smallish man though thick through the shoulders and chest. He wears fringed buckskins decorated with beads like an Indian. He carries a big knife, one of Colt's six-shooters, and a Hawken rifle. He has long, reddish hair. He's a quiet man, but he's able to speak Mexican and a number of Indian languages.

Toward the end of March, one of our patrols met up with the Ollero in the mountains above Peekoorees [Picuris] Pueblo. Major Thompson talked the chiefs into standing hostage for their people. They agreed to come down and camp at Ft. Burgwin. About 300 of them showed up. They looked terrible. Their clothing was ragged. Thin, worn and hungry, they were dispirited. Word had just come of the death of one of the Llanero chiefs, Lobo Blanco, the White Wolf.

Blanco and his band had been on the plains across the mountains. They had stolen a herd of cattle destined for Ft. Union. Dragoons were out hunting them and in frequent contact. Later, we learned the details of the fight that took the chief's life. He had tried to turn a meeting into an ambush. In March, all anyone knew was that Lobo Blanco had been killed when he came in to talk to the dragoons.

Kit Carson came down to talk to Chief Chakone [Chacón]. They talked a long time. Two years ago, the governor made a treaty with the Jicarilla. The chief accepted in good faith. The government was to provide farming implements, teach the Jicarilla to farm, and feed them until the farms began to produce. In exchange, the Apaches gave up their claims to hunting grounds along the Santa Fe Trail. The hunting grounds are occupied by whites, but Congress, after two years, still has not looked at the treaty.

I heard Kit say to his assistant, "Stay here with Chief Chacón. He has promised to wait here for my return. I'm going to Santa Fe to talk to the governor. He must send food, or we will have a war. This time he must listen!"

With that, Mr. Carson rode off. A short time later, Major Blake ordered us to move the Jicarilla into our barracks and store rooms and lock them in. We fixed bayonets and surrounded them. The major told their chiefs to stack arms and move inside. The Olleros became very agitated. It looked like we might have a fight on our hands.

Chacón argued with Blake that this was not according to the agreement. This was not what Kit had promised Chacón.

"Jicarilla will camp outside the fort," the chief of the Ollero said. "We will stay. We will keep our guns."

Major Blake had to give in. The Indians only had about 60 warriors, but mingled together we were in no position to start a fight. We posted guards inside the Cantonment (we have no walls or stockade) and left the Indians unmolested outside. I was on guard at dusk. I could see the Ollero preparing to eat and bed down. On guard again just before sunup, I saw their campfires still burning, but at dawn it became clear no one was near. The Jicarilla had slipped away.

Major Blake flew into a rage. He passed a few injudicious remarks as he worried about his career. "Nasty, lying Redskins have broken their parole! It's my responsibility. I'll look a fool for trusting them. They must be recaptured." As he calmed down, he called for Lieutenant Davidson.

"Lieutenant," Major Blake said, "I've heard you think you know how to whip Indians." The major didn't give the lieutenant time to reply. He'd heard Davidson bragging about how easy it was to defeat savages. "Take Companies F and I. Gain and maintain contact with Chacón's band. Stay with them, but don't attack them. Avoid a fight unless you are attacked."

We were in the field by noon, passed by Ranchos de Taos and descended into the Rio Grande gorge. That night we camped near Cieneguilla, a tiny collection of adobe houses, on the big river, the Rio Grande. We slept without tents despite the early spring chill. We didn't make fires lest we alert the Apache. At dawn's first light, without the cheerful bleat of bugles, we rose to a cold breakfast.

Lieutenant Davidson sent our scout, Jesus Silva - we call him Chewy [Chuy] - and a handful of men south along the river. His orders were, "See if the Indians have escaped across the river at Emboodoe [Embudo] Ford." The high San Juan Mountains are on the other side.

I was one of those chosen to go with Chuy. Silva is a mountain man who has worked as a guide for the dragoons many times. He speaks English as well as any mountain man, which is to say, not very well at all. He's wiry and tough and dresses like an Indian in greasy buckskins.

After an hour's ride, we discovered Embudo Ford had not been used.

"You two," Chuy said with a wave of his arm, "Ride quick back to the Lieutenant and tell him the ford has not been crossed. We will follow."

We worked our way back to the campsite checking canyons and trails. At one canyon, I spotted campfires burning a few miles distant.

"Chuy, look!" I said. "Fires."

"*Bueno, amigo*," Chuy replied. "This is the trail to Peerooris [Picuris] Pueblo. It's the Apache for sure. You," he pointed at a soldier, "ride to Davidson. Tell him what we have found and to come quick. We will go ahead."

We worked our way up the canyon for more than three miles until we could see tepees above us on a low ridge between two higher ridges close by. Behind us, we heard the sound of approaching dragoons: steel horseshoes beating on stone, sabers rattling along with canteens, and other loose stuff a soldier carries. We saw the glitter of brass and shiny weapons as two troops of dragoons, 60 men in all, caught up with us. Lieutenant Davidson seemed cheerful as he rode close to take Silva's report. I guess he thought all that noise and glitter would "strike terror in savage hearts."

The Wildest West

All the fuss made the Ollero Jicarilla aware of our presence. I don't think I heard terror in the voice that called out in English from the Ollero camp above, "Come on up if you want to fight!"

The lieutenant's face went red, and veins stood out and pulsed in his temples and neck. Clearly this was too much for him. "We attack!" he yelled. He split his command and sent one troop up each side of the ridge. First Sergeant Holbrook led one column and Sergeant Kent the other.

We rode as far as we were able on the steep slope, then dismounted and pulled our horses along behind us as the hill got steeper. In the end, we were stumbling and pulling reins but not moving forward.

Davidson called out, "Fourth men and doctor to the rear." We handed over the reins of our horses to the fourth man in each squad. If we dismount to fight, it is the fourth man's responsibility to take the reins of his squad-mates horses and lead them to cover behind our lines. We left our horses and fourth men in a little pine tree-lined hollow on the ridge. The two columns continued up the steep hill. I'd like to say we went with weapons ready, but it's hard to hold a weapon when both hands are grasping at roots, brush and grass as you try not to slide back down the hill. Bugles blaring, guidon leading, pennants waving, the glorious 1st Dragoons charged up the hill on all fours. In truth, we clung to the slope unable to lift pennant or raise bugle to lips.

The heroic 1st entered and conquered the Indian camp. We moved cautiously at first, spread out as skirmishers, musketoons at the ready.

"They're fleeing before us," howled Lieutenant Davidson. "Charge!"

The Wildest West

The bugler, with hands finally free to lift his instrument, echoed the order in song. 50 empty tepees stood before us. Dragoons scattered, poking into them looking for whiskey, women, and loot, returning with armloads of booty. Sergeant Kent tried to restore order. A shot rang out, and Kent fell dead a bullet square through the forehead.

Nobody panicked, and only those few closest to him seemed to notice. No other shots came from the piney hillsides around the village. It was quiet except for the sounds of looters and First Sergeant Holbrook trying to restore order.

A cry came from the hollow below us where we'd left the horses.

The doctor was shouting, "They're attacking the horses!"

Holbrook looked at Lieutenant Davidson who pointed down the slope and called, "Follow me!"

We followed him descending into hell. As the last dragoon went over the precipice to save our horses, the arrows arrived. We scrambled down using hands and feet to slow our descent, unable to get to our weapons. The Apaches fired from behind trees and rocks. We never saw them. It is a horrible thing to watch comrades die when you can't fight back. Dragoons, wounded and dead, never left that hillside.

If anything, the hollow where we left the horses was worse than the hill. When we arrived, Jicarilla had already taken half the horses and left two of our men down, *hors de combat*. Holbrook quickly formed us in a square with the horses inside and our fire controlled. Half our weapons were always loaded and ready to keep the Apache at bay. All we lacked was targets. After a few volleys, we'd so filled the little dell with powder smoke that we couldn't see more than an arm's length. The Olleros continued to fire from hiding, aiming at our shadows in the man-made fog. It was enough. They fired six shots to our one, and men were falling.

Fear set in. Nervous men dropped their paper cartridges while trying to reload. They littered the ground with tiny percussion caps. We came in with 40 rounds per musketoon and 20 for horse pistol. We left with far, far less and fewer men, too.

The Jicarilla had rifles and used them, but it was the bows that gave them advantage. Arrows don't usually kill immediately. Hit, you may find a limb immobile, but you will bleed. The loss of blood weakens you and eventually kills you. I saw men hit, bristling with arrows. Pull the arrow out, you leave the arrowhead inside. Uncork the wound, it bleeds the more. So, you leave it in and break off the fletched end hoping the stub is less likely to get bumped.

I don't know how long we fought from the dell. It seemed like hours, but the sun said it was still morning when we left. From the time we dismounted, no more than an hour had passed.

Lieutenant Davidson's report said after fighting most of the day we "fell back in good order" at his command. That command, as I remember it, was given, "Mount and save yourselves!" Davidson was shaken, as was I, and I was a bit deafened from Bennett firing his musketoon next to my ear.

We had lost most of our horses. We didn't have enough for all to ride, even riding double. Those who could climbed onto horses. Others clung to stirrups and grips on the saddles of horses ridden by friends. I saw five who lay still behind us.

We stopped at a low ridge half a mile distant. Bodies lay on the trail behind us. Some still moved. Holbrook organized the dragoons for defense. But our position was bad. Jicarilla made off with all but 10 horses. Apache shadows flitted from tree to tree. We seldom caught more than a fleeting glance, even though the smoke cleared more quickly here. Arrows arrived at a quickening pace.

The position had looked good, but it was impossible. The Apache got above us on both sides and rained arrows down on us. I saw a dragoon hit in the arm. The man next to him turned to help and took an arrow through the throat. Lieutenant Davidson raised a hand to signal, and the hand sprouted an arrow. It seemed like everyone was hit, most more than once.

The lieutenant rallied us. "We've got to move. Help the wounded." We all were wounded. "Follow me!"

Ten horses, we had, all mounted double. Men clung to stirrup and strap. I didn't count how many we left behind. More than a few. I'm not sure they were all dead. If you couldn't mount a horse or stagger along beside one, you didn't make the move. We moved a long way, more than a mile. Cieneguilla might offer safety, we thought. Lieutenant Davidson led us in that direction. Men were hit and fell along the way. Injured, limping, and faint, we could do little to help them. We carried some and helped all we could. Beside me a man who had been walking was hit again and fell. Still he grasped a stirrup and hung on. Dragged this way for a mile, his strength gave out. He fell and remained in the dust.

Another low ridge close to the mouth of the canyon offered shelter. Our backs were covered, we hoped. We could go no further in any event. I watched Davidson ride back four times to bring in wounded who had fallen. Those men owe him their lives; he brought them in despite the odds and arrows. He went back one more time collecting cartridge cases from the dead.

"Check ammunition," he cried above the din and moans. Those who could still aim a weapon, 16 of us, each ended up with three rounds for musketoon and two for pistol. That was all the powder and shot we had. We had no ammunition train, no pack animals, only what we carried. 42 of us made it to the last ridge. Four breathed their last in that place.

I looked back along our trail, watched as the women came out to collect arrows, cartridge cases, and weapons. I saw bodies still moving. So did the women. They selected large rocks and bashed in the skulls of our wounded until they moved no more.

I turned away retching.

"Take as a kindness, lad," said an old soldier beside me. He was a German, I think, who had fought in armies in Europe.

"Take it for the kindness that it is," he continued. "In Deutschland, peasant women come out and strip them of all they possess, even the gold teeth of the wounded, leaving them naked. I've seen the wounded fall between armies unable to move staring as the ravens peck out their eyes. Their screams are hideous. Wolves eat their living flesh and buzzards tear out their guts. They scream until your flesh crawls, and your blood goes cold. This is a kindness to have your skull bashed in."

We watched as the grizzly work continued.

I'm told I was one of four selected to ride to Fort Burgwin and call out the garrison. I don't know. I do not recall. When they tied me to a horse, I was in pain from my wounds. My head was light with loss of blood. The broken stumps of arrows protruded from my arm and from my leg near the groin. The rubbing and jostling brought intolerable pain, then all was black. I awoke days later in the hospital.

I think I hit one Apache. I saw him go down. Moments later the spot was empty. Apache sham being hit, fall behind cover, and reappear elsewhere unhurt. Not many Jicarilla were killed; we never saw any fallen Apaches. We seldom saw Apaches at all. They flitted from cover to cover, mere wraiths. 24 dragoons died at Cieneguilla, and 38 more are in the hospital recovering from wounds, some will yet die. The Jicarilla had no more men than the dragoons, no more than 60. That many came to Fort Burgwin. When we fought at Cieneguilla, troops from Fort Union were pursuing Llanero Jicarilla on the plains across the mountains. Llanero could not have been at Cieneguilla as the lieutenant claimed. There could not have been 300 warriors fighting us, and we did not kill many. The Mexicans at Velarde, a village the Jicarilla passed through after the battle, said the Jicarilla told them they had two killed and one wounded. With only three rounds left and our horses gone, no reserves and no resupply possible, it was only through Chacón's mercy any dragoons survived. If he had made one final attack, we would all have perished.

I'll write again if I get out of hospital. I have made out a will and left it with companions to forward in the event of my death.

Jicarilla were seen today very near the fort. Our companies are in the field hunting them, but the Apache hunt us here where only the wounded are left. Unable to rise, I fear I shall die in my bed. We expect an attack any minute. I hope this letter will find its way to you.

God Bless,

Garry J. Joseph

Garrett Ian Joseph
Private, 1st Dragoons

Escape from Mesilla

The fringe of his buckskin shirt flapped in the light April breeze. "This way. The stage went this way, mules on the run, out of control." Long strides of his knee-high moccasins carried him along a trail obvious to him if not to his comrades. He led his riding mule.

"Hey, wait! Shouldn't we bury them?" Two bodies pierced by arrows lay on the ground many yards apart.

"Sure, kid, but it can wait. They've been lying here a week, and they'll keep. They're swollen. It's gonna be nasty." This pronouncement came from a big, broad-shouldered, soft-spoken man.

The kid gulped. He was slight but strong having been in the west for a time. He gulped again holding something back in his throat. He tried to mat down his hair without success. It stuck out from his head, and he settled for jamming his hat down over it. "I guess. If you say so, Matt."

A tall, lithe man looked up from a body at the frontiersman's receding back. "Emmitt, I think Jack's right," he said to the kid. "We can bury them later." He seemed to be the leader. Matt and the kid, Emmitt, followed him. Behind them came a dark man, a bit taller than average, and well dressed. His eyes shifted from side to side as he watched.

"Sure, Free," said the kid gulping again.

They hurried after the frontiersman, Jack, walking rapidly away from the big stone building that had been the Stein's Peak Station in the shadow of pyramidal Steen's Peak. The trail followed the course the Overland Road, along the banks an arroyo that cut deep along the mountain's flank. They found the celerity wagon, a kind of coach with three seats on a flat foundation with canvas top and sides. It was over on its side in the deep wash. There was one naked, mutilated body inside.

Matt whistled. "They didn't like him much. I'll bet Sam accounted for a few of them before they got him."

The kid turned green but said nothing.

Jack nodded up toward the peak where buzzards surrounded a clump of trees. They headed uphill but carrion birds and coyotes unwilling to surrender their prey repulsed them. The dark man trailing fired a shot, and the eaters departed in haste revealing two bodies hung by their ankles in the tree. Charcoal and ash showed where the Apache had lighted small fires under their heads. The bodies lacked hair and had little skin left on what had been faces.

Jack scowled at him. "Avaline, yer gonna alert the 'Paches."

"That makes five," said Matt. "Can't tell who they are, but we've accounted for everybody except J.J. Giddings. This must be him."

The kid hurried away and was soon heard retching.

The tall, dark man looked at the bodies. "Does this mean we're out of work?"

Free looked at Avaline a moment and responded. "Reckon not. His brother will still want the Jackass Mail to run from San Antonio to San Diego for the Confederacy."

Jack spat.

Matt nodded. "Got that right. I didn't sign on with Butterfield to work for no Confederacy."

"Maybe the rebellion will die out," said Free. "Then we're keeping the road open for the Union."

The kid, gone dry, returned. "I don't ever want to end up like that," said Emmitt Mills.

"You got that right," replied Free Thomas. "You got that right." Except for Avaline who looked sidelong at the hanging bodies, all nodded and agreed. "Time to get to work."

April became May. The news from the east was not encouraging. There were rumors of a Confederate Army coming to conquer New Mexico. The mail ran sporadically. Drivers never knew if they'd find a station occupied and fresh mules waiting or empty the hostlers having decided to depart with the stock and go into business for themselves. There were more rumors of Apache attacks than there were signs of Indians. The mail was unmolested, but drivers, conductors, and station keepers were well behind in their pay.

In a dry spring, Mesilla slowly returned to the dust from which it was built. In the *Santa Guadalupe* Cantina, Avaline dealt Monte to a hard featured man of medium height. His clothes were dusty but well made, frontier clothes, suitable for the trail. Knife and pistol were stuck in his belt. He had admirers. His eyes were unsteady as he knocked back another cup of cactus whiskey and laid a bet.

Avaline dealt the next card. "I see you've lost again, my friend."

"It's okay, Capn' Mastin. Yuse the capn' o' the Arizona Guards. You can take this tinhorn," cried one of the admirers.

Mastin looked hard at the gambler. "You talk like a Yankee. You a Yankee, tinhorn?"

Another of Mastin's followers spoke up. "He's a Butterfield man, come from up north. I knows him."

Unnoticed by those surrounding Avaline, a man entered and ordered a drink. His clothes were dusty and worn, his broad-brimmed hat pulled low shading his eyes. He was large and powerful and wore his Colt .44 holstered and slung for a fast draw. Had anyone been watching, they might have seen him slip the loop from the hammer of his weapon as he watched the growing excitement around Avaline.

"Kill the Yankee, sumbitch."

Mastin straightened and squared on the man with the cards. "What's a matter with you? Yankee gambler? You don't believe in our rights? We won't put up with that."

"There's another Yankee sumbitch!" howled another of Mastin's Arizona Guards pointing at the newcomer.

Mastin turned from the gambler. "You lookin' fer trouble, too?"

"Me? Not a bit."

Mastin growled. "Coward? You sound like more Yankee, trouble-making scum."

The man in the hat stood his ground. "I don't take kindly to being called a coward or scum."

Mastin's men offered their own insults to the hated Yankees.

The gambler tried to calm them. "Listen here, we don't want no trouble."

Mastin jerked out his pistol. The hammer clicked loudly into place as he drew it back and leveled it on Avaline. "Goodbye, Yankee. I'll see you crap your pants or die."

A bullet crashed across the room creasing Mastin's thigh. He groaned, dropped his weapon, and fell to the floor. The man in the hat stood, the smoking pistol in hand. "Come on, gambler. Time to leave."

The Wildest West

They backed out the door as calls came from within. "You'll pay for this!" "We'll get up a reward." "You can't shoot the capn' and expect to live."

In the street, Avaline spoke. "Name's Tom Avaline. Thanks for your help."

"Name's Jack Portall. Friends call me Port. Is there another cantina in this dust bowl where a man can drink in peace?"

Avaline nodded leading the way. "They'll come for you, ya know. They'll have reward posters up by tomorrow."

"Don't much care."

"I wouldn't worry though." The gambler smiled for the first time. Port thought that crooked smile a bit crooked and evil, but what the hell? "Joke's on them. They ain't got a sheriff or marshal. There's no law to bring you in."

Port laughed. In the next few months of growing Confederate excitement, they were seldom seen apart, one watching the other's back. The wanted posters appeared the next day as Avaline predicted. Confederate sympathizers offered $200 for Port dead or alive. No one seemed to have the courage to make an attempt to collect.

The dust blew May away, and June heat arrived with sweat and grit. Hides toughened as grit chafed, and sweat salted tender spots until nothing soft was left. Thunderclouds built on the horizon promising violent storms that never came.

Avaline approached Freeman Thomas near the Overland Mail Station, now the offices of the San Antonio and San Diego Mail. "Free, you got work for me and my friend, Port?" the gambler asked the Jackass Mail conductor.

"Maybe." Free shrugged. "Can't hardly keep the line open. Giddings don't send half what we need, and station keepers steal half of that and abandon their stations. Don't know from one day to the next which stations are manned."

Matt Champion joined them. "Do you really care? Do you really want to keep the road open for the Confederacy?"

A passing stranger spat at their feet. "Watch what you say about the Confederacy, damn Yankees."

Port turned and lowered a hand to his holster. The man scurried away.

"It's getting worse," said Free.

From down the street came sounds of a fight. They ran to see what was happening. In an alley between buildings, three men had Emmitt on the ground and were stomping the kid who lay curled trying to protect himself. Matt rushed in taking one unawares by collar and belt, tossing him ten feet into the dust. Port kicked a boot out from under another and sent him tumbling. Avaline's revolver clicked. The third man ran, and collecting themselves from the ground, the other two followed.

The Fourth of July arrived with a celestial fireworks display. Black clouds rose high and bristled and glowed with lightning. The rains struck with violence, soaking the world, melting adobe walls, and driving men from the streets. At the old Butterfield Station, Jackass Mail employees huddled in the dark watching the roof leak.

Big Matt commented. "Colonel Baylor's in Franklin with a Confederate mounted regiment."

Avaline whispered, "Rumors. Confederates make it sound big. Just a battalion."

The kid got excited. "Still, it's a lot! And they're close!"

113

Jack entered, his buckskins wet and dripping.

A German sat with them. "Ja. But President Lincoln, he keep Union together, for sure. We gots nodding to worry about. Is good country, Amerika. Nothing bad gonna happen, Gott in Himmel."

Matt shifted in his chair. "Free, what happens to us when the Confederates come?"

Free cocked his head. "We'll be okay. We work for the Jackass Confederate Mail."

"You sure?" asked Avaline frowning. "Don't seem like there's been a mail wagon in a while."

"Yeah," said the kid. "You sure you want to work for Confederates, enemies of the Union? We've got to fight 'em!"

Port looked at Emmitt with narrowed eyes. "Kid, you talk more'n that German muleskinner."

"Ja, ja, we got to fight Sesech for sure, Gott mit uns."

Free glanced around the group. "Major Lynde has got the road blocked. There's no Confederate mail going anywhere. And Colonel Baylor's regiment won't get passed Fort Fillmore."

A rock crashed loudly into the door startling the group. Outside in the rain, someone yelled. "Damn Yankees!"

"Right, Free." The gambler grinned. "All we got to worry about is the neighbors."

Emmitt jumped to his feet and ran to the door.

Matt blocked his way. "Relax, kid."

On July 19, a stage came in from the west.

The driver was heated. "How soon can you get me some stock and get me going? I've got mail for San Antonio. What a trip! Never knew if there'd be anyone or any water from one station to the next! Station keepers deserting right and left. Rumors of Apaches. But we made it, and we'll make San Antonio."

Matt shook his head. "'fraid not. Nothing's going south from here. Major Lynde has got the road blocked. He's afraid of spies. Colonel Baylor's on the march. You're stuck here."

That night the friends met for dinner. They found traveling singly an invitation to a beating by Southern sympathizers.

From the next table, they overheard conversation. "Damn Yankees. Ought to be hung."

"Baylor gets here, maybe they will." There was a laugh.

Port spoke quietly. "California's soundin' better all the time."

"How would you get there?" Free asked. "Is the road even open?"

Matt nodded. "Stage came in, Free. From the west."

Freeman Thomas looked directly at him. "Are you suggesting we steal the stage?"

"Why not?" said Port. "Most of us are owed wages."

Jack looked thoughtful. "We'd need some things. Guns, grain, water."

Free responded. "There's a Sharps for each of us at the station and probably two Colt's revolvers, and there's grain and containers for water as well as canteens."

Emmett spoke for the first time. "I can round up some food."

Free nodded. "That's good, kid. There's plenty of ammunition at the station, too. Maybe 2,000 rounds."

Avaline smiled. "Now there's a bet I like, Sharps rifles and plenty of ammo."

Wrapped in buckskin, Jack folded his arms and frowned. "We need cover, or these Rebs will shoot us."

Free's eyes brightened. "We'll leave at midday during the next storm."

Jack raised a fist in triumph. "They'll be plenty of water in the sinks and holes. We won't have to worry about the stock."

Port smiled. "And if we get shot at, what the hell!"

Avaline grinned crookedly. "What do you care? Wanted posters are still up on you."

July 21st dawned clear and blue, but by late morning thunderheads were crowding the sky. By noon, they'd built up taller and blacker than basalt cliffs, and then with a crash they fell with rain as thick as standing corn turning the streets to rivers. Wind roared and drove the rain before it slantwise.

A wanted poster blew by. "That was one of yours, Port," yelled the gambler, Avaline. "I think they've raised the reward."

Port set two more Sharps rifles into the bed of the celerity wagon and pushed them under a seat. The wagon was a stagecoach with a canvas top and sides. Driver and conductor sat on the same level as the passengers while the first seat faced backwards so that the riders had their backs to them with a sheet of canvas in between. There were two more seats barely 42 inches wide so that with nine passengers aboard, they sat hip to hip, legs interlocked, and those on the outside edge rode with a foot in the air. With only five passengers and two operators, it was going to be more comfortable, but not much. The road was "improved" just enough for the stage to pass over it, but its body was supported on leather straps in the place of springs. Riders would feel every bump and rock personally.

Emmitt emerged into the rain with a sack of grain over his shoulder while Matt and Joseph, the German, struggled to harness four half-wild mules.

Free looked at the load and then climbed into his seat next to the driver while Joseph joined him. "Mount up. Let's get out of here before the storm breaks!"

They headed out. As they passed the cantina, Free heard voices. "What was that? Sounded like a coach." A head emerged, and the shouting began in earnest. "They're stealing a stage!"

"Damn Yankees!"

Someone in the knot of men emerging from the cantina drew a revolver and fired a shot.

Emmitt leaned out, crooking one arm around the pole supporting the canvas roof of the stage. In the other, he held a Sharps. From 100 yards away in a moving wagon, the kid fired a shot striking the cantina sign. It fell. He reloaded and fired again. The knot of men disappeared back into the building, each vying to be first through the door.

"Gotta love the Sharps," howled the kid. "Breech loading, lower the breech and throw in the next cartridge. It's faster and easier to load than any rifle and accurate just as far. Accurate twice as far as a musket or fusil. This is firepower. They'd better run."

"Sit down, kid," said Matt smiling. "You're getting more talkative than Joseph."

Up front Joseph was talking to his mules.

At Picacho, the station keeper was suspicious. Free waved the empty mailbag at him. "Mail's gotta get through."

"Ja. Gott in Himmel, mail's gotta get tru! Patches out der gonna kill somebody sure."

The hostler changed the mules for fresh ones.

There was no one at Rough and Ready or at Good Sight. They watered and rested the mules a while and pressed on more slowly, arriving at the abandoned Cooke's Spring Station well after midnight.

"We rest here," said Free. "Feed the mules a bait of grain and water 'em."

The man in buckskin shook his head. "Free, we oughta push on and get through the canyon in the dark. 'Patches don't fight at night. We can rest at Mimbres Crossing. There's bound to be someone there. In the dark, Free."

Free spoke firmly. "It's a long hard pull to the pass and miles to Mimbres Crossing. The mules are half dead as it is. They need rest."

The frontiersman stalked off into the dark and made his bed away from the others. He didn't want to be near campfire or anything that might become a target, especially in the predawn light when 'Patches were bound to be active.

Morning came, and Free was still resting the mules, letting them munch grass. With the sun directly overhead, he'd finally rested them enough. "All right. Hitch 'em up and let's get loaded."

Jack mumbled, "The 'Patches know we're here."

They set out with Free and Joseph up front, Free with Sharps across his lap and Joseph chattering about something and talking to his mules. Matt and Jack faced forward from the rear seat, loaded Sharps between their knees and pistols tucked in belts. The gambler and his friend, Port, sat in the front facing the kid who sat on the middle seat. All had their weapons ready. They moved rapidly across the flat, bounding through a small ditch, and then made the hard right turn into the narrow mouth of the canyon.

"Mein Gott, de mules ears touch de valls for sure."

Then shots rang out and arrows flew. Two arrows found Joseph's leg and stomach. Bold and strong, the big man whipped up the mules, and they lurched forward at high speed.

"The only way out is through!" yelled Free encouraging the driver.

The five men in the back returned fire, reloaded, and fired again. Free saved his shot in case anyone tried to block their passage.

They emerged from the narrows, their wagon looking like a porcupine, flying at full tilt up the grade and bouncing wildly over the rocks as they passed through the broad valley. Off to the right, a pony herd stood tended by two young warriors. The kid leaned out and shot one. The other dived for cover as the ponies scattered.

Free looked back. "Take 'em a while to gather those up."

They clattered through the valley on the rising trail. Far behind, angry Apaches tried to catch their ponies. Port laughed. The others, even the kid, knew they'd only gained a little time. Precious little. Free held the German upright and tried to come up with a plan that gave them some hope.

Jack stood and hung out the side, the fringe of his coat flapping. He looked ahead and didn't like what he saw. "Get ready. We're coming to a tight spot on a steep grade."

There had been no need. The others had been here before and, knowing the trail, were already loading and checking their weapons. The coach bounced and careened from rock to stone.

Matt yelled. "Careful, we don't want to break a wheel or an axle."

119

The Wildest West

"Ja, ja, Gott in Himmel. Dem 'Patches gonna take some scalps!" The German didn't slow. The pace of his conversation with the mules increased.

Free called back, "Joseph can't continue. When we clear the pass, we'll be out of sight of the 'Patches. We stop, unload everything, get well off the road, and hide. Then we'll whip the mules and send 'em runnin' downhill. With luck, they'll run all the way to the bottom, and with luck, the 'Patches will follow them. We can make our way on foot back to Cooke's Spring Station."

"Why there?" asked Port.

"Because there's water and stone walls. We can defend it longer than they'll want to stick around."

They passed over the saddle and began their descent. Free helped the German rein in the tired, frightened mules. "Quick, everything out. We'll need it."

The kid looked over the ground. "Free, it's wide open. There's no place to hide!"

"Throw some stones together. They'll have to do."

They had to work with what was already there. Small boulders became a base for a circle ten feet across, big enough for four of them. Two other circles were soon large enough for two men each.

The kid shook his head angrily. "This will never work!"

Jack answered him. "It's good ground. We don't much need the stones. We've got range on the 'Patches by 100 yards at least, and we can fire three times as fast. Looks like they could climb to the top of the pass and up the hill and fire down on us. But we got range on 'em. Soon as they stick their heads over. They're within range of our guns and still have a hundred yards to go before they can reach us.

They'll try to come up the hill from below us to that clump of trees."

Free looked around. They'd done all they could. He heard the thud of unshod hooves pounding up the pass and whipped the mules to action. They ran, and he ran for cover.

The mules kept going at breakneck speed following the road down into Starvation Valley between the Cooke's Peak Range and the Pony Hills. The mules performed just as Free had hoped, and the Apaches, with whoop and yell, charged after the Celerity wagon's dust trail trying to catch up. Free was relieved. In a few moments, he and his friends could grab their gear and start back to the Cooke's Spring Station and safety.

Half a mile below the pass, two Apaches stopped their mounts. One was a tall, well-made man with a bit of gray in his hair. "Cochise," whispered Jack, but there was no need. The others had recognized him.

Beside him sitting comfortably on his horse's back was the largest Indian Free had ever seen, a head taller than Cochise. "And that's his father-in-law, Mangas Coloradas."

"They call him Red Sleeves because he bathes his arms in his enemies' blood," said the kid.

"Hush," answered Matt. "No such thing. He likes vests and red shirts."

Emmitt saw that Matt was right.

The two Indians seemed nervous. Cochise kept looking this way and that as if expecting something bad.

Avaline looked at him with understanding. "It's that feeling you get when someone has a gun pointed at your back." The gambler squinted down his sights centering the bead on Cochise's back.

Port gripped Avaline's sight and shook his head.

Now, Mangus Coloradas began to fidget looking as nervous as Cochise. The latter turned all the way around and looked up the hill. Shading his eyes from the afternoon sun, he scanned the hillside slowly. He moved on far to one side of where Free and his party lay. Free breathed relief. The larger Indian was now looking right at their position. Free could feel the tension in the others. No one moved. Satisfied, the two Apache turned and began to ride downhill around a bend in the trail that took them out of sight.

"That's a relief," said the kid starting to rise.

Jack looked at him. "Hold up a minute."

From around the bend below came two shots.

Free shouted, "Check your caps! Get ready!"

The frontiersman scanned the ground to their front. "Wait 'til I fire. Wait until they're within a hundred yards. We'll give them a surprise."

The German groaned as he rolled into position.

Free glanced at him. "Better let me tend to those wounds." He pushed the arrow in the German's leg all the way through until the arrowhead protruded on the far side. A bit of cut glass, probably cut from a bottle, was tied into a small shaft of hardwood. This had been inserted into a longer shaft of bamboo. Free pulled the hardwood part out one side and the feathered shaft out the other. The wound bled but not much. "Good," Free said. Joseph groaned. "Now I'll wrap it to slow the bleeding."

Free considered the second wound. He sniffed it. It didn't stink of bowel. "Joseph, if I push this through, I might cut your gut. It needs a doctor. I'll break the bamboo shaft so it gets knocked around less." Joseph nodded. Free started cutting the shaft and Joseph passed out. The wound wasn't bleeding much.

The Wildest West

The Apaches had stopped 300 yards away examining the situation. Cochise signaled and a group of ten rode to within 50 yards and then charged laterally across the front, encouraging the white men to shoot at them. None did. It was a good trick to play on tenderfoots. They'd waste shots on hard to hit moving targets, and the Indians would close in while they were reloading.

Mangus Coloradas was disappointed. He encouraged the whole group, fifty or more, to charge at once coming across the front at an angle and then veer to come straight in.

"Hold your fire! We'll give them a double surprise. Volley and reload! Now, fire!"

The Apaches were scarcely 50 yards away when the volley hit them as they turned to come straight in. The men didn't manage a volley with the next round. At 30 yards, the first Sharps fired, and by the time the Indians were within twenty yards, the last of six Sharps had spoken. Now pistols came out and the Apaches backed off having lost horses and men. A few wounded began the long crawl back to their lines.

"Get your rifles!" Free shouted. "Keep firing. It's time to let them know our range and speed."

The Apaches continued to lose riders out to 100 yards. They paused. Three fell to well-placed shots. The Indians continued their withdrawal.

When they passed 200 yards, Jack yelled, "Cease firing. Don't waste ammo."

The afternoon sun was hot. The German lay in it, still unconscious, groaning. The kid, aware they owned the ground and that he was well beyond the range of Apache weapons, went down to a small copse of mesquites. He cut a few branches. Then he stopped and looked down the hill.

Running to Free he said, "There's Apaches crawling up the hill toward those trees!" He waved the cut branches in Free's face.

"What are those for?" asked Free pulling his face away.

"Oh, for the German. To cover him from the sun."

"Injuns comin'," called Jack.

The others were busy gathering stones to building up their shelters. Free, Jack, and Joseph occupied the large circle, about 10 feet in diameter. Off to the west, toward the trail, Avaline and Port had a small circle about 20 yards distant. To the south, closest to the mesquites, Matt and Emmitt, the kid, had a still smaller circle.

Apaches in the copse of mesquite, three small trees in a clump, kept the defenders pinned to the earth for the rest of the afternoon.

"Free," said Jack, "we've got to drive them off. Cochise has got the rest of his men working around behind Frying Pan Mountain to come up on the ridge behind us. We can beat them off the ridge okay, but not with others firing at our backs from the trees. I've got an idea. . . Give me covering fire!"

Jack ran to the circle of rocks where Matt and the kid had taken cover.

"What you gonna do?" asked Matt.

"Give me cover." Jack ran, dropped, crawled, and ran again until he was 100 yards beyond Matt and Emmitt. He had flanked the trees and could see behind them. The Apaches turned to fire at him, but he was, as he had planned, beyond their range.

He sighted carefully on the brave nearest him and fired. The Apache on his belly, lurched, groaned, and was still. Jack reloaded and sighted on a second. The bullet struck the prone man in the top of the head. He neither groaned nor moved. Jack reloaded. The third Apache did not wait for further invitation. He ran back down the hill beyond Jack's range.

Dark clouds gathered, piling high, and with crash of thunder and flash of lightning, the rain fell. Heavenly armies charged, fired on each other, and retreated. Below them six men watched and waited. Jack gathered stones for a new breastwork that flanked the trees. The others shivered as they soaked to the skin and waited sure the Apache would come over the ridge next.

Far off, beyond Starvation Gulch, over at Mimbres Station, the sun set sparking a display of bloodied heavens.

"It's beautiful," mumbled the German. He then fell back into delirium talking incessantly in German.

"Is he praying?" yelled Avaline. "He'd better be praying. Let him play with beads and pray." In the dark, the German's mumbled prayers continued.

In the gloom, Jack walked back over to Free. "We should leave. They don't like to fight at night. 'Fraid of spirits that stalk the dark."

Freeman Thomas was troubled. "We can't leave Joseph, and he can't walk."

"He's dying, and the way to Mimbres Station is open. We could be there by morning."

Free shook his head, a gesture Jack felt more than saw in the dark. He nodded and smiled grimly.

"Free, they'll rush us over the ridge in the gray light before dawn."

"I'll be ready. Tell the others."

Jack disappeared silently into the murky evening, stopping when he heard whispered voices.

"Port, we could slip out of here and away and be at Mimbres Station by dawn."

There was silence for a moment, and then Port replied. "Why not Cooke's Spring?"

The other voice responded. "There's no one there, and two of us can't defend the station alone. Besides, the Apaches have all moved to that side."

"What about the others, Avaline? Do we just leave them?"

"They won't leave Joseph."

In the dark, Jack noticed that Avaline called the driver Joseph and not 'that German.' He said nothing and continued to listen.

Port's voice said, "If we leave them without saying anything, they'll all die. We've got to hold this wing."

"I know, but the odds are poor, and I'd rather be somewhere else. We'll hold the ground."

Jack came closer and spoke from the dark as if he'd heard nothing. He told them to be ready for a rush from the ridge behind them. "We're going to be short one rifle. I have to make sure they don't return to the mesquite, and from over there, I'm out of range of the ridge."

Jack returned to his outpost stopping to talk to Matt and the kid.

The kid had an idea. "If they're so afraid of the dark, why don't we sneak into their camp and light 'em up, like Joshua and the Midianites in the Bible?"

Jack smiled despite himself. "Because they're wily devils. We'd be halfway through their camp before we knew it. They sleep spread out and hidden. It'd be a right hornets' nest with us in the middle."

In the dark, Free heard the others gathering stones to make their parapets just a little higher. He marveled that none of them shot at "ghost Apaches" in the dark or fired at noises. The German continued his one-sided conversation.

Free answered him softly, certain Joseph wouldn't make sense of what was said but hoping calm words might soothe him. "Our companions are calm and steady. I'm proud of them. I'd half expected the others to depart and leave us alone. Jack Wilson is a frontiersman. Even alone, he'd make it to Mimbres Station in the dark. He's tough as they come. I don't know if you'd heard, at Apache Pass Station he killed a Mexican in a knife fight. That one was held captive by the Apache when young, but they trained him, and he was one of their best warriors. Jack took him down anyway. Any weapon will do for Ole Jack.

In the dark, Free continued. "I don't know Port so well. The man can be stiff without no back up. He doesn't back away from fights he should avoid. But that don't mean he'll stay and fight Apaches. I don't want to worry you none, but Port has a price on his head, and going back to Cooke's Spring puts him closer to the Confederates that want him. $200. Did you ever think you'd be fighting alongside a man with a price on his head?

Free took a breath and thought a while. "Who knows if the kid has ever faced a crisis? When crisis comes, and the kid is really frightened, will he hold or run? If anything happens to Matt, the kid might panic. But, for now, they all seem calm and steady. Good men. The best."

Matt made his way to Free's position. "How's the German?"

"About the same."

Matt nodded without complaint. "Kid and I need food, water, and ammo."

"Powder or paper cartridges?"

"Paper cartridges. Didn't use the pistols much, but we need caps."

"Matt, we've enough water for tonight and tomorrow. After that . . ." Free trailed off. "And Matt, would you mind resupplying the others."

"No problem."

The false dawn came, and with it Jack's voice. "Wake up. Matt, are you and the kid okay?"

"We're good."

Free's voice was heard. "I'm good. Joseph is very bad, but he keeps talking."

Then Port's voice was heard. "We're ready."

In the gray light that knew no color, dark figures came over the ridge. Five rifles cracked, and 12 figures hit the ground so many 'possums playing dead. The next volley was fast but ragged.

"Matt," cried Emmitt, "which are hit and which are just playing?"

"Dunno. If it moves, shoot it again. Keep an eye out for the ones that fall out of sight."

Free held the weak center, loading and firing as fast as he could. His pistols lay on the ground in easy reach. If the Apache got close, he'd use them. The Apaches had a long downhill approach to get to him, but coming downhill, they tended to fire high, while his shots were ripping into their legs and bellies.

Jack watched as a dozen braves approached the copse of mesquite shielding from the view of the others. He loaded and fired methodically, hitting a man with every shot. He was firing four aimed rounds a minute, and the warriors would have to cross 200 yards of open ground to get to him. They broke and ran before they got within 50 yards. Some fell where he couldn't see them. He could hear the furious fight behind him, but he couldn't participate. He'd have to watch carefully so that no warrior suddenly rose from the dead when he wasn't looking. If he got a chance, he'd take a pistol and make sure each was dead, but that was dangerous work.

On the flank near the trail, Port and Avaline were closest to the ridge. The Apaches were hidden until they were scarcely 120 yards away, almost in range of their poor guns. The pair loaded and fired rapidly and calmly.

Port looked at his friend, sure both of them were terrified. "Avaline, you got the poker face. You sure can run a bluff."

The Apaches closed, and Avaline drew both pistols. Port jumped to his feet and did the same. Between them, they fired 24 shots in under 10 seconds, each at least wounding a warrior. That broke the advance.

Daylight shone on a field littered with Apache.

Free spoke loud enough for the others to hear. "Don't get up. Don't expose yourself. Some may be wounded, others just playin.' Stay alert. Reload."

Port stood surveying the ground and reloading his pistols, a long, slow process, one pistol at a time. He measured powder for each of six cylinders, and then found a ball for each, and one by one, drove them home. Port reached for the tiny caps, which had to be fitted to the nipple on back of each cylinder.

Just outside the circle of rocks, an Apache leapt up lance in hand. Port drew the hammer back, and it clicked on a capless cylinder. He tried again as the Apache drove the lance into his belly. Rising, Avaline drew his knife and slit the warrior's throat. Blood sprayed all around as the brave twisted and died. Port fell to his back.

"Port!"

"Yeah, Avaline. Pull it out. It hurts."

Avaline looked at the lance. "You'll bleed to death."

Port chuckled and groaned. "I won't do much better with it where it is."

"It's gonna hurt." Avaline pulled. The lance stuck. Port screamed and passed out.

Avaline saw his friend was still alive although the spear was still stuck in his belly. He made Port as comfortable as he could. The wound wasn't bleeding. The spear saw to that. Avaline went back to loading all of their weapons while watching for Apaches he could kill.

Nearby, an Apache moved. Avaline walked to him and with his Sharps inches from the dark head fired. The result was unpleasant. The gambler returned to his friend.

From over the hill came the sounds of a large number of horsemen. The sound slowly receded into the distance toward Cooke's Spring.

"They've left," yelled the kid.

"Get down!" Matt ordered.

A lone horseman appeared atop the ridge. The tall, well-made Apache with grey-shot hair looked down on them.

"Cochise," said Free.

The sun rose hot steaming yesterday's rain from the moist earth. High overhead clouds began to gather. On the ridge, a few Apaches, with long guns gathered, began to fire down on the men in their useless shelters. Most shots went long, a problem for men firing down a steep slope.

A bullet struck Free in the shoulder, and he yelped and fell backward. "Lord, that stings like the devil!" He pulled off his shirt finding only a bruise that bled slightly. "It didn't make a hole."

Jack answered. "They're out of range. Their bullets are falling at random without much power behind them."

Before long, Cochise understood as well and called his men back.

Noon came and went. Jack noticed a "dead" body was much closer than it had been. He put a bullet into its head. The dead man groaned and died again.

Avaline looked at his still unconscious friend and started shooting into all the bodies he could see.

Behind him Port mumbled. "Save your ammo. You might need it." He groaned.

"Port, how are you? Are you okay?"

"How do you think I am? I've got a lance in my belly. Why didn't you take it out?"

"It's stuck. I was afraid I'd drag your guts out with it."

Port nodded. "I'm dying. If you get a chance, go with the others, but make sure my weapons are loaded and in reach first." He coughed, groaned, and went silent.

Avaline thought his friend had died.

"Avaline." It was a pained, hushed voice, barely a murmur. "Avaline, write me a letter to my family. I want them to know what happened to me."

"How can I deliver it?"

"Put it under a stone and hope someone will find it."

"Port, I don't write so well."

"Then tell Free what I say, and he can do it."

"Port, I won't leave you."

And then the arrows came, fired by men standing on the ridge.

Jack's voice came clear. "Slow, easy shots, gents. Drive them off the ridge. Let them know we have range on them."

Avaline, Free, Matt, and the kid began firing. An Apache fell. The others withdrew from the ridge, but the arrows still came now from archers firing blind from beyond the ridge. They were still deadly but no longer coming quite so close.

"Matt, I don't like this," said the kid. Matt saw he was shaking.

"Might as well accept it, Emmett. Nothing we can do about it."

The kid gritted his teeth. "I don't know how you can be so calm about it!"

"It's easy, Emmitt." Matt smiled. "I got on my best new hat. Those arrows ain't got much force behind 'em. They'll stick in my hat."

A warrior appeared suddenly on the ridge and loosed an aimed arrow. The range was much too long, 200 yards, and the weapon designed to work at 25. Matt couldn't get off a shot in time, but he was able to knock the arrow out of the air as it passed close by.

The kid laughed. Matt thought he heard the edge of hysteria in it but said nothing. The afternoon passed. Clouds gathered but were weak and distant. At Cooke's Canyon, they didn't build into thunderheads. The sun beat down hard.

Archers popped up and fired from different positions, never the same place twice in a row. Matt kept trying to get off a shot, but he couldn't anticipate where they'd appear and was slow coming on target. At 200 yards, his aim would have to be perfect. And so, the Apaches spread a kind of terror that denied the hot and tired men any rest.

Free made his way to Avaline and Port. Port sat with his back against stone, lance in his belly, eyes open. Free felt Port's forehead. "He's cold."

Avaline nodded. "Good. I'm burnin' up in this sun."

Free looked at the gambler. "Avaline, Port's not breathing. He's gone."

"No, he's not. He's my friend. He'll stay with me. He said so."

Free spoke softly. "He's dead."

Avaline's eyes cleared, and he looked directly at Free. "I know. He gave me a message for his family. Can you write it down if I tell you?"

"Sure. Why don't you come back with me?"

"No, I'll stay with my friend."

Back with Joseph, Free found a scrap of cardboard and began to write:

> "To the family of John Portall. John wanted you to know he lived and died like a man. He was a boon companion. He said he was sorry he couldn't send any money. We're surrounded by a large force of Apache. Some of us are wounded, and we haven't much water. We've killed a great number of the enemy.
>
> Our names are Freeman Thomas, John Portall, Jack Wilson, Emmett Mills, Matthew Champion, Joseph Roescher, and Robert Avaline. Remember us. The Apache will."

He set the cardboard under a stone where he hoped it would stay dry.

A shot rent the air. Matt cursed. "Damn, I missed."

The kid laughed.

"Stop it, kid! I'll get one."

Matt didn't know if the edge of anger showed in his voice. He hoped not, but he was angry. He didn't like a one-sided fight, especially when he was on the wrong side. Having watched the Apache for hours, he thought he saw a pattern. He aimed carefully at a particular spot and waited. Chance or pattern, an Indian popped up at that spot and loosed his aimed arrow. Matt squeezed the trigger carefully. The Sharps roared. Matt watched and waited. Even traveling express, a bullet would take time to reach its target at this range. A small red hole appeared in the Apache's forehead.

"Got him!" Matt roared. "Did you see that shot? I got him, by damn!"

The kid said nothing.

"Emmitt, did you see that shot? I got him!"

Grinning Matt turned to face the kid and find out why he wasn't cheering Matt's champion shot. Matt's patented Champion shot, Matt thought. He looked at Emmitt who lay on his back without expression, a few feathers sprouting from a twig in his chest above his heart.

"Kid, I got him for you." A tear dripped from Matt's eye. He wiped it with a dusty, sunburned arm and then folded Emmett's hands across his chest above the arrow.

The sun sank, and the gray light of dusk crept over the land. "Psst, Free. It's Matt. Can I come in? I can't stay there with Emmett's body any longer."

"Sure. Avaline won't leave Port."

"Port's dead? How's Joseph?"

Free felt for Joseph's pulse. "Weak. He's stopped talking."

"How's Jack?"

Free looked in Jack's direction. "Still in his outpost."

Matt looked up and saw a rider on the ridge watching them. He aimed his Sharps carefully. The man must have seen, Matt thought, but showed no fear. Matt fired. The rider flinched turning abruptly to one side. Then he and horse disappeared from the ridge.

"Dang! You got him! That was Cochise."

Matt blushed unseen in the gray light. "Only winged him."

Time went slowly in the gray twilight. Eerie screams came from Avaline's direction. Matt had been looking toward Jack's position now barely visible. Before he could turn toward Avaline, there were flashes of gunfire all around Jack. Matt saw him silhouetted by gunfire, firing first his rifle and then his pistols. He was surrounded and his attackers were close. The range was great, and there was danger of hitting Jack. Matt turned toward Avaline, who was now firing his pistol at enemies close at hand.

Matt and Free provided supporting fire whenever they could pick out a target. Free's second pistol clicked on an empty cylinder. Matt threw down both his pistols and grabbing his rifle started loading. Silence fell like thunder in the dark.

"Avaline, you okay?"

Silence answered Free.

Matt called out to Jack. Silence. Matt started to rise to go and check on his friends.

Free grabbed his arm. "No. You'll get yourself killed. They're probably gone, but there might be one playin' 'possum."

Matt saw the wisdom in not trusting "dead" Apaches to stay that way.

"Free, how much water we got?"

"'Nough to last the night. No more. Tomorrow will be hot and dry."

Matt thought a while. "What about ammo?"

"We've plenty for the pistols but not more than 20 paper cartridges for the rifles."

"Free." Matt wanted support. He wanted a leader. "What are we going to do?"

"We can't leave Joseph. They'll torture him."

Matt pondered this for nearly an hour. "Free, you think the German is in any condition to know he was being tortured?"

"Matt, I'm not sure."

That satisfied Free's companion for a long while. "We could kill him." In the dark, Matt sounded embarrassed to even suggest the idea.

Free answered without anger. "I don't think that's a good idea."

The stars danced and twisted across the sky. Perhaps beyond the hill the Apache danced, too. Matt thought he heard drums, but it might have been someone's heart. The night was that still and dark. Matt wasn't much given to introspection, but now he thought about life and death, about morals and what a man ought to do and what he ought to be. Matt prayed asking for help for his remaining friends and for forgiveness for his sins. Funny, they'd seemed like a good time when he'd committed them. He'd die well if he had to, Matt thought, but he'd rather go on living. Still, it wouldn't be right to desert Joseph. Matt heard the drums again before he recognized it as a heart beating in time to the drums. Boy, Matt thought, the night is still.

"Still as the grave," said Free.

In the first flickering light of the false dawn, Free grabbed Matt's arm. "Joseph's gone. Now's our chance."

Matt gathered ammo, guns, and water. There wasn't much point in taking more.

He started to rise, but Free said, "Wait a sec." He pulled the piece of cardboard from its hiding place and added to its message:

> "Just Freeman Thomas and Matthew Champion left. We're going to try to make it to Mimbres Crossing. Out of water. The others are dead. July 23, 1861"

He hid it away again. "Let's go."

Several days later, freighters Alejandro Daguerre and J.J. Thibault driving their heavy wagons from Pinos Altos to Mesilla stopped to rest at Cooke's Pass. Their approach caused vultures to rise from their prey.

"Whew," said Alejandro, "there's some bodies here."

Thibault was already off his wagon. "Two here. This one's got a spear in his belly."

Alejandro found the next body in a circle of rocks shielded from the sun by a brush cover. "Apaches must not have liked them much. They stripped 'em and cut their arms to the bone."

"There's another one here. He's young," said Thibault. He noticed vultures flapped 100 yards beyond. "I'm gonna look over there."

Over there, he found another body. "This makes five. Whew-wee, they shot this 'un to pieces and cut him up good. We'd better get out of here!"

"Just a minute," his friend replied. "Maybe they left a message or something. Looking around the large circle, he saw a bit of cardboard sticking out from under a rock. He picked it up. "There were seven of them. You know some of them: Freeman Thomas, Matt Champion, Jack Wilson."

Thibault replied, "I don't see Champion or Free. Maybe they got away. We'd better go before the Apaches come. This was some fight. I think they lost a lot of braves."

Days later Freeman Thomas and Matthew Champion were found not far downhill from their friends.

The Power of Fox and Snake

Peregrino Rojo pulled on his tooled-leather boots, hid a long, thin dagger in one and a .45 caliber pistol in holster in the other, and then folded his black leather trousers down over their tops concealing his arsenal. The pants were open along the sides to the waist but buttoned closed to the knee by large, worked silver buttons called *conchos*. Lifting each foot carefully, he secured his spurs in place. They were elaborate silver decorations with tinkling jingle-bobs and gold filigree. Their large, wicked Spanish rowels were made of sharpened steel. They were a fine and unexpected weapon in a fight. Besides, the others expected a Spanish don to wear spurs.

Rojo thought to himself, "I'd never use these on a horse. That would be sinful." He tasted the word. It was alien to his Jicarilla Apache mind, but it suited the concept. Anyone who would use these on a horse deserved punishment lasting beyond death. Was there something beyond death? Something, perhaps. Darkness, hunger, and wandering for your ghost, if you were bad, all the while you infected others with your evil. But maybe there was something else: a good tipi with a warm fire and old friends to share it with and a warm woman under a buffalo robe.

He stood and pulled his black, velveteen embroidered vest, black on black, with silver buttons on over a clean white ruffled shirt. He adjusted a red sash around his waist and stocked it with a Colt's .36 caliber revolver and a large knife. He twisted his long, black, braided hair around in a ring on top of his head and held it in place with a woman's hat pin. A lady of questionable morals – he smiled recalling her and the epithet – had shown him how to use it to good effect in a fight. Rojo found his black, leather hat with its round, flat crown. Ridiculous, he thought. No one in New Mexico would wear this. Perhaps they did in California. The river people expected it. He looked inside and checked the tiny .30 caliber, two barreled pistol concealed on a metal clip. Carefully, he settled the hat onto his head. He smiled admiring himself in the mirror. He felt like a preening, overdressed Cheyenne.

Rojo thought of himself as having Fox Power, a power not much admired among his people. The fox seemed weak, and they admired the strong. But the fox was clever and able to move about undetected, taking small things when no one was looking. The coyote was strong, but he was chaotic and the People, the Jicarilla, did not like chaotic. It caused trouble and made things come out wrong often to the detriment of the coyote. Fox Power was less chaotic, but unless he developed another power, found another powerful mentor in the natural world, he could never return to his people as a great warrior, leader, nor would he be viewed as wise or strong in medicine.

He felt the *Princess Caraboo* lurch slightly and he rolled with it as the captain brought her in for the first stop for wood and water at some Cajun town on the edge the endless bayous. He listened as Negro slaves manhandled wood for the engine aboard and stacked it on deck. They sang as they worked. Slavery was part of this strange, soggy world where moss dripped from trees to the ground. So were the Cajuns and the Creoles, upper-class French who despised their country cousins.

But he was ready. He was now Don Manuel Alexandro San Xavier Carvajal y Jaramillo Armijo, Don Manuel Armijo to those who met this fine Spanish grandee at the gaming tables. The name always sounded familiar to these Southern gentlemen of the green felt. It should. He'd borrowed it. Manuel Armijo had been governor of New Mexico until General Kearney sent him on his way ten years ago in 1846. He looked into his gambler's box. Cards, mother of pearl dice, markers of various sizes, weapons, and layout for *monte* and faro presented themselves. He didn't think he'd need them this first night north out of New Orleans. Rojo hung a large gold device about his neck. It was a tiny roulette wheel and a come-on to others to gamble. He took it off and buried it in the gambler's box. It was too obvious for the first night. The ship was full of planters returning home rich with cash from the crops they'd sold. They'd be flush. It was better to look the scene over the first night. There was time, and the hunt shouldn't be rushed. He preferred that the others see him as Don Manuel returning to Santa Fe by way of St. Louis and not as a gambler.

All of the river men cheated; Don Manuel did not. Gambling was a religious experience for the Apache. There was Power in the world, in rocks and springs, birds and animals, mountains and trees. Power came from spirit helpers, and if he behaved properly, they assisted him giving insight to the cards and players and wisdom about what was coming each in its own way. Rock power could make a man impassive and unreadable, an advantage in poker. Hawk power could help him see things too distant or small for other men to discern. But a man had to treat Power properly. He had to live as it wanted, had to be moral as an Apache and his gods understood morality. To cheat was a violation of morality and offended Power. Gambling was a test. If you gambled and won, Power was with you. If you lost, perhaps it was testing you or worse had abandoned you. If you caught others cheating, that was a different matter. It opened a new game, a new kind of gambling where old rules no longer applied, but the rules of Power remained.

The powers of the hawk and owl assisted a man in observing and understanding. Cheaters opened themselves to a new game without knowing it. There were new rules, ones most gamblers didn't understand. But the Apache did, and a good man could take them and beat them without offending Power.

The game had many levels, and one had to be prepared. There were those who could not abide losing and sought the return of their wealth with knife and gun. Others cried foul and accused the other players of cheating. They had to be dealt with and reputation preserved. Still others were mere thugs who did not enter in the games themselves but observed who had won and sought to relieve them of their purse. Rojo attached his purse, jingling and fat with Mexican pesos and gold. The United States was short of specie, and on the Mississippi Mexican money served. He was ready, ready to seek out the saloon, the hunt, the adventure.

The *Princess Caraboo* lurched again as her powerful side-wheels pushed her away from shore. Rojo stepped out into the cool night of the river just as far above the ship's calliope sounded the call to dinner. Fancy, he thought. And strange. It was a musical instrument run on steam from the boilers. It bellowed. I know that tune, he thought. The name wouldn't come to him. He looked down over the railing and spoke, quietly, to himself, "From here, I can see more water than I have ever seen in my life." He said it in English. It would be a very un-Apache thing to speak aloud to himself. *Mangani*, whites, were very strange, and they were rubbing off on him. He chuckled. He smiled, a face to make a shark proud. Looking up and down along the railing of the *Princess*, he marveled. It was bigger than the Taos pueblo, five stories high, bigger than both the north and south pueblo combined. And it floated on more water than he could imagine as it swam north toward St. Louis.

Rojo reentered his stateroom. A door on the far side opened directly into the saloon which ran the length of the ship with staterooms on both sides. All of the flush passengers dined here on the best the ship had to offer. Tables were set with linen and silver. Somewhere below not so well to do passengers would dine on tin plates. A liveried Negro maître'd directed him to a table where three men were already seated. The room was crowded, and candles were lit in brass fixtures that glittered. Across from Rojo was a young man in a black frock coat and boiled shirt with a string tie in the Southern fashion. He rose and extended his hand. "Timothy Sutton, at your service."

Rojo bowed. "Don Manuel Armijo." He took the young man's hand as he appraised him. The suit was new and clean but not of high quality. The young man was not wealthy. His hands as he shook were strong but not callused.

The man on his left rose and extended his hand. "George Devol." He was a big man, powerfully built with large hands that engulfed Rojo's. The fingers were long and finely shaped like the hands of a piano player. Devol was impeccably dressed in a fine suit that looked new and a ruffled shirt. His hands were softer than a woman's. Rojo knew that feel, gamblers hands. They had to be smooth and soft to feel the tiny bumps or shaved edges of marked cards. And such hands had to be supple to manipulate the cards and bring out the hidden hold card without being noticed. "I'm in investments." Yes, of course, thought Rojo. He invested in cards and dice.

The man on the right snorted but didn't rise. "They call me Canada Bill."

"*Señor*, are you from that northern country?"

"Nope. Worked a season along the Canadian River." He wore a fringed buckskin shirt with fancy beadwork. Rojo knew this meant he'd probably shared quarters with an Indian woman for a season. The color and pattern looked Southern Cheyenne. Figured, if he'd worked along the Canadian. Bill's hat shaded his eyes. Rojo's hat stayed on his head even in the dining saloon. It hid his hair and he could get away with it because he was a Spanish grandee, and no one really knew what to expect from him. Rojo liked that freedom. Bill, on the other hand, was simply a frontiersman.

The waiter brought menus. "Gentlemen, we are in luck," said Devol. "I saw the chef dickering on the dock with some Cajuns. He bought fresh fish, shrimp, and crawfish."

"And a bear, they kilt," Bill cut in. "I'm gonna have me some bear roast. How 'bout you, Don?"

"No, *señor*, no bear for me," said Rojo. "My people do not eat *el oso*."

"What? I been in Taos plenty of times, and everybody there ate el oso."

"Ah." Rojo nodded. "That explains it. I am from the *abjo*, the southland. We consider *el oso* our *hermano*, our brother, and we do not eat out brothers."

"Well, then," said Devol, "how about some fish? It's fresh."

"No, *señor*, I think not. I will try the roast beef."

"Me, too," piped Timothy Sutton.

Through the meal, Rojo tried not to look at what Canada Bill and Devol were eating. Bill was, to the Jicarilla's way of thinking a cannibal eating a brother, and Rojo dared not think about the fish. It was cousin to the snake, and touching or eating such a thing could paralyze a man, give him arthritis. It was hard to eat around these people and even harder because Timothy Sutton kept on talking. Anglos were afraid of silence. They had to fill it, and it made a man nervous.

"I was selected to be the broker for three farms and sell our tobacco in New Orleans. I'll get a commission. We got a lot more for it in the Crescent City than we'd have gotten if we'd sold in Louisville." Timothy pronounced it Loo uh vul. "And I'll get a fine commission. A few more like this and I'll have enough to marry Betsy Sue. She's the most beautiful girl in Hardin County, and I love her, and she loves me. They trusted me, and I made good money for them. And soon we'll be able to wed."

If they'd been someplace private, Rojo might have slit his throat in self-defense. He didn't dislike the boy. He just wanted him to shut up. There was only so much an Apache could take.

A man approached their table. He was young and well dressed. "Would you care to join us? We're getting up a game."

There was no overt sign, but Rojo seemed to notice something pass between the man and Devol. Perhaps they were accomplices. He'd have to watch closely.

Timothy spoke up. "No, no, I have to be careful and guard my master's money."

"But surely you have some of your own," said Devol.

"Yes, but I'm saving to wed Betsy Sue."

The Wildest West

"Lad," the gambler smiled, "haven't you heard of beginner's luck? Perhaps you'll win enough to marry as soon as you arrive home. Be a man. This is a man's sport. Besides, it's just a friendly game, not high stakes. And it would be rude to refuse such a kind invitation."

The boy was swayed.

Canada Bill closed one eye and cocked his head. "Guess I'm just rude. I'll watch."

They moved to a new and larger table. Rojo knew that reading the room was as important as reading the cards. Two of the men at the table were probably planters on their way home. Two more, including the man who invited them, seemed to be professional gamblers. Two men, not at all well dressed, watched the game intently from another table. Rojo saw them as trouble, bummers.

Devol introduced a deck and asked, "What shall we play?"

The other man that Rojo had taken for a gambler was slender and middle aged. He suggested, "Draw poker." He was referred to as Doc.

As the cards were dealt, Rojo realized that the deck was cold. He was surprised that Devol would be so obvious. He'd watched for a shiner, a mirror-like object that would reflect the face of the card back to the dealer as he dealt, but George Devol didn't wear a ring. He looked for anything that might indicate a mechanical holdout, but saw nothing. He felt the cards carefully and they were neither shaved nor did they bear tiny lumps that shouldn't be there. A gambler learns to study the cards and see what others miss, and this deck was cold, marked. In the upper right and lower left hand corners the back of each card was a figure like a 7 with a dot in it. The direction the dot faced was different on each card. It stood straight up on an ace and 30 degrees to the right on a king and so on. There was no indication of suit that he could tell. If he happened to draw a flush, Devol would think he was bluffing. Otherwise, the gambler would know his hand and every other hand at the table.

Devol ordered whiskey for everyone. Raising his glass, Rojo nodded and said, "*Salud.*" He then brought his glass to his lips and threw his head back without opening his mouth. Then, concealing the glass with his hand, he brought it down and emptied it on the deck. Finally, he turned the glass upside down on the table. "*Muy bueno.*" Everyone at the table would have to buy a round before the evening was over, but it didn't pay to gamble drunk.

Doc lit a cigar as one of the others lit a pipe. Soon the air around the table was thick with smoke and the smell of whiskey.

Betting was light. Despite the rigged deck, Devol seemed to be treating their first meeting at cards as a friendly game. The two planters and both the younger gambler and Doc lost steadily. Rojo could easily have gotten way ahead, but that would have giving away his secret, that he knew the deck was cold. The surprise was that Timothy, clearly not a good player, was winning steadily. Rojo thought about his resolve to observe only on the first night, but a low stakes game like this was a means of observing, telling him more than he would have learned on the sidelines. It was the perfect way to learn about the other gamblers habits at low risk

"My gracious, young man, but you do have the beginner's luck." Devol encouraged him.

"It seems so," said Timothy smiling. Rojo knew he was hooked. Rojo had seen snakes charm a mouse this way, convince it that it was safe before it struck. Perhaps Devol had Snake Power. Having it made sense for a gambler whose quick hands tossing cards were like a snake striking.

"Why, you'll soon have enough to marry that girl! What was her name? Betsy Sue."

So that was the play, thought Rojo. Get him hooked on gambling today; clean him out tomorrow. Show him how easy it was to win. Get his hopes up. This was none of the Apache's concern. He would have liked to have gambled honestly, but since the game was fixed, he was now the hunter and played another game to out-cheat the cheater. There was no room in this game for sentiment or feeling sorry for pigeons. If the mountain lion was busy hunting a rabbit, he was less likely to notice the Apache approaching from behind.

Rojo held a pair of tens and bet $2. He tugged his ear giving the gamblers a false tell. He wanted them to think he always tugged his ear when he was bluffing. He had to stay in long enough to get called so they'd see his cards.

How rare was a flush? Rare, but Rojo held one. The gamblers would think he was bluffing on garbage. "I'll raise you $5."

Doc looked at him. "That's a big raise for this table." The gambler studied the backs of Rojo's cards. "I'll see it and raise you a dollar."

And so it went around the table. Rojo raised slowly not wanting to frighten the fish. And he tugged his ear. They stayed with him. The pot reached $100, and Rojo owned it. It was his big score for the evening.

Meanwhile, Sutton took pot after pot. The Apache figured he was $200 ahead when they quit at 3 a.m.

"You have to give us a chance to win our money back," said Devol. "Shall we meet tomorrow night?"

"Tomorrow night, then," said Timothy. He stowed his money away in a money bag. Sharp eyes watched from another table. "I'm going to get some air, clear my lungs of this smoke, and get to bed." He headed for the companionway up to the Texas and a few minutes later Rojo followed.

"Hand over your purse, boy," a gruff voice demanded.

The two bummers Rojo had noticed earlier had Timothy braced against the rail. Both brandished knives. As he thought, they'd been watching for the big winner. They'd kill him and dump the body over the side. They'd leave the ship at the next wood stop before the missing Sutton was noticed. No one would pursue. There would be confusion over jurisdiction and the body might never be found. Ah well, the Apache thought, it's none of my business.

Then he realized that cheap killers like these weren't good for anyone's business.

Rojo staggered a bit and swayed from side to side as he softly began to sing a mournful New Mexican love song. With effort, he straightened himself and looked ahead. "*Señor*, have you got a light for my *cigarito*?" He played a convincing drunk.

Quietly, he drew his knife keeping it concealed within his clothing.

"Back off you! This is none of your affair!"

"*Señor*?" Rojo staggered and bumped into the man hard pricking him deep with his knife.

The bummer jerked away stumbling and hit the railing violently shattering it. He went through and fell to the water.

The other man turned. "What the!" Involuntarily he took his eyes off Rojo and looked after his partner.

149

"Better get in after him! I don't think he can swim," howled Canada Bill tossing the man in after his partner. Rojo hadn't seen or heard Bill's approach.

Far below, the paddle-wheel thumped a few times as bones, necks, and heads cracked.

Bill chuckled. Timothy Sutton, recognizing that the sounds meant his assailants were dead, bent and wretched over the side. It is not easy to see men killed or to kill. It breaks a deep seated taboo. Men like Rojo and Canada Bill had long since gotten over it. A willingness to kill when threatened made them dangerous.

"*Señor* Armijo, thank you," cried Timothy Sutton rising and wiping his mouth. "You've saved my purse, and it isn't just my money. Oh, thank you." Apparently, he didn't realize how close to death he had come.

Rojo spoke. "*Señor* Sutton, I saw them watching you all evening and suspected they planned something like this. If you are not familiar with the ways of riverboats, you should keep to your cabin, avoid the gaming tables, and guard your purse with care."

"Hey wait, you're not drunk."

"That is correct. Avoid the gaming tables."

Sutton thought about not returning to card playing and wondered if he could avoid the tables, after all he was doing quite well. The others would be offended if he didn't give them a chance to win their money back. "I have to play them one more time. It would be impolite not to."

Canada Bill growled. "He's giving you good advice, boy. There's bad men on this boat."

"Honor demands that I play. Thanks you, again." He turned and headed toward his cabin.

"A drink, perhaps, *amigo*?"

"A drink is always good." Bill grinned. They went below.

The Apache thought about Bill. He could not trust him as an ally. He did not know him. He was not a friend. Anyone so stealthy deserved being watched.

Rojo retired to his stateroom and carefully put away his fine clothing. He slept until well past noon. While he slumbered, the river slid away below. The thrum of the engines was constant. The paddles splashed and groaned with rising and falling pitch as the ship slowed, turned, and pulled into shore where they were silent a while. The noises of the deck replaced them. The gangplanks thumped into place as men shouted, especially the mate, giving directions on where and how to stow the cargo. In narrow passages, moss draped trees scraped the sides of the upper decks. Shallows made the ship shuddered as it passed over them. The smell of the river was always there, smoke from the boilers, mud, moss, and things slowly rotting.

Awaking, the Apache thought, "I won't get fat on this trip with only one meal per day and that taken between a cannibal and a man who eats snake-kin." He strolled from deck to deck to get the blood pumping. On the main deck nearest the river, some of the black deckhands had roped an animal and hauled it abroad. It writhed and whipped about like a huge fat snake, ugly and scaled. It bit one of the men, and he screamed in pain before it released him. The thing had huge jaws with teeth as long as a man's hand. The man bled as he scrambled away from the terror. The hands got a rope on the great jaws and held them shut.

"What kind of fish is that?"

"No fish, suh. We calls that uh gator. Plenty mean, too, but good eatin.'"

Rojo gagged and continued his rounds thinking of George Devol eating fish. All these things were some kind of snake, and snakes were bad. How could a man eat them? he wondered. Why didn't Devol have arthritis? His hands were suppled and quick. Perhaps Devol derived power from them. He had Snake Power and struck in a flash with a poisoned card, the way a snake strikes.

He found himself with the same dinner companions and Devol ordered fish again. "It's good fresh from the river, and chef knows how to prepare it." He grinned showing teeth. Rojo was reminded of the gator.

Canada Bill was amused. "I sought you out. I want to watch the rematch where Mr. Devol tries to win some of his money back."

Doc returned to the game with Sutton, Rojo, and Devol, and they were joined by three well-dressed men who seemed to be planters or businessmen. The kid was there standing behind Rojo. A small crowd gathered to watch the play. In the warm, smoky, stuffy environment they drew in uncomfortably close to the gamblers. Too close for Rojo who had been raised in wide open spaces among a people who kept greater distance between themselves, The cards were not cold. They had not been marked. Nonetheless, Rojo soon caught on. They were iteming, that is to say, the kid and another of the spectators were signaling Devol concerning what hands the players held. The signals were subtle, puffs of cigar smoke or the angle at which the kid held his newly acquired walking stick.

The kid crowded in close behind Rojo who kicked back with his spur catching the man above the instep. The kid howled. Rojo rose suddenly to his feet digging the spur in much deeper. "You must forgive me, amigo. I am so sorry. I did not realize." Rojo lifted his foot and the kid backed off. The rest of the evening no one dared to come in close behind him.

Rojo was free to play an honest game and able to hold his own. He watched as Devol played Sutton like a snake with a mouse. Sutton's pile of chips went up, and then he bet heavily on what Rojo assumed must be a good hand only to lose his previous winnings and most of his winnings from the night before. He hovered a while there at the boundary between his own money and that which he was taking back home to others.

All the while, Devol encouraged him. "You'll do well again. I'm sure. One good hand and you'll get it all back. Soon you'll have enough to marry."

Sutton won a little and lost again, and then his face brightened. He held an excellent hand, Rojo thought. Timothy Sutton dipped into the money of others. The pot grew and grew. Everyone dropped out except Devol. "This is the hand, Mr. Sutton. You'll win enough to marry." Sutton dipped deeper and deeper, needing to win the pot or face ruin.

Rojo's sharp eyes caught the subtle movement of George Devol's wrist and a momentary flash from his sleeve. "*Dios mio*," Rojo thought, "on top of it all, Devol's using a holdout." The gambler had a mechanical device up his sleeve that presented him with extra cards he had reserved for this moment.

"Call," said Timothy Sutton, a victorious gleam in his eye. He lay down four jacks.

"My pot," said Devol showing his gator teeth and laying down four aces.

Sutton was devastated as George raked in the pot.

The game continued, Sutton now desperate. He continued to play with other's money and continued to lose. Finally, he rose from the table hollow eyed and broke. Without a word, he stumbled toward the outer deck.

Rojo rose. "*Señores*, that is enough for me. You will excuse me."

He sought the night air, even if it smelled of river and swamp. It was better than thick cigar smoke. As he went, he heard the kid, still limping and now needing the silver tipped walking stick. "That Devol, he his sharp. He's good at poker, but he loses it all at Faro. He's fascinated by Faro but just can't win or quit. He'll leave here with a fortune and lose it all at Natchez Under the Hill to a Faro dealer."

On deck, Rojo saw a dark form mount the railing.

"*Señor* Sutton, *buenos noches*. Is the view better from up there? Did you wish to look down into the paddles? The two gentlemen from last night are long gone eaten by the river creatures, I think."

Sutton looked up. "Please go away. I want to be alone. I've lost all my money and the money of my friends."

"*Si*, that is the way of poker. Win today, lose tomorrow. You might win it all again *mañana*."

"No! I have been foolish. I think I was cheated. Please go away, *Señor* Armijo."

Rojo nodded. "*Si*, men who have lost often think they have been cheated."

"But I cheated, too. I played with my friends' and employers' money. And now I've surely lost Betsy Sue!" Sutton wailed.

Rojo thought, this *mangani* is no affair of mine. If he wants to kill himself, I should let him." He started to turn away and then thought, But, I do not like snakes and those who eat them. This cheating gator should learn a hard lesson.

He turned to Sutton. "Timothy, come along with me. The sun will shine tomorrow and things will look better. Tomorrow I will propose a new game, Spanish Monte. *Señor* Devol will not be able to resist. In addition, we will let you be the bank. The bank always wins, at least a little. The odds say it must be so."

"I am disgraced. How can I live?"

Rojo smiled. "Go West perhaps. Wouldn't you rather your friends got some money instead of nothing? Besides, you can always kill yourself tomorrow."

Sutton climbed off the railing.

The night and morning passed. The river swam slowly by. Rojo saw that the deck hands had slain and butchered the gator. That was a good sign, he thought. Snake Power was fading.

At dinner, Rojo proposed a game of Spanish Monte.

"I don't know that game," said Devol.

"It is much like your Faro, *Señor* Jorge, uh George, but played with a *Baraja Española*, a Spanish deck of 44 cards. We'll let Mr. Sutton be the bank for in Monte, like Faro, the bank often comes out a bit ahead. He can recoup some of last night's losses." Rojo noted that Devol's eyes lit up at the mention of Faro.

Rojo went on, "The suits are *oros* coins, *bastos* cudgels, *copas* cups and *espadas* swords, but they do not matter because we play to match the face value. And the cards count one to seven and four cards of royalty, face cards. Simple, no."

Rojo laid out a cloth with the printed pictures of the cards on the table. This was the spread on which they would place their wagers.

The Wildest West

"I shuffle the cards and place them face up on the table. You place your bets on the card you think will come up next. You can bet on as many cards as you like. Once you have placed your bets, I pull off the top card and reveal the winner. If you have won, bet on the card that came up, and the banker pays you. All other bets remain in place. I then take away the winning card and place it on the first *monte*, mountain, for which the game is named. The third card, thus revealed is the loser, and if you have bet on that card, the banker takes your money. If the cards are the same, we have a split, and the banker takes half the value of the bets on those cards. This is his advantage, and it is small. We then go on to the next card placing the losing card on the second monte. And so on. The odds are almost even. Everything depends on the quality of your luck and skill in guessing. You may string your bets by placing a coin between two adjacent cards to win or bet on the entire high or low row. And you may copper your bets by placing a penny on your money and betting on that card to lose. Do you understand?"

The men nodded. They understood. Monte resembled Faro although it was played with Spanish cards. It would be no problem.

Rojo smiled. "*Bueno*! Since I have not the banker, I will merely deal for the amusement of my amigos. I cannot win or lose. Let us try a few turns in a friendly manner before we count in a fresh 44-card deck and begin in earnest."

He was faced by George Devol, Doc, the kid and two men of apparent means who wanted to try the new game with an honest dealer who had no stake in the play. Everyone looked forward to a new and interesting game. It was rare for a game to be honest on the Princess Caraboo.

156

The Wildest West

"Don Armijo, please begin," said Devol.

"Si, Don Jorge," Rojo replied and dealt the cards placing them face up on the table.

Tentative bets were placed, and Canada Bill watched from the sidelines. Devol won on the first turn, and the kid lost when the third card was shown. With more courage, Devol bet the lower set and coppered his bets on the upper. He won again, and so did some of the others. There were more losses, especially among those who bet on the face cards to win or lose.

As in all games of monte, much excitement and much cheering and a great deal of noise were heard as bets were made and paid. The players were enjoying themselves, especially Devol who was winning for a change. That wasn't his habit at Faro. He lost regularly.

Rojo heard the kid whisper that Devol would be a rich man if he didn't lose it all on Faro. Devol was excited his was winnings. He kept backing the low cards, and his gamble paid off. What a time he was having. His bets got bigger. Spanish monte was a game he could win without cheating. Caution seemed to leave him. All the players were doing well, except for those who consistently backed the high cards, but this appeared to be just luck. The high cards won as well, though perhaps not as often.

Sutton was pulling in some money as banker, but was losing far more. Soon he was short.

"*Señor* Armijo, I am out of money. I am ruined!" cried Sutton.

"If you will allow me, *mi amigos*," said Rojo, "I will lend him some money that he may continue. He may pay me back when he is able."

Devol nodded his approval. "That is very kind of you. Of course, we know the banker will win sooner or later."

"I have such confidence," said Rojo. "And, if not, I can bear the risk." He passed $100 to Sutton.

"I can't," said Sutton. "I owe too much already."

Rojo glared at him. "You must, or you will insult me."

Continuing, Rojo said, "And now, *señores*, it is time to count in a new deck of 44 cards." He opened a fresh package and handed the cards to Devol to count. Everyone was satisfied, there were 44. Rojo looked around for his old deck and didn't see it. The disappearance of his deck worried him.

Play resumed. And the players began to lose. The banker, Sutton, was taking in money and soon paid off his debt to Rojo.

Devol ground his teeth. "I know I can win at this. I was winning."

"Of course, *señor*, of course. *Doña* Luck, she is a fickle lady, but she always returns to those she loves."

Devol grinned like a gator and play went on. Devol won, and the others won, but somehow the splits, pairs, were coming up more often than before, and the high cards had grown lucky. They strung their bets, bet high and low, coppered them and won, but the players were losing consistently to the bank.

"That's how it is, *señores*. The banker always comes a little ahead. But there are other winners, too. Always. Lady Luck always loves someone best."

The night went long. Cigar smoke grew thick. The gamblers were more quiet now, intent on winning. When one took a bet, he cheered a little, but not like before.

Rojo had been taking chances in how he laid the cards down. To give Sutton an edge, he placed a low card unevenly on the *montes*. This action of the dealer looked merely careless. When its mate came up, he placed it unevenly as well. When he shuffled, it was easy to keep the cards together so they would come up as a pair. He could only chance this trick occasionally and not enough to account for all of Sutton's luck. This obvious form of cheating was a dangerous thing to do in front of experienced gamblers, but he was good at it, and they trusted him. After all, he was a Spanish don whose name they knew, and he was not the banker and thus was not winning anything.

Toward dawn, they broke up. Devol was down heavily. Sutton had recovered his previous losses and then some. He hugged Rojo.

Rojo stepped out onto the deck for some fresh morning air even if it did stink of the river.

Canada Bill stepped up behind him. "I found your cards. And by the way, this deck has only 36 cards."

Rojo remained calm. "Thank you. I must have dropped some."

Bill smiled. "A short deck would give an advantage to the players over the banker. There wouldn't be as many splits. Oh, and by the way, a Spanish deck has only 40 cards, not 44. Forty-four cards, I'd allow, would make for a lot more splits where the banker would win."

Rojo grinned. He'd foxed Devol at his own game. He had Fox Power, and it had beat Snake Power. His grin broadened. He had gambled and won. "Can I buy you a drink, amigo?"

The Lady was a Gunfighter

"Doña Tules, please, you don't understand!" cried Jack Tremayne. "Don't be taking her away."

"Calm down, Hack," said the lady. "I am your friend and hers."

"It's Jack."

"Si, Hack.

"I know she's a bit wild. She's Ann White's daughter, Virginia, taken by the Jicarilla in '49 and sold and sold again until the Mojave got her over on the Rio Colorado where they taught her to run about in the heat without a stitch on."

"Si, Chack, and she is still wild. You've dressed her in half-cured skins. I must teach her to be a lady. She is *cimarron*, wild."

"I've treated her good. I taught her to shoot, and she's good with rifle and pistol. Saved my bacon twice. I'll take care of her."

"She must learn to be a lady."

The frontiersman and sometimes prospector was out of arguments that he was willing to make. He didn't want to tell Doña Tules that he didn't think that Virginia would learn the right things in a gambling *sala* run by Santa Fe's most famous courtesan. Nor was he willing to admit even to himself that he loved the girl. When Tules expressed love for him, he had rejected her.

Tules had seen Jack's lack of interest and enthusiasm as she lay with Jack, white and naked in the filtered moonlight on the bed in an inner chamber of her home. "Hack! Your mind is not on me. You are thinking of another." She pushed him away. "I will not have a lover who does not think of me alone at times like these! It must be that girl."

"No," he replied, "I don't love the girl. She is only a friend and someone I protect. I cannot consider her as a lover. She is much too crude. She has no manners, no graces, unlike yourself. I want a lady, not a squaw who doesn't know how to act."

"Hack, I am surprised. You are a man of the mountains and deserts. You are certainly no gentleman."

He blushed. "My mother taught me to want a lady."

The confrontation in the street came soon after. There was nothing more Jack could say. Doña Tules led the girl away into her great house on Burro Alley near the Palace of the Governors. There she dressed Virginia in her own clothing. A white blouse exposed most of her breast and upper arms. If she leaned forward too far her nipples winked at the world. A full black skirt covered her legs to mid-calf. Tules decided she could keep her moccasins for now.

"After all," she told the girl, "most everyone in Santa Fe wears moccasins." She didn't speak of undergarments. They were still foreign in New Mexico in 1862.

Virginia was still somewhat confused. She'd only been learning English for a few months since Jack had taken her, at great risk, from the Mojave. Now, she was learning Spanish as well. It was all very confusing. The white Spanish, who really looked like Indians, spoke a different language from the Americans but acted like them in many ways.

"We must do something with your hair," said the older woman. "I will let you have my *tortuga* shell comb to hold it in place."

The Wildest West

Doña Tules undertook the girl's instruction. "Ah, I see you recognize the *Baraja Española*, the Spanish deck of cards. Do you know how to shuffle?" Virginia nodded, and Tules handed her the deck. She demonstrated. "Let me show you a new way." The girl learned quickly.

"Let me show you how to deal Monte. It is a good game, and one women can play to make a little money. The suits are *oros* coins, *bastos* cudgels, *copas* cups, and *espadas* swords, but they do not matter because we play to match the face value. And the cards count one to nine and three cards of royalty, face cards, so there are 48 cards. Simple, no." Virginia nodded.

Tules took the girl to the gambling *sala* entering from her home into the large room that fronted Burro Alley. It was 14 feet deep and 40 or more feet long, with blackened *vigas*, pine log roof beams, overhead. There were three tables for Monte with the special spread painted on their tops, three more for *pokar* with chairs, and a bar where Tules' servants served *pulque*, *mescal*, *aquardiente*, *tequila*, and American brandies and whiskey. The painted spread on the Monte tables showed the 12 cards of the deck in two rows, high and low, plus three places for the dealer's cards. The dealer handled the bank.

Doña Tules continued the instructions. "I shuffle the cards and place them face up on the table in this spot where you see the outline of the deck painted. Yes?" The girl nodded. "Gamblers will place their bets on the outline of the card in the two rows they want to bet on, the card that will be drawn next. They can bet on as many cards as they like. Once they have placed their bets, the dealer pulls off the top card and reveals the winner. If they have won, bet on the card that came up, the banker pays them. All other bets remain in place. The dealer then takes away the

162

winning card and places it on the first monte, mountain, for which the game is named. The third card, thus revealed is the loser, and if they have bet on that card, the banker takes their money. If the cards are the same, we have a split, and the banker takes half the value of the bets on those cards. This is his advantage, but it is small. We then go on to the next card, placing the losing card on the second monte. And so on. The odds are almost even. Everything depends on the quality of your luck and skill in guessing. Gamblers may string their bets by placing a coin between two adjacent cards to win or bet on the entire high or low row. And they may copper their bets by placing a penny on their money and betting on that card to lose. Do you understand?" Virginia smiled. She did. "Good. Then let us play a few hands, and you can practice being the dealer and banker." Virginia learned quickly.

Learning to play an honest game is not as hard as learning to cheat. Tules thought the girl would make good money playing honestly. Many men would want to play at the pretty girl's table. She was *muy bonita* and an *Americana*, a novelty. Word would travel fast. Unlike most dealers, she would play silently, for she did not yet have the language skills to interact with the players. That, too, would be a novelty. The men would like a silent woman. Tules knew they would find her silence mysterious and alluring.

A week later, Jack entered the gambling *sala* in search of the girl. He found Virginia dealing monte with a 48-card Spanish deck. She stood behind her table and bent well forward to deal, thrilling the men who crowded her table. Tules didn't seem to mind. She also had admirers even if her crowd was somewhat smaller.

Jack held his temper. "Doña Tules, I think we may need some help with her training."

"*Que? Porque*, Chack?" replied the woman who retained her charms despite being in her late 30s.

Jack tried hard to be diplomatic. Ladies where he came from didn't expose their form to throngs of men, nor did they deal cards in smoky *salas*. "Perhaps we should get some help from one of the officer's wives at Fort Marcy."

"Why? Aren't Mexican ways good enough?"

Jack nodded. "Good enough but different. She should learn both."

"*Si.* And perhaps I can learn to please the officers, too." She grinned wickedly.

Jack recruited Mrs. Alice Emory, wife of a dragoon captain, and brought her offer to meet Doňa Tules.

Mrs. Emory had trepidations about meeting Santa Fe's most famous courtesan and gambler. "I'm not sure I should be seen with a woman like this. It would destroy my reputation."

Jack tried to calm her. "I'll take you in the back way. Besides, this is Santa Fe. Things are different here." Mrs. Emory wasn't much reassured.

They entered the interior courtyard, and Mrs. Emory was amazed, for it was a garden surrounded by two-story adobe rooms with balconies and doors facing inward. "My goodness, this is lovely."

Tules made an entrance with Virginia in tow. Jack introduced them, and Alice offered her hand first to Tules and then to Virginia, who stared at it, uncertain for a few moments before she took it.

Jack left, and Alice, looking around, noticed a beautifully made clock on wall. She also noticed it wasn't running. "Your clock is beautiful but it appears to have run down."

"*Si*. He is run down. I let him rest and wind him up so guests can see him on saints' days."

Alice absorbed this information and considered the girl. "First thing we need to do is bathe her and wash her hair and then get her into some makeup and proper clothing. Do you have a tub?"

"Si, I have a wonderful copper slipper tub, the pride of Santa Fe, *muy bonita*. But, what is wrong with her clothing?"

Alice was unthinkingly blunt. "Why she has no foundation garments and no hoop-skirt. I will get some things from my quarters and return tomorrow. Can we have her bath ready and perhaps a meal so we can teach her to eat properly?"

The next day when Alice returned, the copper slipper was set up in the middle of the courtyard of Doña Tules home. Servants came and went about the courtyard.

Tules smiled and said to Alice, "You shall have the first bath. It is an honor. The water will be fresh and hot."

Alice was horrified. "Not in the middle of the courtyard! Everyone can see!"

Tules was puzzled. "We all bathe in the open in the river. It is good for the skin to let it feel the air. No one is ashamed. It has always been so."

Alice tried to compose herself. "We are more modest. Please move it to a place where it will be shielded by the shrubbery." And so Tules' servants were called to move the tub to a sheltered corner.

Tules and Virginia were startled by Alice's screams. They ran to her to find her standing in the slipper, one arm across her breasts and a hand shading a darker region.

Tules whispered to Virginia. "See, her hair is all blonde." Then she asked Alice, "What is the problem?"

"This, this man..." Alice pointed at Pedro, a servant, who stood there with a bucket of water.

"He has brought you more hot water. What is the problem?"

Tremulously Alice said, "He is a he! Make him go away."

Alice dressed, and Tules enjoyed her bath singing Spanish love songs the whole time.

Then it was Virginia's turn.

Alice said, "I think we need to scrub her and show her how it's done."

From years of going barefoot and naked, Virginia had ingrained dirt under her nails and in her palms, elbows, and knees. Her hair was still matted and dirty. The Mojave coated their hair with mud to keep out the numerous tiny insects of their hot, riparian homeland.

"*Si*. She will need some work."

They helped her out of the clothing Tules had provided, stood the girl in the tub, and proceeded to scrub. They then had her sit and soak while they worked on their hair. Soon the three were giggling like schoolgirls. Virginia showed no sign of inhibition as servants came and went with buckets of hot water and towels. She had spent her life on the Colorado River amongst a people who went naked most of the time.

They dried her off and Alice produced a bundle of clothing. They started with bloomers and a chemise, followed by a hoop skirt and petticoats. Finally, a dress was added covering all. The skirt came all the way to the ground and would have to be lifted if she encountered mud puddles. Shoes were a problem. None would fit over the calloused feet.

The Wildest West

Alice frowned. "We'll have to take her to a shoemaker. For now, she can wear moccasins."

Tules looked on in amazement. "But how will she do her business?"

"What do you mean?" Alice was puzzled. "Oh, she'll head for a privy, lift her skirts, and lower the bloomers."

"*Muy* awkward. Our way is much better. Just squat by the side of the road, and the skirt conceals you. When you stand, the skirt is short enough that it doesn't drag in anything."

Alice tried hard not to show her disgust. "It is not our way. We are more modest."

Tules shook her head. Taking out her tobacco pouch, she rolled two *cigaritos* from tobacco and corn husk. She lit her own and offered one to the girl who took it happily. "Would you like one?" she asked Alice.

"Heavens no! We can't teach the girl to smoke! It's unladylike."

"*Que*? I have smoked since I was a little girl, and I assure you, I am a lady."

Alice rolled her eyes and tried to grab the *cigarito* from Virginia.

The women giggled again as they brushed and combed Virginia's hair. Alice twisted and curled it and pinned it up in the current style.

"What?" said Tules. "No shawl or scarf to cover her head?"

"Not indoors. I have a bonnet for her for outside."

Tules shook her head. "It is not good for a woman to go uncovered. It is against God, I think. The priest said something like that."

Alice pondered the need for headgear. It seemed strange to her. "I suppose we must decide if she is

Protestant or Catholic. Her mother was Protestant and probably had her baptized. So I think we'll be okay. There isn't a Protestant minister in Santa Fe that I can check with."

"Si," agreed Tules, "Such things can wait."

They spent some time teaching Virginia to shake hands, to bow and curtsy and then to say "Pleased to meet you," "Pardon me," "Please," and "Thank you." It was exhausting work even though Virginia was a quick study.

Alice smiled. "Tomorrow we can work on 'Pass the salt.' We should teach her how to eat tomorrow. I'll bet her table manners are atrocious. We need to take her shopping for her own clothes, and then we can teach her to dance and show her some party games so she'll fit in. We haven't time to teach her a musical instrument. I wonder if she can sing."

Tules nodded happily. "Of course she can sing. *Indios* sing all the time."

Alice was not reassured.

"Tomorrow, I will have my *cociñero* make up many foods so we can teach her to eat. And I know some musicians so we can teach her to dance." With the new clothes and new hairdo, Tules could hardly wait to get the girl back into the gambling *sala*. She would be a wonderful novelty and draw many new patrons.

Alice turned before she left. "Doña Tules, I hope you don't mind me asking. Why do they call you Tules? Are you from a rural area?"

"It is my name. My full name is Gertrudes. Tules is, how you say, a nickname."

"Oh, like Trudy for Gertrude."

"*Que?*"

The Wildest West

The *sala* was crowded and smoky that evening and stank of too many unwashed bodies too close together. Virginia smelled wonderful. Lilac water in the bath and a bit of perfume from Tules along with rouge on lips and cheeks made her stunning even in the very conservative dress Alice had provided. She worked her table silently substituting a smile for banter. Men crowded in. There were few American women in Santa Fe other than the officers' wives and a few traders' wives. Even the imperial Colonel Carleton, only recently made military governor, came by to bet a few coins. The word went round that her table was honest, but it wouldn't have mattered. Men were happy to lose money to her. The *sala* drew Mexicans and Indians, mountain men in buckskin, rich and poor, traders in fine suits and silk cravats, and the military, Colorado volunteers, California Column men who had marched across the desert and regulars.

The next day, Alice came again, and they practiced the polite phrases until lunchtime. Tules' servants brought a table into the courtyard and set it with an array of food.

They walked over to look at the array of *chili rellenos, posole, enchiladas, tortillas, refritos, sopapillas* and *chili con carne.*

"Let us sit and begin," said Tules.

Virginia dug into a bowl of *refritos* with two fingers as she had always done and brought them to her mouth so she could lick off the goo. She burned her fingers on the chili con carne and on the *rellenos* and then turned to the *posole* which she found too thin to dip, so she lifted the large bowl, meant for everyone, to her lips and sipped.

Alice nearly fainted. "Oh my, this will never do."

Tules took charge. "Here child, use a tortilla. Dip it in the *refritos* and bite off a piece and do the same with the *chili con carne*. Use the *sopapilla* to get the *posole*. That's it. You've got the idea. Now you're eating like a proper lady."

Alice was aghast. "Tomorrow I will bring my servant and have him prepare a meal. We will also bring a proper table setting with knives, forks, and spoons and plates for everyone instead of common bowls."

"*Que?*"

In the late afternoon, Virginia and Tules went into the *sala* so that the young woman could practice with her cards. Four men   led by Patrick Sloan, a gambler, let themselves in. He was dressed is a fine, russet frock coat with black velvet cuffs and collar. Under it, he wore a red Chinese silk vest and a cravat with a diamond stick pin.

Tules looked up. "I'm sorry. We are closed. *Cerrado.*"

Sloan smiled behind his mustache. "What a pity. Hope it stays that way. I've come to make you an offer. I'll buy you out for, shall we say, $200."

Tules was puzzled. "The gambling *sala* is part of my home, and my home is not for sale." She went to Sloan to escort him out.

His men fanned out across the room. One approached Virginia, a man in dirty clothing that had seen too much of the range and trail. He was long overdue to a shave and a bath.

"All right, then, $300. Or perhaps you would just close your gambling *sala* and keep the house."

"*Porque?*"

Sloan chuckled. "Because I don't like competition.

One of Sloan's men was a giant in buckskin with Bowie and tomahawk tucked in his belt. He leaned heavily on a Monte table and it collapsed under his weight.

170

"Murphy, don't be doing that. I'm trying to buy this place. He gets carried away."

The dirty man reached out a filthy hand and stroked Virginia's cheek. She recoiled. Leaving the hand where it was, he reached out with the other and pinched her breast. She turned her head suddenly and bit him. The dirty man screamed. Virginia spat out a chunk of flesh and blood.

"Virginia!" roared Doña Tules. "Don't do that! It's unladylike. What have I told you about putting dirty fingers in your mouth." She turned to Sloan. "Get out. I've nothing more to say to you!" She produced a revolver from the folds of her skirt and the click of the hammer got everyone's attention.

"This isn't over, Tules. Your customers may find dark Burro Alley a very dangerous place." He left and his men followed one holding a bleeding hand.

Sloan and his men returned to the *sala* in the late evening. The house was packed and Virginia's table crowded with would be beaus. Jack was there, gambling a little, looking sad and forlorn. The dirty man was there with his hand bandaged and looking hate at the girl. Sloan and his men didn't gamble but watched the action closely. Around midnight they left.

There was a shout from Burro Alley loud enough that it was heard by the gamblers. A man with a bloodied head staggered in. "I've been robbed!" He'd been a big winner earlier.

Around 3 a.m., there were screams. Jack went out and found another winner bloodied and unconscious in the alley.

After the *sala* closed, Virginia retired to the room Tules had provided for her. It was a nice room on the ground floor, and Tules had decorated with a *trastero*, a cabinet for hanging her new clothes, a side table with a mirror and her brush, a bed, and a *bulto* of Saint Francis. The girl didn't know who he was but he seemed nice and liked animals. There was no window, but she did have a wooden door, and there was an *horno*, a fireplace, in the corner. She was troubled and couldn't sleep. She didn't understand everything that was going on with the strange men, but her friend seemed to be in trouble.

That man had assaulted here, but she fixed that, but was shamed that Doña Tules had called it unladylike. She thought Tules was her friend. Tules was good to her, and so was Alice. They had taught her many strange things and seemed to contradict each other. They wanted her to be a lady and she did, too. Her other friend was Jack, and he said he would only have a lady. He had rejected her, but Virginia thought he wanted her. He said things she did not understand about honor and protecting her and not taking advantage of her. She wanted to be a lady for him because he wanted a lady. Perhaps, she would be if she learned everything Tules and Alice taught.

Thinking of Jack, she went to the *trastero* and took down the holster and pistol Jack had given her. He said it was a .44 caliber Dragoon Colt. She didn't know what that meant, but she treasured it anyway because Jack had given it to her, and a man only gives gifts to a woman he wants. She fondled the pistol and then loaded it carefully the way Jack had taught, greasing the front of the cylinders so they wouldn't chain fire. He'd taught her how to use it on the way from the Colorado River to Santa Fe, and Virginia had become a very good shot. There wasn't anything else to do in the months he spent prospecting but learn to shoot since he wouldn't treat her like a woman. She recalled the lessons that he'd given and for a little while she pictured him there in her room, giving them again.

"Be cool," he had said. "Take your time and aim. You can't do that if you're excited or worried about getting shot. Let the other guy worry. It will ruin his aim." That was easy for her. As a slave to the Mojave, she'd been beaten regularly. She'd learned to ignore it, to set the pain aside. A part of her was very cold when it came to danger and pain.

"Sometime though," he had taught, "you let a shot loose in someone's general direction just to worry him and throw his aim off. Use every advantage you can. Get the sun behind you to make it hard for him to see. Startle him any way you can."

She liked imagining Jack was there. His presence comforted her. She hadn't known much love from men, only lust. Nor had she parents to care for her. They'd been killed when she was very young, and she'd been an Indian slave ever since. But she felt something from Jack, something she wanted to return. She felt protected and something more. In the false dawn, she put the gun away and went to sleep resolved to protect her friends.

At noon, Alice had a table set in the courtyard with new foods and new rules. "These are fork, knife, and spoon. Using them properly is essential. Keep your hands in your lap unless you are using them and don't rest your elbows on the table. Put the napkin in your lap to protect your clothing and use it to wipe your lips before you drink. Pick up the fork with your left hand and turn it downward to hold your meat. Use the knife in your right hand to cut it. Then lay the knife on your plate and pass the fork to your right hand to bring to your mouth.

She went on, "The servants will bring food on your left, and if you nod, will put some on your plate. When you are done with a plate, place knife and fork on it as is they were the hands of a clock at four o'clock. The servant will take them away from the right."

Alice nodded and smiled, for Virginia and Tules seemed to be understanding. "Make all your moves dainty, small sips and small bites. You're a lady."

There was a lot more. Alice showed them how a dinner of many courses was served and how to choose the right fork, knife, and spoon for each course and how to sip soup and to butter bread. It was all very complex. "And if you don't do it right, they will think you an uneducated barbarian, and you may even make people sick. Next time I'll show you some games and dances. Our young lady is coming right along."

Virginia felt happy and proud. Maybe now Jack would accept her.

There were fewer patrons that night, and the *sala* closed early. Nonetheless, there were two more incidents of outlaws robbing the winners.

The next day, Doña Tules was set up in the courtyard to teach Virginia to dance. There were *mariachis* to play the tune. "Like this," said Tules, "put your hands on my shoulders, and I will put mine on yours. Then we bring our hips together to form the *cuna*, the cradle. And we whirl around the floor." They whirled, and Virginia laughed and smiled at the fun.

"No, no, no!" cried Alice, "You are touching where man and woman should never touch! This is horrible."

Tules squatted down and rolled herself a *cigarito*.

"No," said Alice. "Squatting isn't ladylike, nor is smoking. Tomorrow I will bring some soldier musicians from the fort."

The Wildest West

Virginia shook her head. There were so many rules to learn. Even Tules didn't know them all, and men liked her. It was going to take a long time to learn them all so Jack would want her.

In the late afternoon, General Carleton came calling. "Doña Tules, your establishment has become a public nuisance. Last night, one of my soldiers was beaten and robbed just outside. There have been many incidents. If this persists, I will shut you down. I am putting your establishment off-limits to my soldiers as a house of ill-reputation."

Virginia had never seen a man like this. He swirled into the room in the midst of his cape. His uniform was immaculate and creased, and it closely fit the contours of his body. His knee-high black boots gleamed, and his glittering sabre rattled. He spoke with his chin in the air in a voice that demanded instant obedience. He was imperial though Virginia didn't have any word for to express this idea. No Indian, in her experience, acted so haughty. She knew it was something special.

"But *Señor Comandante*, my *sala* has always had a good reputation for fair and honest games."

"No more! One more incident and I will close your *sala*." He clicked his heels, spun about and left.

Virginia thought Tules looked worried. "I will send for Chack."

There were very few customers that night. Word was spreading of the robberies and beatings. But there were no new incidents in the street. Jack was on patrol. He came in after closing. "Tules, I can only do this for a few nights."

"Chack, I know. I will have to think of something."

The next day the soldier band played in the courtyard, and the dance lesson went well. Alice even showed them

175

the military parade dance that started all dances on the post. She had to learn about rank and branch for the engineers came first with their senior officer in the lead, followed by the cavalry and the infantry and artillery. But still Virginia and Tules had fun, and even Alice seemed gay for a change. Some of the soldiers danced with them.

That evening many of their patrons returned to the *sala* aware that there was a patrol, Jack, in Burro Alley. Tules never thought of anything. Fortunately for her, Sloan was an impatient man.

The next day, Alice was busy and Virginia got to take a bath. She liked relaxing in the hot water that came up to her neck in the deep slipper tub. It was still out in the courtyard shielded by a few shrubs. As she splashed happily in the deep water, she heard loud voices coming from the *sala*. One of them sounded like Sloan. Tules screamed. That was enough.

Virginia sprang from the tub soaking wet and ran to her room where she pulled on her bloomers. They clung to her wet body revealing contours below. She hurriedly ran to the *sala*.

"Always scout the situation first," Jack had told her. She listened at the door.

Sloan was speaking. "Tules, Murphy will be happy to cut you a new face if I let him. Would you like to sell me your *sala* now? I'll be fair. I'll still give you $200 despite the additional trouble I've gone to."

Off to the left. Virginia heard two men laughing. Murphy giggled. Was there something wrong with him? Did he like to hurt women? The giggle sounded childish. Perhaps he had a weak mind. Beyond the door, Sloan would be straight ahead and Murphy to the right.

Doña Tules' response was muffled. Someone was holding her. Probably Murphy. There was no more she could learn here, so pulled her Dragoon, cocked the hammer, and threw the door open.

"Shock them and size the situation up quickly. Act without thought," Jack had said.

She took it all in. Off to the right by Tules' Monte table, Murphy held her with a knife to her face. Sloan stood directly across smiling. The other two were, as she'd thought, off to her left. Next to the dirty man was a youngster, lean and spare. He reached for his gun but hesitated at the what had come through the door – a beautiful woman, naked to waist with wet bloomers clinging to her nether parts.

"Shoot the one that poses the most danger first," Jack had said.

The hesitation cost the young man his life. She shot him in the chest and then whirled to face Murphy. He had dropped his knife away from Tules' face and turned to stare. It was enough. She shot him through the eye, and he fell on top of the woman.

Sloan was fumbling in a pocket for a gun and jerked out a derringer. She shot him in the forehead between the eyes.

That left the dirty man. He was slowed witted, and his move for his gun equally slow. Virginia shot him twice in the breast. He took a few minutes to die.

She'd fired five times. Virginia hoped there were no more in the street. She leapt across the room and grabbed up the youngster's gun with her left hand, just in case. Then she looked around the room. Only the dirty man was still moving. Suddenly, Murphy turned over. She almost fired before realizing that Tules was pushing him off her. She rose covered in Murphy's blood and looked around the room.

"*Chiquita*, you can shoot well!"

Virginia looked worried. "Doña Tules, was I unladylike?" Would Jack reject her?

"Perhaps. Go get dressed." Tules smiled. Carleton might close her down for the incident, but all was well.

Penitent Child

Juan Gallegos knelt before the altar in the windowless *morada* of *La Santa Hermandad* (the Holy Brotherhood). He had entered the secret home of the *penitentes* for the first time that day. This was not the *Terciarios de Penitencia* (the Third Order of Penance), a Franciscan lay order with whom they were sometimes confused. The Franciscan lay order had never been strong in New Mexico, but the *Santa Hermandad* had arrived with the Conquistadors in 1540. The men considered Juan, fourteen-years-old, old enough to take on the responsibilities of a man and mature enough to keep the secrets of the *morada*. He could keep the secrets of his *hermanos*, his brothers. He had sworn a long oath to God and his brothers detailing his religious responsibilities and his responsibilities to his new brothers. He wasn't even permitted to tell the priest in confession, if he ever saw a priest to take his confession and shrive him of his sins. Until then he would have to cast away sin in the way of his brothers, the way they had brought with them from Spain centuries ago when the Conquistadors came to the Rio Arriba, New Mexico, north of Santa Fe.

The hooded brothers had shown him how to whip himself with the yucca whip, which now lay beside him on the cold, hard-packed floor. He could use it again on his bare back if he felt the need to keep him from sleep as he made the lonely night-long vigil. He shivered in the cold of the room and the cold of creepy *Doña* Sebastiana's glare. She sat there in her little cart with her bow drawn, a warning that death could strike at any time. The skeleton

179

watched him and reminded him to stay awake and keep watch. He was allowed to prostrate himself on the floor, but he dared not for fear that he might sleep, and the cold take his body. He glanced around the room at the cruel tools of the *penitentes*. Without a priest, there was no other way for a man to shrive himself of sin.

Juan had known them all his life, seen them march on Good Friday when they came with drum and *pito*, a high-pitched wooden flute. They were hooded and barebacked, beating themselves with yucca whips. Some wrapped themselves in pads of cactus and made crowns of the crucifixion thorn. Two men dragged the Doña's little cart now filled with rocks. The axles, which knew not grease, shrieked like monsters. The wheels dragged and did not turn becoming flattened and making the cart harder to pull. Worst of all was the hooded man who carried the cross and wore a crown of thorns. He had already bloodied himself with whips. Now, he carried the heavy wooden cross. At the edge of town, the other men tied him to it and inserting its base into a hole hoisted him aloft. There he would stay and suffer all day. At nightfall, they would bring him down, his penance done. Sometimes he lived.

In the long cold night, Juan had time to think upon these things, on life in the Rio Arriba, and on sin. He had heard that before he was born, there had been priests, Franciscan friars who were sent to the *Indios* by the Spanish Crown. Many were kindly and cared for the Indians, but they charged high fees to perform religious ceremonies for the *pisanos*, the native New Mexicans. People waited to see if a child would live before they went through the expense of baptism, and then they saved all their lives for last rites. They paid only for the important things. Most never went through the expense of a marriage ceremony. The sin could be forgiven, and no one had the money. Juan's parents weren't married.

Now, even the Franciscans were gone. In 1830, Juan had heard, the Mexican government told all the Spanish friars to leave. They couldn't trust them because they were Spanish in the pay of the Crown. That left only two priests for everyone from El Paso to Taos. Priests didn't like to come to New Mexico. The people were too poor, the parishes were too poor, and that meant the priests would be poor. Men with education didn't want to be poor, so the *penitentes* took the place of the church and helped rid men of their sins.

Padre Antonio Martinez in Taos was running a seminary to make new priests, but their training would take time, and the people could do without them. They always had. They had always done for themselves.

In the cold dawn, the hooded men entered the *morada* and greeted Juan. They took off their hoods revealing themselves to him for the first time and greeted him with hugs, which hurt his raw back, as *hermano*, brother. They prayed with him and sang their special hymns. Then they allowed his father to take him home.

Their home was made of adobe with a heavy blanket as the door. The family used on room for storage and the other for everything else. It was where they worked, ate, and slept. In the late winter, there was little to do outside, so they sat on their bedrolls around the *horno*, a beehive-shaped fireplace, in the corner. The fire warmed the earthen bricks, which cast heat into the entire room. Juan's mother stretched and patted balls of dough into *tortillas*. Outside, she had a flat piece of metal set between adobe bricks that she used as a stove. There wasn't enough room to cook in the *horno*.

Nursing his sore back, Juan said, "Father, it seems so cruel, not at all like the forgiveness Jesus seemed to promise."

"*Silencio!* We do not speak of these things outside the *morada.*"

Juan sat in silent contemplation of the stories he had been taught. The church walls were painted with them, but there were more saints than Bible stories, and under the choir loft in the church at Trampas, if you looked up, the wood was scared with the brands all the families in the area used on their sheep, oxen, and burros. At Chimayo in the *Santuario* were the 14 Stations of the Cross. He had prayed at each one and thought about what the stations meant. The Romans did horribly cruel punishments to Christ, but hadn't he suffered so Juan wouldn't have to? Theology was confusing.

Because there was no one to teach him to read, Juan had to depend on the *bultos* and *retablos,* carved and painted saints and stories, at the church to guide him. He recognized the saints from the symbols they carried and knew stories about them. He had heard the Padre Martinez speak a few times, but he lived over in Taos and wasn't around enough to train or guide Juan. Moreover, much of the service was in Latin, which Juan couldn't understand. The priest had baptized Juan when he was five and his parents were sure he would live. Paying the priest for the ceremony was expensive, so they postponed the ceremony until he was no longer an infant and they knew the money for the stole fee wouldn't be wasted. Juan had heard that boys who lived in Santa Cruz de la Canada and Don Fernando de Taos were taught catechism, all the rules and laws of the church. Here in the mountains, Juan wasn't so lucky.

The Wildest West

His mother stepped outside and cooked the tortillas while she heated a dish of chili. It was chili with a little precious salt, some garlic and onion, and made from the dried chilis of the *ristras* that hung from the *vigas*. When it was hot, she broke some eggs into it. They had a few chickens but not enough so that they could have eggs every day, but this was a special day. Juan had been admitted to the *morada*. She took the *tortillas* and the big bowl of chili, his favorite breakfast, inside. They gathered around the bowl and dug in using tortillas as spoons. They didn't have any silverware or enough dishes for everyone to have his own.

"Thank you, Mother. That was very good."

Lunch would include beans or maybe *refritos*, refried beans, made of mashed, cooked beans fried in lard. If he was lucky, Juan's dinner would include a little chicken, mutton, venison, or rabbit. There might also be some squash. The end of winter was coming and they were running low on food.

Every few days, Juan went out to tend the sheep. All of the sheep of the village of Trampas grazed together, so only one or two boys had to be there on any given day. Minding the flocks was nice in the summer when the weather was warm, but in late winter and spring, Juan shivered in his sheepskin vest and blanket poncho. Tending the flock gave him time to think about the things he had learned in church and in the *morada*.

He was also getting lessons from his new brothers, but they seemed very different from what the priest taught. That shouldn't have been so, Juan thought. The brothers claimed they were on the same faith as the church. After several months, he learned a new secret: Padre Martinez was the spiritual guide and protector of the *Santa*

Hermandad. More than that, Bishop Zubiria had outlawed the brotherhood and had even ordered the locally made *bultos*, *santos*, and *retablos* removed from the churches! He said they were too crude and ugly and depicted things that were not right. Padre Martinez ignored him. How strange.

The brothers prepared for Easter. They would make a pilgrimage to the *Santuario* in Chimayo and join the others brothers there in a procession. They walked all night through the mountains by candlelight. Only the senior brother had a candle. They were expensive. The others followed him so they could be in Chimayo at dawn.

The brothers were all hooded, although they had their shirts off. Some wrapped pads of cactus about themselves. Others wore crowns of crucifixion thorns. Three *morada*s had brought their Doña Sebastianas, and they now loaded the carts with stones. The brothers who didn't have cactus pads had yucca whips and beat themselves until they bled. The hooded procession started out, and the crowd hushed in awe and terror. They beat themselves and bled. Padre Martinez and another priest smiled and waved and made the sign of the cross blessing the brothers. The *pitos* and drums sounded; the axles of the carts squealed. In the rear, three hooded brothers, one from each *morada*, dragged a heavy cross. Juan beat himself and bled. Under his hood, he thought, this a scene from hell. Perhaps it was what was needed to get into heaven.

At the edge of town, the men tied the three brothers with crosses to these objects of torture and hoisted the crosses aloft. They would stay up there suffering all day. It was an honor. Meanwhile, down below the people celebrated.

Juan put on his shirt over his sore back thinking that this was more a vision of hell with demons screaming than of heaven. He sought out the padre, trying to get to him alone, a difficult task. The Easter crowd thronged about and pressed heavily on him. They all wanted to be blessed or needed him for one ceremonial event or another. Tables and carts were set up in every space where they would fit. People sold special, and not so special, Easter foods. Some sold religious icons and relics. Business was especially lively around a vendor selling *milagros*, little tin representations of arms, legs, eyes, and hearts. Bought here, at this time, worn with a prayer they could perform miracles in helping people recover from afflictions and injuries. The greedy purveyors of religious artifacts reminded Juan of the story of the moneychangers in the temple. The celebration was all very colorful and lively as the people crowded happily about to spend what little money they had.

Finally, Juan was able to catch Padre Martinez alone resting in a quiet spot. He looked dour and sad as always. There did not seem to be any joy in the man who carried some heavy burden.

"Padre, may I speak to you?"

"Yes, my son."

"Padre, these Holy Brotherhood rites seem so cruel. Isn't life cruel enough? Can this really be what Christ demands so that he can forgive us?"

"My son, it is our way. It has always been our way."

Juan thought about this. "Does that make it right?"

"My son, it is not good to dwell on these things. God makes demands of us, and we must obey. This is our way of seeking forgiveness, and it brings us closer to Christ to understand the wounds that he suffered."

Less than satisfied, the boy returned to Trampas to work alongside his father in the fields. It was spring, and that meant the *acecia madre*, the mother ditch for irrigation, the men of the village gathered to clean out and repair the ditch. They had very few tools, and most of the work was done by hand.

"Father, where is Pancho Griego?"

"Hush, son. He is too important to join us here."

"But isn't he another farmer just like us?"

"Hush. He is a very important officer in the *morada*, and he has sources of wealth other than his farm. If you spit in the sky, you get it back in the face. Now get back to work."

The stream had been diverted from its bed and directed toward the fields below. The *acecia madre* ran parallel to the stream, and the land was divided into long, narrow lots. The road and homes were near the ditch where people drew water. Water released into the fields would flow across them and back into the stream. The ditch had been made to cross a deep gorge, and wooden columns had been set up to support hollowed out logs that the water flowed through. Fed by the melting snows, it was clear, clean, and cold.

"Father, do you think this aqueduct will last another season?"

"Let us pray that with God's will it does."

They returned to plow their fields behind an old ox that pulled a wooden plow. It had been made from a forked oak tree. One end was sharpened and fire hardened while the other served as a guide. It was difficult to keep the furrows straight, and they could not plow very deep.

"Look, father, Carlos Salizar has a metal plow he got from the *Americanos* in Taos. It plows deep and true."

"Bah, the *gavachos* charge a great deal of money for such things, and he will not lend it to us, only to his *primos*, his cousins. I do not want anything from these Protestant heretics, these *gavachos*, who have come to rob us of our religion and our land."

They returned to struggling with the wooden plow. Juan's father said, "The plow is getting old. We will have to make a new one next year."

Carlos Salizar was in his fields every day, weeding and hoeing the hard soil to encourage it to produce. He collected manure from the sheep and oxen in a pile, and when it was ready, added it to his fields. They all did the same thing, but his pile was bigger.

In the summer, Juan's father said, "Let us go down to the Picuris Pueblo. They are celebrating their saint's day."

At the church, they found the Picuris Indians throwing balls of adobe mud at their church. The building was considerably broader at its base and slopped from top to bottom like a pyramid with a flat top. This made it kind of squat and ugly. A priest, visiting from Taos, was smiling and throwing mud.

"Father, it does not seem right to throw mud at a church," said Juan as he hurled another ball of adobe.

"It is their way. We are repairing the winter damage by adding new adobe."

Afterwards, there was a dance involving corn maidens and men dressed as deer. Juan couldn't remember the Holy Corn Maidens or the dancing deer from any of the lessons of the church or from the painted retablos. But, he thought, they must be in there somewhere. God had made the deer, he was pretty sure, and maybe the corn, too.

On the way home, they passed Carlos Salizar's field. "Look, Father, at how well it grows. The corn is already as tall as I am, and everything looks healthy and big."

His father spat. "He is a *brujo*, a witch. He is not of the brotherhood. He must be stealing water from the *acecia madre*. Only an evil *brujo* would do that!" He crossed himself, Juan did the same, and then they both made a sign against the *ojo malo*, evil eye. "We must put some turquoise paint on the lintel over the door to keep out the *brujos*."

A month later, Juan sat on a hillside tending sheep. On the trail from Chimayo, the road to Taos, far below he saw Pancho Griego attack a *gavacho* leading a pack mule. The man rode a fine horse. Pancho approached him, and there was a conversation between them. The man stepped down from the saddle, and as he did so, Pancho hit him again and again with his big knife, almost a small sword. As Juan watched Pancho dumped the body into a deep ravine where it would not be found. There was nothing Juan could do. He was too far away, and there was no time to leave the sheep and get help.

That night Juan told his father. "Pancho Griego murdered a man and stole his goods and horse. I saw him. He hid the body, but I can show you where."

"I know. The man was a *gavacho* and a heretic. He was one of those who would rob us of our religion and our land."

"But, father, how can you know this?"

"Pancho told me."

Juan thought about this. "Father, he took the man's horse and mule and his goods. This is how Pancho gets rich without working."

"He is your sworn brother! He is a powerful officer in the *morada*. You are sworn to keep his secrets. We will speak of this no more!"

"But, father, Pancho is a murderer. We must tell the *alcalde major* so he can be arrested and tried. He must be punished."

"No more! We will speak of this no more. You are sworn to keep Pancho's secrets. The man was a *gavacho* heretic and a danger to us all. *Silencio!* The brothers would kill you if they knew what you have said. You would be an oath-breaker, no better than a *brujo*. And the church tells us we should not suffer a *brujo* to live."

Juan was not satisfied, but he dared not disobey his father. His only hope in life was to someday inherit the little strip of land that they farmed. There was nowhere else to go. There was no city that offered jobs in factories or big ranchos where he could be a *vaquero*. The *haciendado ricos*, the wealthy ranchers, had *peones*, debt slaves, to work for them. There was no other future. He must obey his father, and he must conform to that which the men of the village considered right and just, even if it seemed wrong.

Carlos Salizar had a fine harvest. His crops had done very well. "Because he is a *brujo*," said Juan's father whose own harvest was poor. The winter would be long and hard. "Juan," said his father, "we must take the bow and arrow and hunt for elk and deer, or we will have nothing to eat."

As they hiked up into the high mountains, Juan asked, "Father, why do we not have a gun?"

"You know there is only one gun in the village. You have seen it. It is the one Carlos Rey, King Carlos of Spain, gave to us with this grant of land when he told us to guard the passes against Comanche raiders. He gave us that gun so we could be soldiers."

"Only one?"

"Only one."

"But, father, it does not seem enough to fight Comanche."

His father chuckled. "It always has been. They have not come in many years. They are afraid of us."

Juan looked at his father. "There are other guns. Pancho Griego has the guns he took from the *gavacho*. I saw."

"Do not speak of this!"

The hunt was successful, but they would have to go out many times more to have enough for winter. Hunting with bow and arrow meant getting very close to an animal and often following it for miles while it bled to death.

"Come, Juan, it is nearing Christmas. We will cut some firewood and load it on the burros to take to Taos before the snows close the road. We will make a few coins to buy things." There were places closer to Taos where firewood was harvested so there was no compensation for the long distance they had to travel to get there. "It is our lot," said Juan's father. "God's will. God loves the poor. He made so many of us."

It was hard work cutting wood. Their axe was old and dull. They gathered as much wood as they could by hand, breaking it up, as best they could, without the ax. Then they loaded it onto the donkeys.

The walk to Taos was long and cold. They climbed over the ridge to Picuris, and there the trails divided confusingly. One went up to the highest passes and over to Mora on the Llano Estacado. One went down through the canyons to the Rio Grande, and one went over the pass and down to Fort Burgwin and finally Don Fernando de Taos. Confusion came in because of the many streams with deep gorges that joined in the area. One often had to climb up to go down, and the trails led through dark pine forest where the distance and direction were often hard to discern.

The Wildest West

They loaded their two donkeys and took them over the trail walking all day through light snow.

As they passed Fort Burgwin as soldier cried out, "Hey, *chico*, you got firewood? Come here and sell us some."

Although Juan did not understand, the soldier's intent was clear. Juan was concerned. Soldiers did not protect people. They often hurt them and stole from them. Juan was somewhat reassured because soldiers were gathered around a tree decorating it with candles and ribbons. Decorating trees and wasting candles wasn't Juan's custom, but he understood that it was the *gavachos* Christmas custom. If they celebrated Christmas, perhaps they would be kind. "Father, if we do not stop, they might steal everything from us, even the burros. But if we sell to them, perhaps these ignorant *gavachos* will give us more than we could get in Taos. I understand that when they pay, they pay far more than they should."

"It is true, son. This is what we will do." They got about three times what they would have in Taos. The soldiers paid a peso for each burro load. Father and son continued on happily. It was the Christmas season, and God was giving them a gift.

This was Juan's first trip to Taos, and it was a wonder to him. There were many large homes spread out around the plaza. There were poor people as in Trampas with one and two room houses, but many had haciendas, and the streets spread out from the central plaza with shops where men worked in leather, wood, and iron. Juan saw *trosteros*, wooden cabinets for clothing, and chairs for the first time. There were so many *ricos*, wealthy people, that their number astounded Juan. The plaza was completely enclosed like a *presidio* or a fort, and the buildings around

191

it were of two stories. Most important to Juan were the stores. There were places to buy pots and pan, food, tinned goods, thread and cloth, traps for animals, and more things than Juan could imagine.

Some of the *gavachos* had decorated their shops for Christmas. Christmas decorations were strange to see. They used branches of evergreen trees, bits of cloth, and shiny things. This *gavacho* custom was strange but pretty.

Leaving his father, who had all of the money, Juan made his way to the church. He crossed himself, genuflected, and made his way to the altar to kneel and pray in front of a statue of Christ on the cross suffering as he and his brothers suffered in the Holy Brotherhood. Rising, he looked around to find decorations that told the Christmas story. It was a happy story of God's gift to man. Some gift, Juan thought, he showed us how to suffer so we might have salvation. Gifts were supposed to be free.

That night the church put on a Christmas pageant telling the story all over again. Mary and Joseph went by on their burro looking for a manger in which to have a baby. Children dressed as angels sang, "Glad tidings. Peace, goodwill to men for unto you a child is born, a king is given." The pageant was beautiful and moving. Juan felt carried away by it. He wanted to be part of it. And all he had to do was beat himself bloody a few times a year and keep the secrets of his brothers who murdered men for their goods, and he could have the great gift. It didn't seem right. God said do not murder.

Juan and his father slept in the church and returned home, climbing high into the mountains the next day.

The day after they returned home, the clouds built up dark and menacing over the peaks. The wind blew cold, and the air felt moist with heavy, wet snow. Overhead, dark, low clouds wrestled with each other hiding the peaks. The first big storm of the season would be bitterly cold and drop more than enough snow to close the passes. Trampas would be isolated for a while.

Juan looked up the trail toward the ridge and saw two men riding mules and leading a string of laden pack animals. One was *gavacho*, and the other appeared to be a *paisano*, though oddly dressed. Both wore heavy buffalo coats over trade blanket capotes with hoods. Where the *paisano's* legs showed, he had on trousers that buttoned up the side with large silver *concho*s. They must both be great traders and men of wealth, Juan thought.

The two men rode slowly not wanting to exhaust their mules before what was likely to be a struggle ahead. Dan turned to Roque and said, "Those clouds look angry. Should we stop in Trampas for the night?

Roque looked over the village. "No, push on for Fort Burgwin. The *paisanos* look particularly unfriendly today. See how they gather and whisper to each other? It is not a good sign."

"What about your *primo* who lives here?"

"I do not see him in the crowd and do not wish to bring him trouble. It is all downhill to Fort Burgwin. We should be there just after dark. I look forward to a warm fire and a good meal. The soldiers are likely to have a good celebration."

Dan thought about their route and the warm fire that awaited them at trail's end. "They should have an excellent celebration with lots of food and a big fire. It is Christmas Eve! And they will welcome us even if Trampas does not."

They passed slowly by the church and village of Trampas.

The Wildest West

When the two riders were out of sight, Pancho Griego said to Juan, his father, and three other brothers gathered there, "They are very rich and one is a *gavacho* heretic. Let us run by the short cut to the river crossing where we can attack them!"

One brother demurred. "They looked heavily armed. It will be dangerous."

Pancho sneered. "They will expect nothing if we ambush them. They are encumbered by their heavy clothes and have their hands full with the lead lines for their pack animals."

Juan said, "I don't think we should. It is Christmas Eve."

Pancho looked at him coldly. "You especially must go. You have not yet proven your worth as a brother."

Juan's father whispered, "Juan, you must go. He knows you have seen him do murder. He will kill you and call you a *brujo*."

They took off running by the short cut to a spot overlooking the steep banks of the crossing. Griego put them in position. "Jump from the banks and knock them off their horses when they slow down. I'll give the signal. On the ground, we can finish them with ax and knife."

The angry clouds roiled up above and descended until they could almost be touched. An icy wind blew and cut through Juan's thin clothing. He shivered. He did not want to be here. What they planned to do didn't seem right.

Pancho called out. "Everyone down and quiet. Hide yourselves. Here they come."

And then, the storm descended unleashing its full fury. The cloud came down blotting out the light. Snow blew and swirled, and the world disappeared. Juan couldn't see the riders or the river. He couldn't see his father beside him.

He shivered. This storm was the kind that took men away not to be seen again until the snow melted in the spring. It was a killer storm.

The wind let up slightly, and the river became visible. The travelers were gone. Juan was relieved. He'd been true to his brothers and to himself. He hadn't wanted to kill the heretic and certainly hadn't wanted to kill a *paisano*, even if he was a *rico*.

Pancho yelled, "Quick after them! We'll get them at the next ford."

"Roque, where are we? I got turned around in all that snow at the last ford. I can't see the trail, and there seem to be pine trees all around."

"Danito, I don't know. I can barely see my horse's ears, and I can't see you, only hear your voice and that not so good."

Dan said, "We can't stay here. We'll freeze. I know we have to go uphill a little before we go down toward Fort Burgwin and Taos. Head to your right and keep talking so we don't get separated. I think that's uphill."

"Amigo, I don't know what to say. How can I talk endlessly in all this cold?"

"That never stopped you before."

Juan ran across the river as ordered. He was soon separated from his father and the others. In a world that showed little but cold, white haze, and the occasional tree when he got close enough, the boy heard voices. They spoke what he thought might be English. He knew some of the words. It was not the voices of his father or the men from the *morada*. He had found them. If he obeyed Pancho Griego's instructions, he should follow them to the next ford and jump them.

The Wildest West

The world was hushed and cold with only the soft sound of the voices of the two riders. Juan, more familiar with the area, realized that they were on the trail to Mora, which would take them over the highest passes where the strangers would surely freeze to death. That was good, Juan thought. Not that they would freeze, but that Griego would certainly go to the lower ford. He could turn them onto the upper ford, and his brothers would not see.

As they neared the turnoff, Juan grabbed the reins of both mules and gently urged them toward the ford and the trail to Burgwin. It was so cold, and the snow blew so hard that he could only see the mules' muzzles and the steam rising from their nostrils. That was good. No one must ever know what he had done.

In the white darkness, he led the mules toward Fort Burgwin.

"Danito, I think something is pulling my mule toward one side."

Dan pondered this. "Mine, too, but I can see nothing out there, only snow and more snow and no trail. Now and then, I am brushed by the branches of tree. We are lost. It's been good knowing you. I think we're going to freeze and ride our mules in circles among the high mountains forest all winter until we thaw and fall off in the spring." Dan wasn't that morbid. He was working on Roque's imagination. Both knew they would fight to the end and never give in.

Roque wasn't fazed by Dan's premonition of death. "No, Danito, every now and then I think I see something leading my horse. It is small and very white like it was covered in snow."

"Roque, I'm certain we are headed downhill. We're on the trail to Taos, I think."

Roque tried to see Dan through the snow. "You are very white and covered with snow. We've have been headed downhill for a longtime. I think we are on the trail to Taos."

With the two strangers a few miles down the road to Taos, Juan let go of their mules and slipped away unseen into the snow. He made his way back to Trampas.

"Boy," roared his father, "where have you been?"

"I became lost in the snow and wandered in the dark forest unable to find you."

His father glared at Juan. "Why didn't you call out?"

"I did. The snow must have muffled my cries. I tried to find you."

The old man shook his head. "Pancho Griego is very angry. He blames you for spoiling his ambush because you did not want to be there."

"I cannot help that, Father."

"Juan, you will have to do better next time."

The snow let up a little. When they were still a mile away, Roque and Dan could see light from Fort Burgwin.

Roque spoke earnestly. "We are saved. I tell you I saw it. It was all white. It must have been an angel that led us on the right road. It is a *milagro*, a miracle. We were saved by a Christmas angel. The bible story says they fly around this time of year. It is Christmas Eve, so there are many angels around."

Dan shook his head. "I don't know, Roque. I didn't see anything but snow. Maybe we just found the right road. I'm sure looking forward to a warm fire and some good food, lots of good food. And if we're lucky, maybe they'll have some eggnog with rum."

"I tell you, Danito, it was a miracle. I saw the Christmas Angel."

The Black Legend of Lieutenant George Bascom

The legend is black because it casts Lieutenant George Bascom in the worst possible, unfair light blaming him for starting 11 years of bloody warfare. It is legend because, though it is based in history, it is not history. Although historians now have a better understanding of the true story, the legend persists because it has the power of being the first way folks heard the story.

The legend says that in February 1861, while on patrol near the Whetstone Mountains, Lieutenant Bascom accused Chiricahua Apache chief, Cochise, and his Apache band of kidnapping 12 year-old Felix Ward who had been taken from his stepfather's, Johnny, ranch near modern Patagonia, Arizona, in October 1860. According to legend, Cochise had always been friendly to Americans and even had a contract to guard the Overland Mail. Cochise escaped leaving his wife and brother as Bascom's hostages. He then took his own hostages. The wise sergeant told Bascom to make an exchange, but the lieutenant refused ordering the sergeant court martialed. Bascom then, according to Apache sources, hanged his hostages, Cochise responded by killing his captives, and the war was on.

Who was this wise sergeant? Reuben F. Bernard, the First Sergeant of Company G, 1st Dragoons, was assigned to Fort Breckenridge in 1861. Bascom was commander of Company C, 7th Infantry assigned to Fort Buchanan 90 miles away. Bernard was promoted to captain during the Civil War and returned to Arizona in 1868. Thereafter, stories traceable to Bernard began to circulate with the sergeant as the hero and Bascom as the heel. Bernard said of Cochise, "This Indian was at peace until betrayed and wounded by white men." Bernard's tale of what had happened in 1861 was further embellished when Arizona governor, A.P.K. Safford's conversation was reported by the *Arizona Citizen* on December 7, 1872: "I told him that the conduct of Lieutenant Bascom was disliked by our people, and if he had not gone to war, Bascom would have been punished and many lives would have been saved."

Sidney DeLong, a sutler at Fort Bowie when Bernard commanded the post, wrote an early history of Arizona in 1905 and included Bernard's version of the story. Every verifiable fact is wrong. The only part that DeLong got right was that Bascom and Cochise met in Bascom's tent. Then the author of the first major work on Arizona history, Thomas Edwin Farish, picked up the ball. He reported the start of the Cochise War as 1861 and placed the blame on Bascom. Bascom's two reports, a report by Surgeon Irwin and the account from Sergeant Daniel Robinson, Company C, 7th Infantry, all of whom were there, were not available to historians until much later. The early historians relied on the accounts of old-timers like DeLong, none of whom had been there. Moreover, they knew of the events through the accounts furnished by Bernard.

Where was Bascom when these devastating portrayals of him and his actions came out? He was promoted to captain and died a hero at Valverde in February 1862 during the Civil War. He was not alive to defend his reputation.

Starting about 1960, scholars Robert Utley, Benjamin H. Sacks, and Constance Wynn Altschuler began locating primary documentation, namely the reports of men who had actually been at Apache Pass with Lieutenant Bascom in 1861. They painted a different picture of the Bascom Affair.

Bernard had claimed he advised Lieutenant Bascom to exchange their hostages for Cochise's, only to be ignored and court-martialed, yet no contemporaneous record of this has emerged. The historians concluded Bernard could not have offered this advice because, quite simply, he was not with Bascom's command at Apache Pass.

Bernard was in the wrong unit. Bascom was 7th Infantry, and Bernard was 1st Dragoons. He did not show up as an attachment to Bascom's company. No one else remembered him being there, and he misstated key elements, like the subsequent presence of his own commanding officer, Lieutenant Isaiah Moore. The record showed that Bernard was probably on leave in Tennessee when Bascom confronted Cochise. Sacks concluded that even if Bernard had been present, he wouldn't have arrived until Lieutenant Moore did on February 14, eight days after Bascom had refused to accept Cochise's trade of 16 U.S. Army mules and hostage, James Wallace, for Bascom's captives against the advice of his "wise sergeant."

In the 1990s, historian Doug McChristian and Fort Bowie National Monument Ranger, Larry Ludwig, turned up Daniel Robinson's account. Robinson was Bascom's sergeant at the time and respected the officer. From Robinson, we learned that Bascom had objected to hanging the hostages but four officers who all outranked him, none of whom complained of his behavior, outweighed his opinion. The reconnaissance found the tortured and mutilated bodies of four Americans before anyone talked of hanging the Apache hostages. Cochise had acted first, not the other way around.

With all this negative evidence pointing to Bascom destroyed, we still find those who argue that the Cochise War began with Bascom attempting to take Cochise hostage.

The myth of a peaceful Cochise appeared after the Civil War. Captain Bernard returned to Arizona in 1868 and told his commander, Colonel Thomas Devin, his tale of the wise sergeant who had advised Bascom against his course of action in 1861. Knowing that Bernard had been in Arizona before the Civil War, Devin had turned to him for information about Cochise.

Reuben Bernard included in his account that Cochise had always been friendly until Bascom came into the picture. He even claimed that the prominent Apache leader had a contract to guard the Overland Mail in 1861.

Governor Safford's interview with Cochise in 1872 gave the chief the opportunity to reinforce Bernard's story. Cochise said Bascom had blamed the wrong tribe for kidnapping Felix. He came in peacefully to straighten out the matter, but Bascom had tried to take him prisoner, an act that led Cochise to distrust the U.S. Army.

The historical record shows, however, that Cochise is better described as more prudent than friendly. He did not wish a fight with the American army close at hand. He was drawing annuities from the United States, so his men raided primarily in Mexico, but Sonora offered him a better deal. Times were hard and food scarce, so his men began raiding closer to home. On January 11, 1861, they stole 16 mules from troops of Fort Buchanan. Captain Richard Ewell had been out to Apache Pass several times in 1860, forcing Cochise to return livestock. The captain swore the next time he went, he would "strike a blow."

Cochise found the Overland Mail convenient. The company made gifts and bought firewood and hay from his women, but his warriors had twice threatened to kill all the Overland personnel and drive them from Apache Pass. In a society of individualists where each man decided on his own path, Cochise had the respect of many and was able to call together large numbers of his people in a way no other Apache leader ever did.

If Bascom had been allowed to defend himself against Bernard and Cochise's claims, scholars revealed the following is what the lieutenant would have shared.

Apaches took Felix Ward and twenty head of cattle from the ranch on January 27, 1861. Upon returning home the next day, the stepfather, Johnny, traveled to Fort Buchanan at the head of Sonoita Creek to report the abduction. Lieutenant Colonel Pitcairn Morrison immediately sent Lieutenant George Bascom, commander of Company C, 7th Infantry, to search for the trail.

That morning Lieutenant Bascom could not find the trail. In the afternoon, Lieutenant Richard Lord accompanied him, and together they found a trail that led east along the Babocomari River pointing toward the Apache Pass at the north end of the Chiricahua Mountains where Cochise, the chief, lived.

Experience had taught the two young officers that *Coyoteros* (White Mountain), *Pinals,* and other Western Apache returning from raids in Mexico traveled north along Sonoita Creek and over Redington Pass to the San Pedro River and home. Only Chiricahua's traveled east toward their home at Apache Pass. What the two lieutenants didn't realize was that the activation of Fort Breckenridge with two companies of dragoons, 90 miles to the north at the mouth of Aravaipa Creek on the San Pedro, had caused the other Apache bands to change their route east to the Sulphur Springs Valley and Apache Pass.

On January 29, Bascom led 50 infantrymen and four NCOs of Company C mounted on mules. The troops arrived at Apache Pass on February 3 and were joined by Sergeant Daniel Robinson and 11 more men. Johnny Ward, the boy's stepfather, went along as interpreter. Camped near the Overland Mail Station, Bascom sent messengers to Cochise's camp at Goodwin Canyon to ask the chief to come in for a talk.

Cochise arrived at noon the next day. He brought his wife, two boys, and three adult males. He wasn't expecting trouble, nor was Bascom whose sentries patrolled with bayonets on empty rifles. The woman, children, and two men were fed in the mess tent. Bascom, Ward, Cochise, and his brother, Coyuntura, went into Bascom's to dine and talk. The lieutenant asked for the return of the boy and the cattle. Cochise replied that he did not have the livestock or the boy but thought he knew who did and might arrange for their return if given ten days. Bascom responded that Cochise could remain as a hostage until both boy and cattle were returned.

Enraged, Cochise leapt up and cut his way out of the tent. Coyuntura did the same but stumbled over the guy ropes and fell. A sentry's bayonet pinned him to the ground. Johnny emerged from the tent and fired two shots at the fleeing Cochise.

Historians have criticized Bascom for not using the right mix of sabre rattling and diplomacy. Others had successfully negotiated with Cochise, but in those cases, Cochise had the goods to return. In March 1859, he had denied stealing mules when confronted by Captain Ewell even though he had stolen them. Bascom likely felt Cochise was concealing this theft, too. He wasn't, but Bascom had no way of knowing that Cochise was telling the truth.

With Cochise angry and on the run, Bascom ordered his men into the Overland Mail Station and fortified it against an Apache attack. Troops pulled up wagons in front of the gate and dug fighting positions beneath them. They used grain and flour sacks to form a parapet. They had rations for 20 days but water from the spring was half a mile away. That night they saw signal fires on the peaks.

Late the next morning, Cochise came in for a parlay, bringing with him Francisco of the Coyotero Apache and two others. Bascom came out with Johnny Ward and Sergeants Smith and Robinson.

Robinson observed a large number of Apaches in the arroyo south of the station. Two women signaled to the Overland Mail employees who emerged from the station and moved toward the arroyo. Bascom ordered them back, but they ignored him. Nearing the arroyo, Apache warriors emerged and tackled James Wallace and Charles Culver. Culver broke away and with Robert Walsh ran toward the station. Firing became general from both sides. Between the lines, Walsh ran into a bullet, and Culver was wounded. The meeting broke up.

On February 6, late in the morning, Cochise appeared and offered to trade 16 Army mules and Wallace for Bascom's Apache captives. Bascom declined. Bascom may have been insulted on being offered his own mules. He may have believed that Wallace, who claimed friendship with the Apaches, was in as little danger. The boy's stepfather wanted the boy back and exchanging the hostages would not bring that about.

Cochise, of course, did not have the boy to return. His appearance at the meeting with Coyotero chief, Francisco, suggests that those Apaches had not taken Felix. Cochise would have asked Francisco to return the boy. More than likely, Pinals had Felix, and Cochise was not on friendly terms with them.

Growing increasingly hostile and desperate, Cochise set ambushes for both the east- and west-bound Overland stages on February 6. The westbound came in four hours early by-passing an unmanned barricade without incident. Cochise and his men were busy at the other end of the pass where they stopped an east-bound wagon train, killed six Mexican drivers, tortured two more, and took three new hostages: Sam Whitfield, William Sanders, and Frank Brunner. Cochise had Wallace make out a noted detailing his additional hostages. He left it on a tree branch near the mail station.

On February 7, just after midnight, Moses "King" Lyons was driving the east-bound stage when Apaches attacked, wounding Lyons and killing a lead mule. Passengers cut the animal free while William Buckley, superintendent of the line between Tucson and Mesilla, took over driving. Lieutenant J.R. Cooke, eastbound to resign his commission and join the Confederacy, was among the nine on board.

That morning, 1SG James Huber planned to take the mules to the spring in two herds. He posted a lookout on Overlook Ridge while SGT Robinson and four men took up overwatch positions above the spring. Nine others moved the stock.

SGT Robinson saw King Lyons ride a mule in the midst of the herd, foiling Huber's plan and driving all of the herd toward the spring. Minutes later, a large force of Apaches attacked from the south. Robinson was wounded, Lyons slain.

The Wildest West

At the Overland Mail Station, Bascom saw an even larger force of Chiricahuas in the arroyo on his flank. He believed they were going to attack him if he emerged to rescue his men. Although senior, Lieutenant Cooke placed himself under Bascom's command and took ten men to rescue those at the spring. He succeeded in getting the men out, but most of the mules were lost.

On February 7, in the morning before the fight at the spring, Bascom had two wounded, Charles Culver and King Lyons, and believed himself surrounded by more than 500 Apaches. Mangas Coloradas had arrived with his warriors. Lieutenant Bascom sent messengers to Fort Buchanan, and Buckley sent A.B. Culver, the wounded man's brother, to Tucson. Two infantrymen and Culver traveled that night in snow with mule shoes padded. They parted company on the morning of the 8th and arrived in Tucson and at Buchanan, respectively, that evening.

On February 9, at Fort Buchanan, Asst. Surgeon Bernard John Dowling Irwin volunteered to lead 11 men of Company H, 7th Infantry, all the men available, to the relief of Bascom. Meanwhile, Company B, 8th Infantry, was marching 15 miles away north of the Dos Cabezas Mountains en route to the Rio Grande unaware of Bascom's predicament but in sight of Chiricahua sentinels. Apache Pass lay in the low ground between the Dos Cabezas and the Chiricahua Mountains.

By this point, the Cochise-Mangas-Francisco coalition was stressed. The Apaches had no commissary, and food and water were scarce. They had tried to lure Bascom out and failed. They were not about to conduct a costly frontal assault on the fortified station. The chiefs were aware of Company B and may have thought it an attempt to surround them. They apparently left then because they were not seen thereafter.

On February 10, while crossing the Sulphur Springs Valley, Surgeon Irwin encountered Coyoteros herding stolen stock back to their homeland. He ordered pursuit and captured three braves and 11 steers. Arriving at the Overland Mail Station without further incident, he brought in much needed beef. Surgeon Irwin was the first (chronologically by action) ever to be awarded the Medal of Honor. The MOH wasn't authorized until 1862, and wasn't awarded until 1863. Irwin didn't receive his until 1894, but it was awarded for these events in 1861.

Apache Pass was quiet until February 14, when Lieutenants Isaiah Moore and Richard Lord arrived with 70 dragoons. On the 16th and 17th, they ran a reconnaissance-in-force but did not locate any Apaches. They burned one empty rancheria and found the mutilated bodies of Mexicans and Cochise's four American hostages. On February 18, the stagecoaches departed, and the mail was running again.

The military departed on February 19, leaving behind a small force to guard the mail station. They halted at the site where the wagon train had been burned. Four officers-Bascom, Lord, Moore, and Irwin - met in conclave. Irwin, who was disgusted by the mutilated condition of Cochise's former prisoners, suggested hanging the hostages. All of the officers present were senior to Bascom, but it was he who objected. He didn't think hanging them a good idea. Irwin pointed out that three of the Apache captives were his, and he was going to hang them. Bascom then consented to hanging his three hostages. As commander, Lieutenant Moore authorized the hanging. The Apaches captives having learned their fate sang their death songs.

Coyuntura walked to a noose. The woman and children were later released at Fort Buchanan.

On March 3, 1861, Congress moved the Overland Mail moved north to the California-Oregon Trail, not because of anything that happened at Apache Pass, but because the Great Oxbow Route ran through the Confederate territories of Arkansas and Texas.

Cochise took revenge but it was short lived. In April, at Doubtful Canyon, he killed four teamsters and five men who were trying to reestablish the San Antonio-San Diego Mail for the Confederacy. In July, the seven men of the Freeman Thomas party were slain at Cooke's Canyon. In August, Cochise and Mangas Coloradas trapped a wagon train at Cooke's Canyon and could have slaughtered everyone, but were more interested in livestock than lives. Afterwards, they made attempts to drive Americans out and keep them out that culminated with the Battle of Apache Pass in July 1862. Thereafter, Cochise seems to have desired peace but no one in the Army was authorized to grant it.

In 1869, Cochise was the prominent Apache leader in the southwest, and the U.S. military was trying to reassert its control over the territory. Something of Bernard's self-promotion can be seen in his awarding the Congressional Medal of Honor to 30 of his men in one single action. When Bernard sent Devin his account of the October 20 battle, he wrote of Cochise: "I do not think I exaggerate the fact to say that we are contending with one of the most intelligent, hostile Indians on the continent."

Bernard wanted the world to see him as a hero, one who convinced the dangerous Cochise to put aside his hatred of the army and turn to peace. For the 1861 events,

Bascom became the betrayer of Cochise, and the U.S. Army escaped responsibility.

Beginning in 1867, Cochise indicated to the army that he wanted to negotiate peace. The next year, he sent word to Devin that if the army agreed to a truce, Cochise would "not only remain at peace but be responsible for (protection of) the overland road and stock in its vicinity." Four years and many raids later, Brigadier General Oliver O. Howard finally worked out a treaty with Cochise. By that time, Bernard was in California fighting in the Modoc War.

Cochise retired to the Chiricahua Reservation where he died in 1874. His body is believed to be buried in the Dragoon Mountains in an area known today as "Cochise Stronghold."

When Bernard died in 1903, his body was buried in Arlington National Cemetery, a cemetery the government created in 1864 due to the bloody Civil War and cemeteries growing overcrowded with the bodies of soldiers. Bernard's military exploits were extolled in the book *One Hundred and Three Fights and Scrimmages*.

Bascom who died a hero in 1862 at the hands of the Confederates in the Civil War was buried in a New Mexico cemetery at Fort Craig. When the post closed in 1885, all the bodies were reburied at Santa Fe National Cemetery. Bascom's grave could not be identified, so if his body made it there at all, it lies beneath one of the unknown markers. A fort in New Mexico was named for him.

Nearly 150 years after Bascom's death, Twitter would light up with "this day in the past" tweet: "4/24/1836 George Bascom born (died 1862). Arrested Chief Cochise (the Bascom Affair) who escaped. This arrest triggered the Apache Wars." The Black Legend persists.

The Wildest West

Felix Telles Ward, about 12 years-old when he was taken, was raised as an Apache warrior. In 1872, he enlisted as an Apache Scout under the name Mickey Free. Free was the name of an Irish rogue in the novel, *Charles O'Malley, The Irish Dragoon* by Charles Lever. At the time of enlistment, soldiers needed a name for Felix that they could spell and one of them thought he looked like the character in the novel. Felix was all Mexican. The Irish name and his Irish step-father led to speculation that he was half Irish. Apache Scouts had to be Apache, and Felix was not, so a story circulated that his mother had been a captive and he was half Apache.

His step-father, Johnny, died in 1867. Younger sibling, Santiago, sought him out but Mickey had no desire to return home to siblings who had been babes-in-arms or not yet born when he left. He lived out his life as a White Mountain (Coyotero) Apache with two wives.

Sergeant Robinson became a captain in the Civil War and afterwards instructed junior officers in fighting Indians using the Bascom Affair as an example.

The Life and Times of Tom Jeffords

Tom Jeffords was portrayed by Jimmy Stewart in the 1950 classic film *Broken Arrow*. Although he did ride alone into Cochise's Stronghold to make the peace, events were not quite as portrayed in film, legend, and popular history. The real Tom Jeffords was equally brave, and although often motivated by profit, he was still swiftly able to gain and maintain the respect and trust of a leader, Cochise, from a warrior nation. Tom left only a handful of letters, and these written by partners, clerks, and attorneys, and a few hints as to his past from which we might gage the man and what elements of character made him the key to building peace with Cochise, then 11 years at war.

Thomas Jefferson Jeffords was born January 1, 1832, to Eber and Almira Jeffords, the third of an eventually 12 children. Eber had come from Massachusetts in the early 1820s to the furthest southwest corner of New York, Chautauqua, at that time a land of hardwood stumps. Pioneers had preceded him, clearing and planting the land. There was no industry and no big towns. He came to find farmland but was too late. Instead in 1824, he met and married 16 year-old Almira Woods. In 1825, the Erie Canal opened and so did the asheries, which turned hardwood into pearl ash used in glass, ceramics, and making saleratus, baking soda. The canal tied Chautauqua to New York City and the world, and the lake tied the county to Chicago and New Orleans. It's likely Eber worked in the asheries, but when Tom was seven, Eber concluded he'd never earn enough to raise a family and buy a farm. He took the family west to the nearest corner of Ohio, Ashtabula, in the Western Reserve of Connecticut.

The Wildest West

Ashtabula was a lake port and a town built by New England Yankees. Four of Eber's sons sailed the lakes, and two, Tom and James, rose to be captains while in their early twenties. It's likely Eber worked the docks. Eventually, he bought his farm. All twelve children grew to adulthood, suggesting that this was a loving and well-regulated family. The daughters all married and named their sons for their father and brothers. One brother who went to sea spent his declining years with a nephew's family. The family did not make a mark on Ashtabula society suggesting that they were poor and that the sons went to work early. Lack of funds for school meant the boys went to work at a young age which would also explain how Tom and James achieved captaincies so young. There wasn't enough money for much schooling. In the guest book of a Tucson area ranch, I found Tom Jeffords's signature. In a book of poetry, fancy sentiments, and drawings, one page contains a simple signature, that of a man uncomfortable writing cursive. Set aside the fine letters in the writing of others and see Tom as a rough and crude frontiersman with little education but still a leader. We get the feeling that Eber, who married young, told his sons to make their fortune before they married. Four, including Tom, never did marry. Tom and John went west to the gold rushes. That two of his sons were captains suggests that Eber taught discipline, self-respect, and courage.

In 1856, the bark *John Sweeney* capsized. Her skipper was 24-year-old Captain Jeffords of Ashtabula. Sailing the Great Lakes wasn't like sailing the salt seas. Ships didn't make voyages; they made runs lasting a few days to a few weeks at most. The lakes were frozen in the winter, and sailors stayed home or found other jobs, often as lumberjacks. On reaching port, the crew was paid-off, and the captain remained with the ship while it was unloaded. He then hired a new crew. Land was near, food was fresh, and the cook often a woman. Crews consisted of a captain, an officer, a cook, and two or three deck hands, just enough to raise the fore-and-aft sails. The crew dined with the captain in his cabin. If the water-butts ran dry, the crew could always dip a bucket over the side. The most exotic ports were in Canada. It was a bit like truck driving: repetitious, boring, familiar ports over and over again.

Sailing the lakes did require special qualities in the officers. Faced with constant crew changeover, they had to gain respect and obedience quickly and had to maintain it at close quarters, dining with the men and, therefore, being friendly and accessible while projecting an air of authority and personal discipline. Tom must also have learned to bury fear and remain calm so as to give orders effectively under trying conditions. Crews were drawn from a variety of backgrounds of social class and culture: Germans, Dutch, Swedes, French-Canadians, French-Indian Metis, and backwoods Americans. The officer had to win respect from all and had to be able to live at close quarters with their varying habits. George Hand, who ran a saloon in Tucson during the 1870s, described Tom as a man who arrived in the company of friends and who was always welcome. He held posts of trust and leadership, as superintendent of the mail from Tucson to Socorro in the 1860s and as head of the Tucson Artesian Water Company in the late 1870s. Lessons learned as a sea officer stood him in good stead when he met Cochise.

Tom Jeffords grew bored with the lakes and realized he would be slow in making his fortune sailing other men's ships. In 1859, he laid out the road west to Denver and the

Pike's Peak Gold Rush but soon found he'd arrived too late to claim a good placer and headed south to the short-lived 1860 San Juan Gold Rush. He wrote that he arrived in Arizona in 1860, but didn't see Tucson until 1862. Most roads led to Tucson, which at that time with Tubac and Gila City, was one of three towns in Arizona. Kearney's Route along the Gila River, a trail for pack animals, was the exception. There was insufficient water to work the placers at Gila City. Tom found Sonorans winnowing gold by tossing blanket-loads of earth in the air and letting the wind blow away the lighter elements. Four men breaking their backs could earn $5 or 6 in a day. American prospectors packed up and left for a new gold strike at Pinos Altos near the headwaters of the Gila River, six miles north of where Silver City is today. It was in this vicinity that war found Jeffords in 1862.

He said he was a civilian courier at the Battle of Valverde near Fort Craig on the Rio Grande. Man for man, it was the bloodiest battle of the Civil War with 300 out of 3,000 lost on each side. The weakened Confederates pushed north and took Santa Fe while Colonel Edward Canby remained in control of Fort Craig and Union supplies. Confederates held Mesilla and the road to Tucson. Colonel James Carleton was at Fort Yuma coming with a brigade-sized unit, the California Column, but the two colonels were not in contact. Canby needed someone who knew Kearney's route to carry dispatches. Jeffords made the ride of 500 miles through the Apache country of Cochise and Mangas Coloradas, then hostile to the U.S. The dangers of such a journey are almost beyond belief. The country with poor water, rough ground, and little grazing would weaken or kill a horse, or the Apache might steal it and slay the rider. Without the horse, the rider stood little chance in the Gila deserts.

Tom Jeffords returned to the Rio Grande with the lead elements of the California Column and may have met Cochise when Major Eyre made contact in July 1862. The major provided the chief with enough information to set up the ambush that became the Battle of Apache Pass. Tom remained with the army through the war, scouting and serving as courier; however, we know little of his adventures. Mail to Tucson was cut off in March of 1861 when Congress moved the route north to the Oregon-California Trail out of Confederate control. Thereafter, mail came by Army dispatch from Fort Yuma or, after 1863, from the new capitol, Prescott. The lack of a direct route like the Southern Overland Mail had used meant that mail had to go around the Horn or across the Panama isthmus to San Francisco and then by steamer to the mouth of the Colorado River, thence upriver by steamboat. It was slow and arduous. Mail was the lifeblood of commerce. It was how merchants ordered and paid for shipments.

Mail again ran over the Southern Overland Mail route when Tom Jeffords became superintendent of the mail from Tucson to Socorro from whence the line ran on via Santa Fe to St. Louis. In 1867, the mail was started with two express riders per week. It was so successful that soon a once per week stagecoach (buckboard) was added. Legend and Robert Forbes have added confusion to the story. Tom may have driven the buckboard on the old Butterfield Road, but he did not drive for Butterfield whose Overland Mail relocated out of Arizona in 1861. He may have had scars, but they weren't from Apache arrows. He may have known 22 men killed by Cochise's band, but they weren't express riders. The pony riders had nothing Cochise wanted, and their horses were fast. The stage was attacked only once in 1869 and that caused a stir that led to a month-long pursuit and the Battle of Turtle Mountain where 30 Medals of Honor were awarded.

In 1870, Tom Jeffords partnered with Elias Brevoort as Indian trader at Canada Alamosa. This Chiricahua reservation near modern Truth or Consequences was popular with the Apache, many of whom came in voluntarily. The agent was Lieutenant Charles Drew who was liked by the Indians. Brevoort and Jeffords sent him a letter advising him that it was unwise to drink with Apaches. Drew took it to his commander, accusing the traders of trying to intimidate him to cover for their own misdeeds. Drew was a known alcoholic, and it seems likely the warning was sincere. Nonetheless, they lost their license to trade.

Jeffords returned to prospecting and scouting for the Army. While on a scout, his patrol passed through Cochise's camp in the mountains west of Canada Alamosa. Cochise and his warriors were away raiding in Mexico. The people were rounded up and escorted to the reservation. The Army needed someone to go back and invite Cochise in for talks. The chief was wary of the Army. In 1861, Lieutenant George Bascom had attempted to take him hostage during talks leading to an open break in relations. The man who knew the way, and the one willing to make the trip was Tom Jeffords. He returned alone to Cochise's camp and billed the Army $300. Courage and Jeffords's personality made an impression on the Apache. The chief came in to the reservation to discuss settling there and in subsequent talks called on Jeffords to advise him. While Jeffords did not speak Apache, both he and the chief spoke Spanish.

The Wildest West

The Chiricahua War might have ended then and there, but the Indian service decided that the Canada Alamosa Reservation was too close to whites and Mexicans who were corrupting the Indians. The Apache were moved to the Tularosa Valley in far western New Mexico. The elevation was high, the growing season short, and the Apaches didn't like it and began to leave. Meanwhile, General George Crook had begun a campaign near Prescott moving relentlessly toward the southeast, subjugating Apaches and forcing them onto reservations where various bands hostile to one another were made to live at close quarters. At this point, in 1872, General Oliver O. Howard, the one-armed, Christian general, arrived with a special commission from President Grant to make peace with the Chiricahua. Crook's campaign was put on hold.

The general was told that Tom Jeffords was the only man who could take him to Cochise. He sought Tom out. Jeffords told the general that he could take the officer alone to Cochise's camp but would not lead a column or patrol. In the end, the party consisted of Tom, the general, his aide, Sladen, a cook, and a packer, Streeter. Departing from Canada Alamosa, they picked up two of Cochise's relatives as guides and rode the breadth of Chiricahua country from the Rio Grande to the Dragoon Mountains. There they found Cochise's people camped in a canyon whose description matches Slavin Gulch. The chief was found in a tiny mountain alcove seven miles to the north and there talks began with Cochise, Tom, and the general sitting atop the flat rock that was Cochise's roof.

The chief wanted reassurance from Tom Jeffords that he could trust the general to do as promised. The scout reassured him; he thought Howard could be trusted. Cochise asked for a reservation whose western boundary was the foot of the Mule and Dragoon Mountains running northeast from Dragoon Spring to Doubtful Canyon and then south through the Peloncillos to the Mexican border. He also demanded a reluctant Tom Jeffords as the Indian agent. The general granted all of that Cochise required, and peace was made.

From the start, there were problems. The Army and Cochise kept their word, but Jeffords soon found beef supplier Henry Hooker unwilling to deal with him. The Indian service wouldn't pay for the beef, claiming the Army had created the reservation, and payment should come from the Army budget. The difficulty with the Indian service refusing to pay was straightened out in the first few months but was typical of the challenges Jeffords faced. Three hundred and fifty of Cochise's people came in followed by 250 more of the Juh-Geronimo band. Other smaller bands came in as well. They lived scattered about the reservation. The agency was moved to the San Simon Cienega, about 25 miles south of the San Simon on the today's Interstate. There they were supposed to farm, but they soon began to die of fever, and the agency was moved again. There were visitors on hunting passes from other reservations, some of who continued on to Mexico to hunt Mexicans, claiming a ration going and coming. Eventually, Jeffords was calling for 900 rations. When the reservation was broken up, only 300 of Cochise's band went to San Carlos. The Juh-Geronimo band went to Mexico, and the others scattered like quail. Jeffords's accounting was called into question, but no evidence was ever obtained that he was profiteering, only that he kept the Apache well-fed and happy and spent money from his own pocket. Problems with travelers on the road through Apache Pass resulted in the agency being moved there so that Jeffords would be close at hand to settle disputes.

Cochise died in 1874, and Tom Jeffords was with him the night before he passed. He is said to have asked Tom, "Do you think we'll meet in the afterlife?"

To which the agent replied, "I don't know."

Cochise said, "I think we will." Cochise was buried in a blanket given to him by Henry Hooker. Thus ended a very special relationship between two men of very different backgrounds.

Taza, the chief's son, kept the peace while he lived. In 1876, Apaches bought alcohol from Nicholas Rogers at Sulphur Springs Ranch. Becoming drunk, they murdered two of Apache women of their band and then in company with Geronimo returned to buy more liquor. Rogers refused them, and he and his partner were slain. This band of Apaches then left the reservation and killed three settlers along the San Pedro River. Jeffords was fired as agent. The reservation was broken up and the Apaches escorted to the San Carlos Reservation.

Now in his late 40s, Tom returned to trying to make his fortune. He headed up the Tucson Artesian Water Company, an attempt to bring drinking water to Tucson homes. With Archie McIntosh, he pursued Geronimo into Mexico and brought him in to the San Carlos Reservation. Even while Tom was agent, he had been prospecting and relocated the Brunckow Mine, which he continued to own into the 1880s. Immediately after the reservation closed, he staked claims in Apache Pass, the Huachuca Mountains, and the Dos Cabezas. He owned shares in mines in Tombstone and bought, for $5, George Warren's 1/9th share in the Copper Queen Mine after Warren had lost in the famous footrace against a horse. Tom turned $500 profit by reselling it a few years later. At various times the newspapers reported he'd made $20,000 on the sale of a mine. County records place the amount at closer to $2,000. Perhaps the low figure was to fool the taxman. Jeffords seemed to have money and invested $8,000 in building a new sutler's store for Fort Huachuca where he was sutler, post trader, and postmaster for a number of years.

In 1892, he moved to the Owl Head Buttes on the northwest slope of the Tortillita Mountains, about 35 miles north of Tucson. Today the site seems remote and requires a lengthy, drive by a round-a-bout route. In those days, the road ran direct, and there were neighbors, a stamp mill, and a small village nearby. In 1895, Alice Rollins Crane sought Tom out. She claimed to be a writer and ethnographer who had lived among the Apache for nine years. Later she added the Dakota Sioux. Little can be found to support her claims. She talked Tom into showing her where the peace had been made. In Slavin Gulch, she claimed to have induced Tom to make signal fires to call in the Bronco Apache. When she retold the story in 1914, the Broncos had become the Apache Kid. In 1898, she put together a consortium of Los Angeles women who paid her way to the Yukon Gold Rush where she was to buy mines in her name and pay them dividends. She bought mines, but no dividends were forthcoming. By the time she reached San Francisco on her way north, she claimed her backers were a secret consortium of New York newspapers for which she would write articles. In Seattle, she had been dispatched by the Smithsonian as an ethnographer. In the Yukon, she published an anthology of other people's short stories in her own name leaving out the name of her partner, Captain William Galpin, who tried to kill her. She ran to the protection of Russian Count Moraczewski, who was actually a Polish peasant.

Madam and the Count were associated with Jeffords throughout the rest of his life. They claimed that he was destitute and that they had supported him, but at the same time, they tried to profit from his estate. After Tom's death, Moraczewski displayed a shotgun that he claimed had been given to the agent by Cochise. He said he would give it to the Arizona Pioneers Society, now the Arizona Historical Society. It isn't there. George Oakes saw the weapon and noted that it was a modern breech loading shotgun while those in Cochise's day had been muzzle loading, and moreover, he knew where Tom had bought it.

Tom had neighbors and friends. He built a good-looking frame house with glass windows and a picket fence and continued to work his mines until he died on February 19, 1914. He was buried at Evergreen Cemetery in Tucson. The list of his pallbearers reads like a who's who of frontier Arizona. The entire Pioneers Society turned out in his honor. He was not a loner, but he was a very special man who had been able to win the trust and respect of an Apache chief suspicious of all white men.

Padre Antonio Jose Martinez,
New Mexican Hero

The victors win the honor of writing history. Great heroes can be lost and have even their purist motives denigrated. To make themselves appear great, the triumphant often choose to magnify the villainy of the defeated. In the mid-nineteenth century, Padre Antonio Jose Martinez held power difficult to imagine today, and it made him a target for Anglo leaders and French clergymen. They described him as clutching for power and implied that he was immoral. French-born Jean-Baptiste Salpointe, second archbishop of Santa Fe, omitted Martinez from his history of the Catholic Church in New Mexico despite the fact that the padre had established the region's first school for both genders, printed the first books, educated the first native priests, and bridged a period when New Mexico was almost completely without priests.

To understand the man, we need to comprehend his time and place and what he was defending. In this light, his motives appear purer. Picture New Mexico when Brigadier General Stephen Watts Kearny's army arrived in 1846 as a priest-ridden land full of fat friars who took their ease at the gambling halls and bordellos of Santa Fe. The parish priest of the *Villa Real de la Santa Fe de San Francisco de Aziz* may have taken his ease in this manner, despite being a very old man. The priest of a neighboring town might even have joined him from time to time: however, there were no friars in 1846, fat or otherwise, and very few priests. Controlling religious observances was the mysterious and secretive brotherhood of *Penitentes*, a lay organization proscribed by the Catholic Church for its excesses. During Holy Week (Easter), the brothers whipped and otherwise tortured themselves in public. Others dragged a cart full of heavy stones on which sat the skeleton Doña Sebastiana, representing death, bearing her little bow to remind all that death can strike at any time. The cart's ungreased axle and wheels did not turn but skidded over the road to shrill tunes played on the *pito*, a little flute. In the final ritual, a brother depicting Christ carried a heavy cross, was roped to it, hoisted aloft, and left to suffer for the day. Most years, he was still alive when they brought him down.

The ecclesiastical power struggle had begun centuries before with the *Entrada,* the conquest, when the Spanish crown gave New Mexico to the Franciscan Order as a mission field, paying for the upkeep of the friars from the royal treasury. At first, there were no secular priests (priests who were not associated with a monastic order), only the missionaries who sought out the Pueblo Indians in their villages. Only much later, in 1797, did New Mexico become part of a secular diocese with parish priests at El Paso, Santa Fe, and Santa Cruz de la Cañada. Through 1821, when Mexico won her independence from Spain, these secular priesthoods were seldom filled while at the same time the Franciscan Order found it difficult to find friars for the northern frontier. New Mexico became a land with very few priests and was soon to have even fewer.

A lay brotherhood of obscure origins, *La Santa Hermandad* (the Holy Brotherhood), was known by many names. Anglos called them the *Penitentes* because of their rites of physical self-abuse, penance. The Franciscans disavowed the group, which was often confused with their Third, or lay, brotherhood, *Terciarios de Penitencia* (the

Third Order of Penance). The Friars practiced a private and gentler form of self-flagellation. When the *Hermandad* first became a matter of record after 1800, it was already old, perhaps as old as the *Entrada,* and widespread. Its ritual closely resembles the Holy Week observances of a society in Seville, Spain, but the route of transmission is unknown. This secret society of mutual aid and assistance was, in many ways, like the Freemasons, binding society together beyond family and across class lines. The brotherhood thrived where priests were few and more involved with Indians than Hispanics as a source of succor and religious observance.

The brotherhood had a dark side. A secret society, appearing hooded in processions, their identities hidden from the world, they beat themselves publically until blood ran. Onlookers likely wondered what self-abusing fanatics might do to outsiders. Hoods and secrecy made blood run cold. While they punished brothers severely for minor infractions against other brothers, when the victim was an outsider, they overlooked major crimes, even murder, keeping the secret. They voted as a block, electing officials of their selection.

As times changed, more parishes were created at Albuquerque, Taos, Abiquiu, San Miguel, and Tomé, but the priesthoods often remained unfilled; rarely were there more than two secular priests in all New Mexico. By 1830, more than 80 years had passed since the Bishop of Durango had visited his far flung flock. Distance from the bishop and the lack of regular priests was a mercy for the poor of New Mexico, for the crown was paying the Franciscan's expenses; there was no mandatory tithe. Priests and friars not otherwise compensated by their parishioners charged high stole fees, payments for ceremonies, such as marriage, baptism, and last rites. Still, people found ways to avoid even these. They didn't really need a formal wedding, and a baby, who might soon die, didn't really need a baptism; instead, they saved for the truly necessary, last rites. Then, in 1828, even the friars were gone. Mexico didn't trust the predominately Spanish monks and drove them out, leaving New Mexico with only two priests. In the vacuum of religious leadership, the Brotherhood of Penitentes flourished.

Representing the Catholic Church were a priest in Santa Fe and Padre Antonio Jose Martinez in Taos. The departing Franciscan friars asked Padre Martinez to watch over the Franciscan lay brotherhood, *Terciarios de Penitencia* (the Third Order of Penance, the first two orders were of friars and nuns). In 1833, Padre Martinez asked the *Custos*, head of the Franciscans in New Mexico, to put him in charge of all *Terciarios* there. The *Terciarios* were in disarray while the *Penitentes* were growing in power and political influence. If the *Penitentes* were of Franciscan origin, and lacking priestly supervision after 1800, their ceremonies took on a degree of violence of which the gentle Franciscans would not have approved. Padre Martinez seems to have taken charge of the *Penitentes* perhaps unable to distinguish between the two lay brotherhoods with oddly similar names.

The *Penitentes* were associated with the *Santuario de Chimayo* located about 20 miles north of Santa Fe. Its founder brought a peculiar cult and cross, the cult of Our Lord of Esquipulas, from Guatemala, and along with it came the practice of geophagy, eating clay (considered by pilgrims *tierra bendita*, blessed earth). A leader of the local Penitente group built the chapel after 1802. The *Hermandad* was already coming to prominence, and its symbols appeared prominently on the altar screen. The Santuario became an important pilgrimage center known today as the Lourdes of North America. At Easter the *Penitentes* come to practice their Holy Week rites and pilgrims walk all night from distant towns to hear Mass. Many leave behind their crutches having been healed. Others take home a little clay from an opening in the floor of a room just off the sanctuary. Those who seek blessing mixed the tierra bendita with food or sprinkle it on window and doorsills to ward off *brujos,* witches, and other evil influences. The religion of the *Rio Arriba,* the region north of Santa Fe, is unique in North America. Such beliefs had a powerful hold in early New Mexico.

In the 18th and early 19th centuries, education was under the purview of a few *ricos*, the wealthy, who could afford to bring tutors into their homes. Elsewhere, priests often taught at a village school, but New Mexico lacked priests. There were no printing presses and no newspapers, for there were few who could read them.

Antonio Jose Martinez was born at Abiquiu in 1793 to one of the richest families in the *Rio Arriba*. His family soon moved to Taos. Married in 1812, his wife died soon afterwards leaving him a baby daughter. In 1818, the child installed with family, he entered a seminary in Durango, Mexico, seeking a secular priesthood. He was present for the excitement and hope of the Mexican War of Independence while maintaining an impressive academic record. Mexican leaders framed a new constitution incorporating ideas learned from the *Norte Americano* experience. Soon after he returned home an ordained priest in 1823, his daughter died. The padre immersed himself in his work and within a few years held the parish of Don Fernando de Taos. There he preached the ideals of freedom and castigated Gringo mountain men who finagled Mexican land grants — in competition with his family interests — and who provided *Indios cimarrones*, nomadic Indians, with guns, powder, and Taos Lightning. Chief among these were the Bent brothers, Charles and William, who with partner Ceran St. Vrain, ran Bent's Fort and other interests.

The *Rio Arriba* was not the *Abajo*, the land south of Santa Fe, realm of *haciendados ricos* and debt-slave *peons*. The men of the north were free, if poor, with their own lands sharing water, wood lots, and grazing commons and plowing the land with forked tree limbs. Water and commons governed their lives and their natures. In such circumstances, one who does well must be stealing from his neighbors, and only a *brujo*, a witch, would do that. By politicking among the neighbors, a man might, with their consent, win respect and honor, but there was great disincentive to advancing by success in agriculture or business. Being farther from Mexico City than from St. Louis, the land was cut off from trade. Mexican tariffs were high, and the people were metal poor, denied tools, and discouraged from manufacturing by a system that sought to have all manufactures come from Spain and later from the Valley of Mexico.

The elevation was high and the growing season short. There were few Mexican towns in the early 19th century: Santa Fe, Santa Cruz de la Cañada, Chimayo, and Don Fernando de Taos. Most of the remaining towns were Indian Pueblos: Taos, Picuris, Santa Cruz, San Juan, Pojoaque, Nambe, San Ildefanso, and others. Abiquiu, Trampas, and Truchas were *genizaro* towns. Genizaros were nomadic Indians, captured and held as slaves while they were taught Christianity, then given a grant of land along an Indian raiding trail, and told to farm and defend the colony. The people lived their lives in great isolation from the outside world.

Padre Martinez opened the first enduring school and taught preparatory seminary classes. Within months of his arrival in 1834, he acquired and operated New Mexico's first printing press, using it to create books for his school. As the only press in the region, it continued to turn out books and government documents, including the 1846 Territorial Constitution. He did not publish the first newspaper though. It was published on the press he later bought. *El Crepusculo de la Libertad,* The Twilight of Liberty, lasted only four editions. By 1852, when Frenchman Bishop Jean-Baptiste Lamy arrived to organize the first diocese of New Mexico, 18 of 22 priests were former students of Padre Martinez.

In 1832, in the first visit to New Mexico by a bishop in more than seven decades, Bishop Jose Antonio Zubiria of Durango traversed his far-flung diocese and was shocked by what he found. The *santos* carved by local *santeros,* saint makers, offended him as did the *retablos,* painted saints, of local manufacture. Recognized today as works of art, they were too crudely fashioned to please the bishop, and he ordered them removed from the churches. He was even more shocked by the rites of the *Penitentes* and promptly proscribed the brotherhood. With the bishop safely returned to far away Durango, Padre Martinez chose to ignore his orders and support local custom and art.

Elected in 1831, Presidente Antonio Lopez de Santa Anna suspended the Mexican Constitution of 1824 and replaced it with the Seven Laws of 1835. His action led to rebellion in Texas, New Mexico, and California. New Mexico became a department governed from Mexico City rather than a self-governing territory. It was rumored that high taxes were to follow. The appointed governor, Albino Perez, was subject to excesses of living and spending, calling forth the militia at their own expense, and taking loans he did not repay from the Santa Fe merchants. Padre Martinez spoke out about these abuses from the pulpit, and when the people of the *Rio Arriba* rose in revolt in 1837 literally tearing the governor limb from limb, it was suspected that the priest was behind the revolt. There is, however, no evidence that he was anything but shocked by the violence. As chaplain, he joined General Manuel Armijo, soon to be governor, in its suppression.

Ten years later, Padre Martinez was again suspected of instigating revolt after speaking out against the excesses of the Anglos. The mountain men led outrageous lives and defiled willing Mexican ladies. Through connivance and bribes, Anglos cornered vast land grants in direct competition with the Martinez family. The worst of all villains, the Bents and St. Vrain, sold Taos Lightning, guns, and gunpowder to the wild Indians of the plains who stole from Mexicans and often killed them to gather objects for trade. In 1847, the first American governor, Charles Bent, was killed at Taos, scalped, and mutilated. The priest did not take part in the riots that killed many Americans and their local allies. Instead, he hid Anglos, at great personal risk, in his home. Kit Carson, whom the padre had joined in matrimony to local girl, Josefa Jaramillo, never forgave Martinez for the murder of his friend and brother-in-law, Charles Bent.

Padre Martinez's love of the U.S. Constitution is well known though his understanding that it was both novel and eccentric. In 1846, after the American invasion, he told his seminary students that because the government had changed, they must change their ideas as the genius of this American government traveled in complete harmony with the freedom of worship and complete separation of Church and State. A student asked what form this new government took, and he replied, "Republican. You can say that in comparison the American government is like a burro, but on this burro ride the lawyers and not the clergy."

Martinez saw no conflict in a priest speaking out from the pulpit on political matters. To him "freedom of religion" meant, in part, that the government was free to protect the people from the church. He served in both Mexican and later American legislatures and still found time for his own parish and school. From a position in the new American legislature, Padre Martinez was among the first Native New Mexicans to agitate for New Mexico statehood.

That the padre and the new bishop, Jean-Baptiste Lamy, should clash was inevitable. New Mexico, severed from Durango, was made a diocese within an American archdiocese, and French-born Lamy sent out as bishop. When Lamy arrived in Santa Fe in 1852, the priest was at the height of his power. He enjoyed vast influence among the widespread *Penitentes* who had slipped from Church oversight and control. Most of the priests, the first native clergy in New Mexico, were his former students. At the same time, the bishop's lack of empathy for local customs was astounding. His cathedral and the chapel of the Sisters of Loretto were built in French style.

As the 1850s progressed, the conflict intensified. Vicar General Joseph Machebeuf, serving as the bishop's hammer, circulated to the outlying churches and found immorality and improper handling of church funds everywhere except in Taos. He relieved most of the native clergy and replaced them with mostly French priests. Machebeuf ordered that all church funds should come first to Santa Fe from which priestly stipends would then be dispensed. The vicar's inordinate focus on money shows in his efforts to have himself appointed executor of the estate of Francis Xavier Aubry, the Skimmer of the Plains, and in his actions that a portion of New Mexico was to be called Arizona. Charles Poston, Sonora Mining and Exploring Company at Tubac, had been conducting marriages at no charge for his Mexican workers under the authority of a civil appointment. Machebeuf nullified all of those marriages during his visit in 1859. The matter was settled and the marriages considered sanctified for $775. James Tevis, station keeper for the Butterfield Overland Mail, claimed that Machebeuf showed him the silver altar service he had taken from the Indians at San Xavier del Bac implying he'd put one over on them. Tevis, a teller of tall tales, might otherwise be doubted except that greed fits the vicar's pattern in dealing with New Mexican priests and in collecting money to build the new Santa Fe cathedral and, in 1860, Padre Martinez accused him of selling Church silver. Padre Martinez accused Vicar Machebeuf of betraying the secrets of the confessional from the pulpit, a very serious charge, which had to be answered in Rome.

In 1852, Bishop Lamy reduced the stole fees by half, claiming they were much too high. He did not realize that high stole fees were paid to offset the lack of the tithe had never been paid in New Mexico and that the fees were thus quite reasonable and low. The bishop insisted in the "Christmas Letter," January 14. 1854, that the tithe must be collected before sacraments could be given. Padre Martinez pointed out that if the bishop were successful in collecting the tithe, his treasury would soon exceed that of the territorial government. The cathedral in Santa Fe stands as evidence of Lamy's success. When stole fees were the only fees collected, and tithing was voluntary, the prohibitively high fees still left priests quite poor. In the following years, Padre Martinez consistently spoke out in published letters and tracts against the compulsory tithe. In 1860, he publically denounced the practice as "true simony," a serious religious crime.

By then, Padre Antonio Jose Martinez had been excommunicated by Bishop Lamy. We don't know when except that the excommunication took place secretly sometime after 1857 and before 1860. The record was not kept in Santa Fe; it was concealed in the record of baptisms at Taos in a comment written by the bishop. Padre Martinez questioned the validity of the excommunication, which Lamy had put through without admonition, formal charges, or a hearing. Indeed, the underhanded manner in which the excommunication was handled makes it very unlikely that the reading of the order was done with public fanfare as was claimed many years later. Anglos and French residents were said to have stood with Vicar Machebeuf against a potential rising of the local populace who adored the priest. They were described as "good Catholics," but among those listed were Kit Carson and Ceran St. Vrain who were Freemasons. There is no contemporary record of the vicar's visit, and there was no rising. The charges against the priest would not usually have been considered grounds for excommunication. He stood accused of having conducted a baptism at the oratory in his home because the church was not available to him. Of course, he failed to first collect the tithe.

Despite the rift with Bishop Lamy, arguing that the excommunication had no legal effect because it was not properly undertaken, Padre Martinez continued to minister to the poor and to friends until the end of his life in 1867. Although this created a schism of sorts in the church at Taos, Padre Martinez never sought to teach a new doctrine. He simply felt the bishop had acted improperly.

Although he did not resist the Protestant missionaries who came to the Rio Arriba, he never strayed from the traditions of the Roman Catholic Church. A leader of the church and legislature, at the forefront of printing and education, a defender of the rights and culture of the *Rio Arriba*, Padre Martinez is almost forgotten. Immersed in a tradition few outsiders understood, the priest was reviled by Kit Carson, Ceran St. Vrain, and Bishop Lamy for defending the common people of the north. He surfaces as the villain in Willa Cather's novel *Death Comes for the Archbishop* while his antagonist, a man who unwittingly trod on his parishioners and built a cathedral on their backs, is held up as a saint. In a land where education was almost unknown, his learning and expertise in canon law were renowned. Despite his dour demeanor and opposition to those who would exploit his people, he taught religious tolerance and the American Constitution and was instrumental in preparing New Mexico for democracy.

Sailing the Great Lakes with Tom Jeffords in the 1850s

I wish I could sail the Great Lakes on a wind-driven ship. I've sailed on small lakes, lakes too small to have waves of any size. And I've sailed on the ocean, which is quite a different experience.

On the ocean the wind is in your face, bringing with it the tang and smells of saltwater. In seaports, the smell of fish is always nearby, brought by mounds of clam and oyster shells and fish being processed – dried, salted, and canned. Would Ashtabula in the 1840s when Tom Jeffords was young, have smelt of the sea and dead fish? Probably not. It would have smelled of the products coming through, and in the nineteenth century many of these were much more crude and aromatic than would suit us today. Pitch and tar would have been needed to caulk ships' hulls and protect cordage. There would have been a strong aroma of hemp, for that was the plant from which cordage was made. Lumber was being shipped, and it would have smelled of pine forest and resin. The ship might also stink of damp and moldy things that had settled to the bilges but perhaps in fresh water on short runs, not as much as salt water craft on long voyages.

On the lakes, ships would slide along to the gentle shoosh of water passing underneath. Square sails on the foremast pulled the ship along, while triangular sails aft tilted the decks to one side, allowing the ship to sail closer to the winds eye. That advantage could kill a ship, especially in the narrow channels around harbors and between lakes where the wind could shift suddenly. Ships were built nearly flat bottomed with no great, deep keel to provide resistance, a sudden shift in wind would capsize a ship as witness the accounts of Captain James Jeffords's ship coming to the rescue.

Another danger came from cargo, which could shift if not properly stowed. It could also be flammable. Even grain was a risk. If the hull leaked, and the grain became wet, it would swell and tear a ship apart from the inside. Flour, too, was an explosive risk, for the dust it brought was combustible. The crews were small, three or four deck hands, just enough to hoist the sails. In danger, there were few hands to respond.

Ships of the Great Lakes didn't make long voyages. They made short runs from port to port. The small crew departed after the run leaving the captain to recruit anew. He'd need another officer to stand watch, three or four deckhands, and a cook, often a woman. The cook was important. Without a good one the captain would never find deckhands. The ship would also smell of the cooking of fresh food and bread, not the hard meals of long voyages on salt water. Descriptions of sailing on the Lakes from the Canadian side compare it to the hard life of sailors in the Royal Navy. Perhaps, but on the American side, conditions are said to have been much better.

The small crew huddled together and ate at the captain's table. Although their time together was short, officers and crew would have been much closer than on blue water ships where the quarterdeck kept far aloof from foremast jacks. Relations would have to build quickly. Respect would need to be earned and discipline enforced even as the ship left port for the first time. On the Lakes, they were thrown together. Officers needed to be guarded in their behavior; they couldn't unwind in front of the men, or they'd never be successfully obeyed. At the same time, they had to be on companionable terms with the deckhands. Meals at the captain's table would have been horribly uncomfortable if they'd tried to keep Royal Navy rules for dinner in the captain's cabin: don't speak until the captain speaks to you. Dinnertime, when sailors could relax, needed to be polite and easy. Men needed to feel they could speak freely even as officers maintained much of their reserve.

Tom Jeffords rose to command before he was 25. He would have been giving orders to men much older than himself, so he must have been sure to maintain his reserve, appear wise, and earn respect. He would have lacked the natural respect that comes with age. He would have needed to earn respect across cultural barriers with crews of Dutch, German, English, French-Canadian, and Swedes. This would serve him well in later years, earning swift respect from Apaches who called themselves *Indeh*, the people, implying that everyone else wasn't quite human and deserved little or no respect.

The Great Lakes offered some terror of sudden sinking against a backdrop of familiar peoples – Americans or at least Northern Europeans -, familiar lands, fresh water, and fresh food. The Lakes lacked the charm of exotic ports and peoples, of colorful parrots and strange goods. Lacking as well was the terror of long, violent storms, of being becalmed on a salt-sea – water, water everywhere but not a drop to drink. To an active, intelligent young man in search of wealth, captaining a ship on the Lake must have felt a bit like driving a semi-truck today. He'd have seen the same ports, the same cargos, and the same people in a land as bland as the water. Adventure and fortune lay further west where there were Indians, mountains, and, in California, gold, gold that could be picked up off the ground. In 1858, the adventure drew closer with news of gold at Pike's Peak and Cherry Creek.

Go Jii Ya,
Christmas for Jicarilla Apaches
Relay Race to Balance Nature

The annual Go Jii Ya, or Harvest Relay Race, was being run 200 years ago, and this most important ceremonial of the Jicarillas (*hic ah ree yahs*), the northernmost band of Apaches, continues to be run each September. The annual footrace pits the Sun, which is represented by the Red Clan (***Llaneros***, *yahn erh ohs,* Plains People) who controls animals, against the Moon, represented by the White Clan (***Olleros***, *oy erh ohs,* Water Vessel People) who controls plants and growing things. When the White Clan wins, the "losing" Sun releases his animals to the People and the hunting is good. When the Red Clan wins, the "losing" Moon allows for strong crop growth and the abundant harvest of wild foods— chokecherries, acorns and piñon nuts. Before the Jicarilla began racing, nature would get out of balance with too much of one kind of food and not enough of the other. In the old days, top runners also won maidens as brides. Against all odds, the Red Clan has won the relay race for the past 15 years, resulting in cooler, wetter weather, which is good for crops.

More about food than foot speed, the race, now held at Stone Lake on the Jicarilla Reservation in northwest New Mexico, is both a ceremony and harvest festival. It is a great insult to refuse food offered as one wanders from camp to camp. Tortillas are roasted on the grill together with chili, lamb ribs, and legs of mutton. Sausages, stew, and posole sizzle and bubble on an open oak-wood fire. The camp is bathed in wood smoke and the aroma of roasting meat.

In 1850, the Jicarillas, never a large tribe, numbered about 800. The Olleros lived along the Rio Grande from Abiquiu (northwest of Santa Fe) to Alamosa (in Colorado). They hunted game, planted crops in the river bottoms, and were friendly with Taos and Picuris Pueblos, whose word for the Jicarillas meant "the protectors." The Llaneros hunted buffalo on the Llano Estacado, or Staked Plains, of northeastern New Mexico and were well known to travelers on the Santa Fe Trail.

The Jicarillas' great enemies were the Kiowa Apaches, whose language is almost identical to theirs, and the Comanches. In the fall of 1849, Jicarillas ambushed an advance party of a trade caravan and abducted Ann White, the only white woman in the territory, and her daughter Virginia. Celebrated frontiersman Kit Carson tried in vain to rescue the women (see "Kit Carson's Ride" in the April 2007 *Wild West*). In March 1854, in the Battle of Cieneguilla (see story in the February 2008 *Wild West*), a band of Jicarillas (estimates range from about 100 to more than 200 warriors) defeated a 60-man force of the 1st Dragoon Regiment, killing almost half the men and wounding the rest. By the late 1850s, the Jicarillas were starving and had to resort to begging for food at agencies or else preying on travelers. The tribe did not get its own reservation until 1887.

Through the good times and bad, the Jicarillas continued to hold Go Jii Ya and two other ceremonies. The Holiness Rite, sometimes called Bear Dance, was suppressed by the Bureau of Indian Affairs in the 1920s, but it survives today as a private, quiet, healing ceremony attended by family members. The *Keezdah*, or Adolescence Rite, is a feast held soon after a girl reaches puberty, though it involves both boys and girls proving themselves worthy of a place in the adult world through singing, dancing, and work-related tasks. At great expense, the family feeds all visitors on beef stew, fried bread, and *tizwin* (corn beer).

No other Apache tribe has a ceremony similar to Go Jii Ya. The Pueblos—Taos, Picuris and San Juan—practice a harvest rite, but it is of less importance among them. Jicarillas take the ceremony seriously; men begin learning its secrets in childhood. For instance, walking across the racetrack is taboo, and runners must prepare by staying away from women, meat, and tobacco. No photography is allowed.

Before the reservation, the race track was located between Santa Cruz and Abiquiu on the Chama River. Jicarilla then and now assembled to camp together, share food, dance, sing, and prepare for the ceremony. Today an informal rodeo and powwow (competitive dance) occur afterwards. At night, soft drumbeats and singing can be heard in the camps, which vie with each other in rending war hoops.

There is much to do before the race. The track must be leveled and purified. Kivas (brush corrals) must be built of aspen and cottonwood branches at each end of the track as private staging-points for each clan. A tepee pole above each kiva flies the banner of the clan. Inside, realistic sand paintings of Sandhill cranes, eagles, hummingbirds, and other swift birds adorn the center of the floor. The day before the race, the clan elders prepare, and when they are ready, they emerge singing—with their banner leading and drum beating—as they shuffle down the track toward the other clan. They meet in the middle, approaching and backing off three times, their singing growing to a shout as they vie to outdo each other. Advancing to the end of the track, they soon reverse course and head for their home kiva. There, the drum beats at four intervals summoning the runners.

Traditionally, mounted tribesmen followed the elders and the drum. Today, the participants travel by pickup trucks, driving through camp, with much honking and war hoops, to their practice tracks: White Clan by the lake and Red Clan over the hill to the north. The elders then choose the runners, putting the fastest in key positions. It is not important that the teams be of equal size. The fastest will be sent into the relay again.

The participants wander back to camp by twos and threes while the pickups are parked tailgate toward the track, lining its quarter-mile length from end to end. Old photos show Model-Ts and horse-drawn wagons lined up in the same way. Still older photos show women on horseback, cheering for the runners. The pickups serve as box seats.

The morning of the race is busy as elders prepare runners, painting their bodies red and white with ochre and clay in opposite patterns for the different clans. A headband is fitted in clan color with a circlet of yucca leaves on the forehead to which the wing feathers of fast birds are attached with a long ribbon in blue, red, or white at the tip. Bodies are daubed with down. Two elders jog down the track and wave eagle feathers to purify it. The runners, led by their elders, finally emerge from the kivas and dance and sing down the track, each clan taking position by the other clan's kiva and mounting its banner there. Half of the runners return to the end near their clans' kivas. Four referees armed with aspen fronds take positions along the track, and the race begins.

In the 2010 race, the fastest runners raced neck and neck down the track as referees enforced the rules, kept spectators back, and encouraged their clans' men with strokes of the aspen frond as they passed. Red Clan partisans told the White Clan runners to "slow down" and their own to run faster. As the White Clan fell behind, a fast runner was put in for a second lap. The elders recycling runners is how it has always been done. The Red Clan led by a season (one lap) when a Red runner developed cramps and fell again and again—four times—as the White runner gained ground. An elder said to me, "I told them not to let him run." The race continued until Red was two seasons ahead, and White admitted defeat once again. It seemed like hours had passed. Somewhere from 60 to 100 men and boys had run, and the cheering never faltered. After the race came the turn of the small boys, painted and adorned like their elder brothers. They raced together in one group and afterward were admonished by their parents that they must wear the paint until sundown like their brothers.

Led by their banners and the drums, the clans formed up again. They sang, danced, and shuffled down the track toward each other. Approaching each other three times, they shuffled backward and repeated until the two clans were abreast. Suddenly, the air was full of gifts as the clans tossed presents high into the air for the other clan to catch. Ears of corn, chili peppers, packaged candies, and jerked meat sailed by overhead. The competition continued until the members of each side and the spectators had filled their hands and arms with groceries.

With the formal ceremony over, informal and casual events began. The plaza south of the track, ringed by the stalls of vendors of food and finery, became a dance floor for an impromptu powwow. Men showed off their dancing skills, and women in their fine costumes danced displaying intricate footwork. Across the hill to the west, a rodeo formed as the men and boys competed to see whose horse was the fastest or who could ride the bucking horse the longest. These contests have gone on as long as Apaches have had horses. As night fell, singing and drumbeats began again; the Round Dance continued till dawn.

Fandango on the Fourth of July
At Isolated Fort Massachusetts

The post was as isolated as any in the United States in 1856. Located in the high country of New Mexico Territory (in what today is southern Colorado) some 90 miles north of Taos over roads that ranged from rough to nonexistent, Fort Massachusetts was manned by a single company of artillerymen, serving as infantry. The U.S. Army was no longer risking its valuable dragoons and their horses there. The nearly 9,000-foot elevation meant a short growing season (too short for vegetables) and long winters with deep snows and sub-zero temperatures. The frigid winter of 1855-56 had kept the men indoors. Many of them, including post surgeon Dr. DeWitt Peters, had come down with scurvy. There was nothing to be done except to await summer "green-up." But when the warmer weather finally did arrive, the occupants of the fort were ready to let off some steam. Post Commander Lieutenant Lloyd Beall, 2nd Artillery, assigned Dr. Peters and Lieutenant John R. Smead the pleasant task of preparing a fandango for what Peters described as the "Glorious Fourth." The guest list, thanks mainly to the fact that the Army was in the process of looking to replace Fort Massachusetts, was impressive.

Fort Massachusetts had been established on June 22, 1852, on the west bank of Utah (or Ute) Creek primarily to protect settlers in the San Luis Valley. It was a log structure 320 feet long by 270 feet wide, constructed of vertical poles 10 feet in length, chinked with mud, and built to accommodate two companies. The sutler's store stood about 150 feet south of the entrance across Sand Creek from the corral. Utah Creek ran on the other side of the fort, and the forested arms of the mountain embraced all closely. It soon became apparent that the location, built in a swampy area that was subjected to paralyzing winter storms, was less than ideal.

In the summer of 1856, Brevet Brig. Gen. John Garland, in command of the Department of New Mexico came to the area with his staff to survey better ground at a lower altitude and nearer the new settlements of the San Luis Valley for a new post to replace Fort Massachusetts. Providing escort duty thorough Jicarilla Apache country for the general was Troop G of the 1st U.S. dragoons, headed by Captain Richard S. "Old Baldy" Ewell, who would rise in the upcoming Civil War to lieutenant general in command of a corps under Confederate General Robert E. Lee. As agent for the Utes and Jicarillas, former mountain man Kit Carson, along with some of Carson's friends and allies, including large land grant holder Carlos Beaubien, his son-in-law Lucien Maxwell and Ceran St. Vrain, rode at Garland's side. Vicar General Joseph P. Machebeuf, Bishop Jean-Baptiste Lamy's ramrod, made a trip to Fort Massachusetts and led services there during this period, and he may well have accompanied this large party. At the old fort's fandango, these "guests" would share in the holiday celebration, not only with Lieutenant Beall and his command but also with invited *señoras y señoritas* from the San Luis and Costilla settlements.

As it turned out, only 17 of these Mexican settlers attended. Apparently, threatening rumors kept some of them away. Kit Carson had overheard a man in San Luis passing the word that the American soldiers planned to kill the local men and steal their women. Other settlers might have been discouraged from attending the fandango by the distance to the fort, a 24-mile full-day journey by burro and *carreta*. The Mexican women who did attend in their finest clothes were certainly noticed. They wore colorful *rebozos* about their shoulders against the high altitude evening chill over low cut white cotton blouses that revealed their shoulders and more. Long pleated skirts left their shapely ankles exposed above moccasined feet. The men likewise wore moccasins. Dark wool trousers fastened up the side with silver *conchos* were left open below the knee, exposing shins covered by rawhide *botas*. At the waist, a red sash often hid a knife, or if one could afford it, a gun. The men wore light-colored shirts and dark vests. It is hard to imagine poor folks dressed so well, and surely these were among the poorest in the north, but so they are described.

Dr. Peters, who wrote of the event and was avid in noticing Mexican women, never mentioned any American women in attendance. He noted that the previous Christmas (1855) on a trip to Santa Fe he encountered the first American ladies he had seen in 18 months. If Dr. Peters and Lieutenants Beall and Smead were married, their wives were not present at the fandango. Although unmentioned by Peters, there almost certainly were some other women at the event. Each company was authorized at least four laundresses and could not manage without them. These women were often the wives of non-commissioned officers. Some commanders insisted they be wed, for unmarried women tended toward profitable temporary liaisons. It would have been difficult to solemnize one's vows at Fort Massachusetts, for the nearest cleric was a priest at distant Taos, so arrangements may have ranged from casual to extremely casual, enduring only the evening.

The Wildest West

They were women of independent means and thinking. Assigned their own private quarters, they were issued a food ration as well as being paid for their labor. Another class of "camp followers" was less fortunate. Enlisted wives who were not laundresses did not draw rations, receive pay, or get assigned quarters. They had only their husband's pay, rations, and whatever house he could erect outside the post. There is an extensive area of such homes at Fort Garland, the fort built twelve miles away in 1858 to replace Fort Massachusetts, but none has yet been discovered at Fort Massachusetts. It is possible that most such women had better sense than to accompany their men to this desolate mountain post, but artifacts found at the site indicate that women were there.

Dr. Peters and Lieutenant Smead worked hard to make the fort's corral presentable for the fandango. They converted a stable for the event, hiding the unsightly with evergreens and flags. The table was laden with pies, cakes, and venison. Evidence on site suggests the party also enjoyed tinned oysters, imported French sardines, and tinned ham, all delicacies sold at the sutler's store.

The soldiers arrived at this "grand ball" in undress uniform, that is to say neither in work clothing nor in their fanciest uniforms, ready to drink and be merry. Beer was difficult to brew and did not travel well. Distilled spirits took up less space in a wagon and were easier to make. Taos Lightning, Mexican *aguardiente,* and Mexican wines would have been available. American spirits came over the Santa Fe Trail from the States. A few soldiers drank too much at the fandango and soon found themselves lodged in the guardhouse to sleep it off. The ladies, according to Dr. Peters, gorged on this feast until they were sick with gourmandizing, but they didn't allow upset stomachs to impede their dancing, as "they [were] never set back by trifles." The *cuna*, cradle, was a popular dance in New Mexico Territory. Men and women placed their hands on each other's hips and leaned back at the shoulder forming the cradle, they "rocked" about the dance floor.

Before the Civil War, bugles were not yet in vogue, and each company was provided with a drummer, but he would not have been much use on this occasion. Because Fort Massachusetts was not a regimental headquarters, there were no bandsmen (and certainly nothing nearly as fancy as the bands seen in John Ford's John Wayne cavalry trilogy). Ordinary soldiers carried instruments and even formed small musical bands. There were guitars, fiddles, and various squeezeboxes. Music and musicians came from Germany, England, Ireland, and the American countryside. They had differing ideas about which types of music and which dance tunes were best. Indeed, fighting among the members of these informal bands often broke up dances, but not at Fort Massachusetts on the Fourth of July, 1856. The soldiers did themselves proud for General Garland and the other dignitaries who gathered at this lonely fort for the fandango. "The music," wrote Dr. Peters, "was good, and everything passed off very creditable." For a few hours, isolation, suffering, and boredom lifted as the soldiers shared the Glorious Forth with important visitors and ladies.

Tom Jeffords, Sutler at Fort Huachuca
Life after the Chiricahua Agency

In 1950, Jimmy Stewart played Tom Jeffords in *Broken Arrow*. He rode alone into Cochise's Stronghold and became the chief's friend and advisor. The Apache called him brother and sought his council. In 1872, he helped General O.O. Howard, the one-armed Christian general, negotiate the peace with Cochise. The reservation included most of modern Cochise County, and Cochise demanded that Jeffords be his agent. The peace held while Cochise lived. A minor outbreak led to the Chiricahua being moved to the San Carlos Reservation in 1876 with John Clum, of *Tombstone Epitaph* fame as agent.

With his job gone, Tom Jeffords went back to prospecting and scouting. He owned mines including the Brunckow, the Yellow Jacket in Tombstone, and a 9th share of the Copper Queen, and he held a contract to supply artesian water to the City of Tucson. On April 15, 1880, Tom Jeffords was appointed Post Sutler and postmaster for Fort Huachuca. His store was located at the mouth of Huachuca Canyon near the road to Reservoir Hill on ground that has since been graded so that only a few foundations remained. The curator at the Fort Huachuca Museum has located a photo of a building from 1888 labelled simply "where we go to drink." The sutler's store was the principle provider of alcohol on military posts. It's in the right place and seems "large and commodious" as Jeffords described it.

The Wildest West

The sutler was the post trader, a precursor to the modern Post Exchange (PX). It supplied the needs of the soldier that weren't provided as military issue and rations. A soldier could get new socks, a sewing kit, polish, and tinned meats and sardines. The sutler's store was also the canteen (snack bar) and the equivalent of an enlisted man's club. The store had card rooms, a pool table, and a bar. The sutler operated on credit in a time when paydays were sporadic and irregular; he served as a high-risk banker to officer and enlisted clientele alike.

Tom took the lucrative post at a difficult time. Two executive orders had complicated the life of sutlers. One forbad holding an Indian trading license at the same time as a sutler's appointment. Jeffords had to surrender the one he held for Fort Bowie and Apache Pass. The other forbad selling alcoholic spirits. A great part of a sutler's income came from the sale of liquor, and enlisted men expected the sutler to be the supplier. Post commanders looked the other way to keep the men happy as long as there weren't too many incidents at the store. The anti-alcohol policy left the sutler under the thumb of the commander who could crack down at any time.

Fort Huachuca was a two-company post. Companies were supposed to have 100 men so there should have been no more than 200 men assigned to the fort. There were actually about 70. The Old Post and Parade Field we see today were built in the 1890s, after Jeffords's time, to be occupied by two regiments, 20 companies. In December 1881, a complaint was made against Jeffords by men unhappy with high prices and inferior goods. The post officers found against him. There are indications that the post commander had a friend who wanted to be sutler, and these machinations were an attempt to get him the job. New prices were set for beer, wine, and liquor. Tom agreed to some changes.

In June 1882, Captain Madden had the post council remove Jeffords. Madden's friend, M.W. Stewart, was nominated to replace Tom. In the ensuing struggle, Jeffords agreed to stock his store with an amount of goods appropriate for a five-company post. Stocking for five companies was expensive and was a significant overstock. The overstock gave customers broad choice at Jeffords's expense. Jeffords asked help from Granville Oury, the Territory of Arizona's representative to Congress. In November, at Oury's behest, Robert Lincoln, Secretary of War, decided in Jeffords's favor, and Tom was reinstated. October 1883 brought more intrigue, and Jeffords was again removed. In his letter of rebuttal, he noted that he had built a "large and commodious store at an expense of between eight and nine thousand dollars."

Tom Jeffords returned to his mining interests, and they occupied him throughout the rest of the 1880s. In 1892, he moved to the Owl Head Buttes north of the Tortollita Mountains 25 miles north of Tucson. There he spent the rest of his life working some small gold mines.

The Mystery of Chaco Canyon, A Review by Rahm E. Sandoux

The story of Doug Hocking's new historical novel, *The Mystery of Chaco Canyon*, takes place ten years after them events described in his earlier book, *Massacre at Point of Rocks*.

At the bequest of a dying Masonic brother, Dan and his friends Roque, Doña Loca, and Peregrino Rojo, embark on a search for the Los Lunas Decalogue Stone, a boulder with an inscription believed to be an abridged version of the Decalogue (Ten Commandments) in Paleo-Hebrew. The clues lead them all over the Southwest, including the Estancia Valley, Acoma, Zuni, El Morro, the Hopi mesas, the Grand Canyon, Chaco, Chimayo, Chihuahua, and Casas Grandes. They finally locate Rough Hurech's grave in a mountain cave in southwest Arizona and then return to Chaco Canyon.

Along their twisting route, they meet so many minor characters that, to be honest, it was hard for this reader to keep track of them all. Many of these figures are drawn from history, including George Bascom, Padre Antonio Jose Martinez, Kit Carson, and Albert Pike. There are also Danites, Masons Texas Rangers, and Apaches.

Although the plot is motivated by the fictional search, Hocking manages to discuss dozens of historical incidents. These events are described with limited detail, but they might spark a reader's interest to investigate certain incidents more deeply.

The Mystery of Chaco Canyon has all the elements that endeared Hocking's previous book to Southern Trails

Chapter readers: short chapters broken into even shorter scenes that make it easy to say to yourself, "I'll just read one more chapter," and before you know it, you are swept up in another bit of exciting action.

Hocking clearly loves history, and in *The Mystery of Chaco Canyon*, he demonstrates a knowledge of and appreciation for the various cultures inhabiting the Southwest.

Rahm E. Sandoux

A page from
Massacre at Point of Rocks

Going West on the Santa Fe Trail

The affair ended in blood and icy death for Indian and white alike. How strange that chance meetings and hasty words of no more weight than seeds of *chamisa* dusting the fall breeze should bring so many to calamity. Bad acts and actors abounded. Small things, done by people meaning well enough, led to disaster for everyone, but through it all, a boy grew and moved toward manhood.

He was tall for his age and broad shouldered, nearly a man and working his first real job. Insulated by school and native intelligence, he used his wits to escape the lessons apprenticed boys and laborers learned early working with men. Possessing the body of an adult he had not yet fully matured as many younger than he had already done. Still expecting men to be the bold, perfect heroes in his books, he was disappointed by the imperfections of real men. The West was the land of his heroes. He would find a man to look up to on the Frontier. He was called Danny

Trelawney, or more often by the men of the slow moving caravan, *Danito*. They trudged, their wagons four abreast, through dust and sweat following the long, dry road to Santa Fe, which stood in imagination and dreams a gleaming citadel of wealth and exotic sight, sounds, and smells. Santa Fe was where men made their fortunes. Danito thought of it as the home of Kit Carson and a place where folks met wild Indians.

He walked behind an ox team, whip in hand and cracking it now and then above a beast's back as warning to keep moving. He was lucky to have this job occasioned by a man's demise. The sickness was a mystery to those in the caravan. Fortunately, it took no one else, but death on the trail was all too common. The men who ran the *ramuda*, the horse and mule herd, were all New Mexicans, so the boy wouldn't fit there. The cooks were Cajuns and Quebec French speaking a language few but they could understand. The boy replaced the one who had died walking beside an ox team.

What kind folks have said about
Massacre at Point of Rocks

Historian Will Gorenfeld said: Very readable and informative. Your knowledge and description of Aubrey's train, the men, the countryside is, thus far, superb as is Grier's failed attempt to rescue Mrs. White.

Author Gerald Summers said: Doug Hocking has done himself proud. His writing flows smoothly, his historical references are spot on, and his action exciting. I recently read Kit Carson's autobiography and found it to be one of the most interesting historical presentations I've ever read. And that is saying something, for I have studied western history for many years. Doug has captured much of this famous man and his exploits and deserves much credit for bringing him and his other wonderful characters to life. I thoroughly enjoyed this book.

Jicarilla Apache teacher from Dulce, NM, on the Jicarilla Reservation said: Written by a resident of the community - interesting story line. Reading parts to my Middle and High School classes in hopes to spark their reading interests.

Shar Porier of the Sierra Vista Herald said: It [reveals] an historical view of the life and times in New Mexico in the 1840s and '50s in a novel story, written just as one produced by western authors of the past. It is hard to set the book aside.

Greg Coar: Just finished your book. Saved it for the trip home. Loved it. Hope there is more to come. Great to meet you and your wife in Tombstone. Keep the history coming.

Dac Crassley of the Old West Daily Reader: As you know, I have a considerable interest in Western History and enough knowledge to make me dangerous. And I read a lot because of my research for Old West Daily Reader. This book was comfortable, like worn in buckskins or one's favorite Levis. Everything felt right. The story unfolded in a coherent and, for me, personal fashion. I truly appreciated and enjoyed your obvious care in building the historical background of the tale. Characters were fleshed out, real, believable. I could picture the landscapes. The trail dust...Ok, I really liked the book! Great accomplishment and a fine telling!

Rahm E. Sandoux, *Desert Tracks* **(OCTA) reviewer:** Doug Hocking's *Massacre at Point of Rocks* is a fascinating story of historic events along the Santa Fe Trail in 1849. Setting the White massacre and captivity in context, Hocking reveals to readers the ethnic side of of the frontier, showing how Indians, Mexicans, and blacks were just as much a part of that historical tapestry as the white men were. He brings characters like Kit Carson, Grier, Comancheros, and the Jicarilla Apaches to life, revealing how tough life was on the frontier for all of its inhabitants. *Massacre at Point of Rocks* will definitely be of interest to readers who want to learn more about the history of New Mexico and the Santa Fe Trail.

About the Author

Doug Hocking grew up on the Jicarilla Apache Reservation in the Rio Arriba (Northern New Mexico). He attended reservation schools, an Ivy League prep school, and graduated from high school in Santa Cruz, New Mexico, in the Penitente heartland among *paisonos* and *Indios*. Doug enlisted in Army Intelligence out of high school and worked in Taiwan, Thailand and at the Pentagon. Returning home he studied Social Anthropology (Ethnography) and then returned to the Army as an Armored Cavalry officer (scout) completing his career by instructing Military Intelligence lieutenants in intelligence analysis and the art of war.

He has earned a master's degree with honors in American History and completed field school in Historical Archaeology. Since retiring he has worked with allied officers and taught at Cochise College. He is now an independent scholar residing in southern Arizona near Tombstone with his wife, dogs, a feral cat and a friendly coyote. In 2016, Arizona Governor Doug Ducey appointed him to the board of the Arizona Historical Society. He is Vice President for Arizona of the Southern Trails Chapter of the Oregon-California Trails Association, a Road Scholar for Arizona Humanities and Sheriff of the Cochise County Corral of the Westerners.

Doug has published in *Wild West*, *True West*, *Buckskin Bulletin* and *Roundup Magazine*. He has three novels in print: ***Massacre at Point of Rocks*** about Kit Carson and the White wagon train massacre, ***The Mystery of Chaco Canyon*** concerning mystery, archaeology and lost treasure, and ***Devil on the Loose***, a story of love and adventure in 1860 Arizona. The is also an anthology of short material,

The Wildest West. He is working on a biography of *Tom Jeffords, Cochise's Friend.*

All books are available at www.doughocking.com , on Amazon.com and through Ingram.